Susie Boyt was born in London in 1969. She is the author of two acclaimed novels, *The Normal Man* and *The Characters of Love*. She lives in London with her family.

The Last Hope of Girls

Susie Boyt

review

First published in Great Britain in 2001
by REVIEW

An imprint of Headline Book Publishing

First published in paperback in 2002
10 9 8 7 6 5 4 3 2 1

ISBN 0 7472 6515 1

Typeset by Palimpsest Book Production Limited,
Polmont, Stirlingshire

Printed and bound in Great Britain by
Clays Ltd, St Ives plc.

Headline Book Publishing
A division of Hodder Headline
338 Euston Road
London NW1 3BH

www.reviewbooks.co.uk
www.hodderheadline.com

For Tom and Mary with love

Acknowledgements

With thanks to:

Kate Mackenzie Davey
Leonard Rau
Tom Astor
Joseph O'Neill
Michael Gormley
Caroline Dawnay
Mary-Anne Harrington
Charlotte Mendelson
Geraldine Cooke

&

Jeannie Milligan

dead has a smile like the nicest man you've never
   met who maybe winks
at you in a streetcar and you pretend you don't but
   really you do
see and you are My how glad he winked and hope
   he'll do it again

to be careless, dauntless to create havoc — that was
   the last hope of girls

e.e. cummings

One

Complete darkness.

The kindly man was saying things again. 'After you. That's right. Do be careful. It's rather rough down here. Do mind how you go, won't you?'

It seemed to Martha, for a second, that she had embarked on some kind of breathless adolescent game involving body swerves and winking and murders. She felt oddly conscious, suddenly, of the outline of her body beneath its many layers of clothes. Just then a floorboard creaked theatrically, and she gasped and froze. Only it wasn't a game.

'So sorry about all this mess. I did ask them to have a tidy, but . . .'

'Well, I was warned that things might be slightly . . . on the muddly side.'

'You were? Oh, that *is* good news.' Mr Quinn's long-legged footsteps were tentative, but there was a certain speed to them. 'Another thing. I'd much rather you said straight away if you don't think it's going to work. Please don't stand on any kind of ceremony, will you? It's just I've got to get it sorted out by the end of the week, one way or another. Thing is if you said yes now and then changed your mind further down the line, I can't pretend it wouldn't be an enormous inconvenience. Although, I don't mean to put you under any pressure at all.'

'I do realise that. And I am sure.'

'You are? Well, that's marvellous news.'

'Oh, good.' Was that all it was going to take? She had prepared a catalogue of sketchy illustrations of her conscientious side. The very least she expected was a salty taking-to-task of her character traits, her previous habits.

'I'm sorry it's so dark. Do mind — there's a low step just coming up ahead. The light is just — don't know what your dad told you exactly . . .'

'Well, hardly anything, I mean . . .'

Mr Quinn snapped on the light switch, only nothing at all changed. He sighed humorously, his voice retaining its note of buoyancy. 'So sorry. I'll see to it this afternoon. I've got some spare bulbs upstairs.'

Martha inhaled. The entrance smelt woody and thick with dust. She shivered and folded her arms across her chest.

'You wait here. I won't be a moment. There's a flashlight in the car. Don't move an inch. I'm afraid some of the floor in front of you isn't terribly . . . I'll . . . I'll be back in *one* second.' Mr Quinn struck a match, then another. Martha breathed in the scent of sulphur and listened to his footsteps, the thick-soled, pudgy American sports-shoe soles, making their way out of the shallow gloom down the narrow corridor, and then came the click of the latch. The door opened and a brief triangle of light illuminated her surroundings — Mr Quinn's huge form disappearing out of the ghostly hall or reception area or vestibule, she supposed it was, with its roughly textured floor, the ceilings high and flaky, the colour of hospital walls, the small hill of damp-smelling, steel-coloured rubble that lay to the left of the door. Under the broad slope of the stone staircase were piled-up wedges of wooden decking. Split bags of sand

and more dusty grey powder lay against the front wall, black rubbish sacks filled with discarded musty wallpaper scrolls, tiny ancient wreaths of flowers winking delicately from their yellowed insides. There were paint-pots, electrical cables, large steel tools, plugs, spanners, some polystyrene cups with shallow ancient orange tea, the tea-bags crisp and rust-coloured, poking out like fins. Two sandwiches cut into quarters, their ancient tops matted and snarl-edged, lay in an unlidded white plastic container. Out of the corner of her eye, in the very last of the light, Martha glimpsed a few small slabs of grey and white marble propped up against the bottom step and next to them two or three pale batons of parquet flooring arranged in a herringbone design.

For a few moments thick, juddering sounds of traffic assaulted her ears: clotted, honking delivery vehicles, snarling taxis, shuddering overheated buses back to back, the low, angry, strangulated noises lurching wildly in the cool dark air above her head.

What was it her father had said in the restaurant? Martha cast her mind back, her eyes stung, her ears crimson. His expression of deliberate mildness, the subtle, grey-blue eyes, the sharp bones, the thin, grey-pink lips. She could not quite remember his words — for some reason when he spoke she never quite felt inclined to listen. Of one thing she was certain, however. As he had raised his eyes slightly and batted away some swirls of cigarette smoke that curled their way from a neighbouring table, the word *luxury* had come into it. 'An acquaintance who has acquired a luxury block of flats, luxury mansion block. West End. De luxe accommodation.' Something like that.

What did he think he was doing making these wild suggestions? How did it occur to him she would manage? He didn't think. It didn't occur.

Earlier, while she had waited outside for Quinn to arrive and scoop her into her new dwelling, twenty minutes she had stood there, concentrating on staying cheerful, she had examined the entrance to the building, which was at the western end of Oxford Street. The slim mahogany-framed door was low and narrow, the letters RAVEN COURT etched in proud, uppercase gold letters in the rectangular sooty slit of window above the door-frame. The door itself bordered a huge shop window at the top of which the bedraggled plastic legs of can-can dancers in green skirts and nylon petticoats jerkily lifted up and down, to no particular rhythm. Red stuck-on letters above the dancers' legs announced the name of the shop: WORLD OF LONDON. It was filled with stacks of dazzling tourist bric-à-brac: paperweights depicting Big Ben surrounded by luminous, quivering green fern and silver-blue snowflakes; gold plastic models of tower Bridge; glossy red telephone-box key-rings; ashtrays embossed with navy-blue royal silhouettes; quite a wide range of Sherlock Holmes memorabilia and some garish Beefeater statuettes, in a variety of sizes, with detachable red flock coats. 'You've fallen on your feet here,' she'd mouthed to herself, watching her lips going in the dark reflective glass, flinching as one of the orange plastic legs skimmed the tip of her pony-tail. 'Oh, yes.'

Plunged in darkness again, as the door closed on her, Martha pursed her lips and put a hand, thoughtfully, to her forehead. The room was quiet now apart from muffled, assorted street sounds and she took a couple of small paces, trailing her fingers along the powdery walls for safety, watching her step. Smells of clay and kindling rose up as she lifted and placed each foot. Just then her fingers brushed a thin tangle of wires and she withdrew them speedily. Suddenly the adventure she was embarking on made her feel madcap and a little dizzy, but her spirits were high.

It was not looking ideal, this glorified building site, but you couldn't argue with the potential. Her present accomodation situation, she had resolved that morning, was unendurable, even for another night, and in a frenzy of hope and shaky adrenaline she had handed in her notice and two weeks' rent, citing Raven Court as her new address. It wasn't just Stacey's thin walls and her all-night high-octave sexual gymnastics with Lukey that got Martha down, nor Lukey's aversion to clothing, even in the most common areas of the tiny flat. It wasn't even the lack of space so pronounced that Martha had to see to her college work on the grey flaky surface of an ancient ironing-board under the window-sill, sat on her bed, knees jammed flush with the party wall . . . nor Stacey's pneumatic psychological insights that lashed and flattered by turns. No, the last straw was seeing her flatmate careering past her, through a thick, murky puddle, on her Vespa in Martha's brand-new (unworn) high-heeled black suede peep-toe mules. No, the very last straw was when Lukey's pet iguana had moved into the flat, a huge, evil-eyed, ancient-looking speciality lizard who threw filthy looks at her and kept her captive in her own room. The rent was low, but still . . .

The latch clicked again and in flooded the newly familiar roar of excruciated, furious traffic noises, standstill groaning-engine sounds, but these were broken up by some larky teenage voices from the street, and there was Mr Quinn, light-haired and pink-faced in his dark, baggy suit and running-shoes shining a bright torchlight on her face, on her nose. A lighter kind of air flew into the room with him, air that was thinner, more transparent. 'There we are, then,' he was saying now, and other such soothing expressions, a huge, rounded smile of unexpected radiance lighting his face. The torch-beam dipped to Martha's shoes, exposing the bald patches where the suede had worn thin round the toes.

Martha felt her face, which was already irregular in many

ways, become even more lopsided with anxiety. It is an old-fashioned sort of face of the type that people do not really have any more: her mouth is small in length but her lips are full so that the shape it makes is more square than round. When she speaks it does quirky, unplanned things, expressing more than she means. Her eyelashes are long but extremely thin. Her face is oval and very pale, and this she remedies by applying roses to the apples of her cheeks with a light translucent blush, as often as she remembers. Of the fact that Martha has an unusual figure also, she is quite aware. Her top half is slightly heavy-looking, she has broad, square shoulders, a large bust and a high waist, but her bottom half is made on a different scale, slight and narrow. Sometimes, at low moments, she fears she has the build of an American sportsman.

Martha shuffles her feet out of view and tries to adopt an attitude with her body, with her eyes and inclined head that is casual and hyper-relaxed. She shakes her hair, which in sunshine is dark blonde and on dull days very light brown, and tucks a small wing of it that has escaped her pony-tail firmly behind her ear. The odder the situation you found yourself in — and this was something she had learned a long long time ago — the more ordinary your behaviour needed to be.

Mr Quinn shone the light on the staircase. 'I'll lead the way, shall I?' he said, standing intrepid and humorous on the first powder-flecked step, the torch beaming out of his chest, his massive glossy eyebrows, two shiny chestnut brushes over squinty eyes. On the back of his broad, curly-haired scalp, where the curls were thin and wiry, slightly anxious-seeming (his hair was the only part of him that wasn't luxuriant) there hung a little disc of spider's web that fluttered like lace.

It struck Martha then that Quinn resembled nothing so much as someone's huge, nervous uncle: well-meaning and enthusiastic, with abundant ruddy cheeks, smiles, reserves of flesh, but possibly lacking the morale to see things through. She observed him closely for a second, admiringly. He scarcely had the confidence to carry off his height, but if you straightened out the stoop, he was probably nudging six four. There was something dignified and sentimental about him. Martha tried to reckon it up . . . He was the kind of person who would inspire in children – any who came his way – huge affection.

('A self-made man, large, foolish, nervy, good-natured who laughs easily,' was her father's character sketch. 'Kind almost to the point of imbecility.'

'Loves easily, did you say?'

'I actually said laughs, but it's an interesting idea.')

'Assumed we'd see you last night at the book launch,' Mr Quinn was saying cheerily. 'Thought we might have had a chat about the arrangements then. Not a bad do, as these things go. Drank too much, not that that's at all unusual. Bit surprised your father didn't put in an appearance. Too grand to show at his own party, heh heh! Won't even play tennis with me now, hasn't for twenty years. People don't like to when they reach a certain level. They're afraid I'll bring down their standard. What they don't understand is that they bring up mine!' Mr Quinn swivelled round his torso and shone the torch down the staircase on to Martha's embarrassed knees. 'Rather thought *you* might have been there, though.'

'I had been meaning to go,' Martha said, 'but – but, when it came to it, it – it seemed like I didn't quite make it.' She rigged up a soft, beamy smile on her face, by way of apology, in case he should think of picking out her features with his torch again. 'You . . . er know what it's like!'

'Yes, of course. Well. Let's see. We bought the book, in any case, Linda said we ought, so that when your pa arrived we could get it signed, but then when he didn't show . . .'

'No.' Martha's steps were more confident now. She found there was less debris on the inside edge of the staircase, next to the wall with its brown gloss-painted rose-relief wallpaper, so that was where she positioned her feet as she climbed.

'Might leave the book with you and you can get him to scribble in it next time you see him. If that's all right. Linda was very definite about it.' Quinn waved it at her in his right hand, to emphasise the point, having fished it out of his jacket pocket. His mouth softened, fondly. 'She does get these ideas in her head, and it's always best to go along with them.'

'I s'pose.' How could she say she did not actually want that thin, dry brick he was brandishing in her new home, squaring her off day and night with its tight corners and sharp edges? That sort of sentiment would strike someone of Quinn's sensibilities as a sort of violence.

'In any case,' his voice dragged on each of the three words, 'I don't know what you've been told but there's four flats, on the top floor, your floor.'

'Right.'

'The rest of the building is used for storage at the moment, by the tourist shop and some of the adjacent offices. The owners are applying for planning permission to convert it to residential use in order to make it more attractive to me. I've got first refusal written into my contract. Everything's on three-month rentals at the moment. It's just a question of price now. Well, I say "just". We're trying to agree on a deal at the moment. Meanwhile they're sorting out the rest of the building. Some of the lower floors are practically derelict. There used to be some kind of . . . *clinic* operating on the second and third floors . . .'

'What kind of clinic?'

'Oh, well, you really don't want to know. It's closed now. Been closed best part of a year.'

'Oh, I see.' Mr Quinn was edging cautiously up to the landing at the top of the first flight. 'All right?' he called down to her, 'careful with this last bit,' illuminating again each step as she climbed in order that her foot didn't go into anything it oughtn't.

'Mmm,' she answered. She was thinking of the procedures such a clinic might offer without the proper safeguards: the rapid abortions, the botched plastic surgery. She envisaged its sorry-looking clientele, the jittery, staggering patients insane with grief, with wounds. Then some kind of saving-scolding mechanism came into play as it always did when she betrayed herself and she quickly shunted these pictures from her mind.

'I'll say now that one of the flats isn't in a great state. Some squatters were living there, we just saw the back of them last week. They had bad habits, you might say. Jim, the foreman, sorted it out, but their — their things are still there, though I'm sure it'll clean up all right. There's rather a nice pair of windows in the main room, and one of the other properties is still full of the last tenant's things, just accumulated family effects, toys and so on, and then the larger one is being done up now. An Iranian family is very interested in it, pretty much made a commitment to it, and then there's your flat, which is, well, you can see for yourself in a moment. It's no palace, but I do think it's got an awful lot of character.'

Martha quickened her pace.

They walked up another flight and another. The steps were broad and hard and Martha felt a heavy, fluid ache solidifying gradually at the base of her calves as her feet made shuffling noises. But her head was dancing. Mr Quinn's hands held the torch, the pure, white light, round and frilly-edged, marking out their journey ahead. His other hand gripped the banisters. The higher they got, the neater and cleaner things became. 'Nearly there now.' On the last flight the stone steps were slick and shiny, a dry scent of lemon pine detergent or disinfectant lingered in the air, bitter and overripe all at once. It made Martha gag. Two spider plants in wicker planters sat, sentry-like, on either side of the top step. 'Had a punk-rocker neighbour when I lived at home,' Mr Quinn was saying, shaking his head in a manner that suggested incredulity. 'Used to wear Dettol as perfume, would you believe?'

'No!' Martha's eyes opened wide.

'Oh, yes!'

'How funny.'

'I'll show you the worst first, if you don't mind. Get it out of the way, sort of thing.' Mr Quinn took her through the fire door at the top of the landing and into a small hall, off which four celery-coloured gloss-painted doors led. 'This is us,' he said, smiling at her. 'Mind the step.' He lit it up for her with the search light, pinning back the fire door.

The lock on the entrance to the first flat was broken and Mr Quinn put his huge bunch of keys back into his inside pocket, gingerly edging the door ajar. Martha peered round his shoulder, but almost immediately, before she could get a glimpse of it, he grabbed at the letter-box with the crook of his index finger, and tried to slam the door shut. But it would not shut, it just hung eerily on its hinges, an inch or two from the cracked latch. He switched off the torch. Martha reached for the wall, but there was nothing there and in her confusion her hand mistakenly grabbed Mr Quinn. 'Ooh,' she said, 'lost my balance. Sorry.'

Mr Quinn shone the torch on her upper body. She felt her clothes smarting with all sorts of ancient stains under its scrutiny, and she made to take a step back to get out of its glare, but there was nothing to step on where she trod and she stumbled and was thrown backwards. Her arms flailed wildly for something to secure her as she hurtled towards the staircase.

Mr Quinn grabbed at her as she lurched past, his fingers weaving tight red marks on her upper arm, through her clothes, his other hand pressing hard across her, on the front of her shoulder, on her throat. She closed her eyes and concentrated on her breathing for a few moments, eventually smiling her thank-you as he loosened his grasp. Twelve stone steps – that could see you off. She considered it for a half-moment.

Mr Quinn looked thoughtful. 'Ah,' he said, 'bit of a problem. On second thoughts, perhaps you better not go in there.'

'No?'

'It's a little bit worse than I've been led to believe. I think we'll get it cleaned up for you. There's no need, just now, to – I think we might leave it for now. I don't think it's really suitable for – for—'

'I don't mind. I'm a bit on the squeamish side but it couldn't be worse than – than . . .' She thought better of unravelling to him her present accommodation situation. It would sound garish, shaming: the lizard's ancient hostility, Stacey's menthol-smelling petroleum-jelly face cream that got everywhere, on the kettle, on the telephone handset. If you spent the evening with her, you'd have fibrous sticky patches on your ears, on your shoes, on your head when she wished you, greasily, good night. Stacey was a very physical person. She was all over Martha's friends, when she had visitors, even if they kept to her room. Also, she did like to speak her mind, waggling her strawberry blonde head, narrowing her eyes. 'You do know what your problem is, don't you, Martha?' chimed from her several times a week: the shrill, insightful curses.

Martha fixed her eyes on Quinn. 'I mean, it can't be as bad as all that.' Then, proudly: 'What with one thing and another, I . . . er . . . have seen quite a lot of life, you know.'

'Well . . . well . . .'

Mr Quinn peeled back the door and shone the torch in an

empty corner of the room so that the dark space was filled with a ghostly, dappled half-light. 'Perhaps, it does just need a woman's touch,' he murmured, nervously.

Martha blinked. The splintery raw floorboards were awash with lager cans and ashtrays brimming with cigarette ends, and dotted about the room were a few rotten-looking raggedy items of clothing, and little dried piles of cat-shit and a knot of twisted bedding – and the smell that came at her! It took her breath away. In the middle of the room sat a bobbly brown and orange sofa that had some kind of murky crust to it; it bristled, it crawled with dirt. At the back of the room crumpled sheets were tacked up at the windows for curtains, and these were covered with deep, crusted, oval stains, dark and intense at their middles, opening out into paler and paler rings of brown and light brown and yellow, right up to the hemming at the edges. These stains were so vivid, they were probably alive.

Martha turned her back and folded her arms tightly across her chest. Ridiculously, she felt the prickle of wet heat in her eyelids. She looked round briefly to make sure she had taken it all in fully, but there was worse: scattered randomly among the amassed debris on the floor, she suddenly made out, shiny and menacing, small piles of hypodermic syringes and needles. Her heart was stinging now, and there was a sharp-cornered lump at the back of her mouth.

She faced her father with it squarely. This was the first time she had ever accepted any kind of help from him and now she saw it had been an enormous mistake. She found him in her head, dressed in the quietest of grey suits, sitting on a complacent, pale sofa in one of the sunny upper rooms of his house, legs arranged elegantly in a double slant, streaked with sunlight, a newspaper raised high around him, like a shield. The words smarted in her throat, took shape on her lips. 'For someone of such a supposedly [was that too much?]

creative persuasion, you have a *staggering* lack of imagination.'
Both her mother and her father displayed parenting techniques
that bordered on the surreal, but what could you do? Some
people! was how she referred to them in her mind, her mother
and her father when they occasionally crept in, barged, even.
Some people!

Mr Quinn was talking on, clasping the fingers of his left hand
tightly with those of his right. Martha saw the knuckles whiten
and the fingertips turn a sharp crimson colour. 'Of course, I did
originally think this was more of a job for a . . . a young man.
I said as much to your father, on the fax I sent. In fact, I had
thought that your brother might be interested . . .'

'You see, he's not at all well,' Martha began. 'He's, for a
while now – he's . . . he's just not really himself and he—'

'I know. Your father outlined the situation,' Mr Quinn
offered gently, and as he spoke his eyes flooded with brilliant
kindness and a huge bolt of sympathy was suddenly launched
in her direction, a sort of appeal from his whole face including
his mouth and his chin and his large, sincere ears and it was so
entirely sheer and soft that the effect was slightly hard to bear.

'Thank you,' Martha mumbled, dizzy, off-balance.

A thought crashed rudely into her brain. If she telephoned
Stacey now and ate a bumper portion of humble pie, she might
just be able to get her old room back. She peered at Mr Quinn's
watch. It might not be too late. Stacey was out of control,
but she was in no way intentionally vindictive. Mr Quinn was
shooing her out of the room. 'Let's press on, shall we?' Martha
nodded seriously.

It came at Martha suddenly, stark and bare and with some
force, that she might end the day without quite having anywhere
to stay. She exhaled loudly, watching her breath gather and
disperse in the air. It was not the end of the world – that was
something that was always worth remembering at such times.

These days she was fairly strict with her feelings. A parent, who had an idea about such things, might ignore a child when it was behaving badly or oddly, only to pay it all the attention in the world when it was being useful or engaging, thus imparting fundamental lessons about discipline. Martha had begun to adopt this kind of approach with herself, some years ago, following a teenage that was so raw it had almost seen her off – and how her skin had thickened as a result! So she would turn her gaze abruptly from herself when she was stung now, or stumbling or flailing about – she would switch off, cutting out, making a diversion down a stillish slip-road, until it was a suitable time for things to be resumed. Low moments, by means of this rigorous kind of training, were so much rarer these days. She noted each occasion when she came up hard against something sharp and painful and it didn't get to her, celebrating the incidents dimly in her mind as little triumphs of courage over personality. She could almost shrug off these stinging things now, they were like water off a duck. That was progress and steps forward.

The only bad thing was, as you grew older and evened out in yourself and your sharpest corners were sanded down a little bit by ordinary civilian wear and tear, you expected these great strides to be reflected in the world around you, but in fact the world around grew more huffy and imperious by the day!

Quinn was fidgeting with the bunch of keys, fingers long and nimble, twirling and clacking the silver- and gold-coloured metal, and it took him a while to undo the series of locks on the door of the next flat. Once inside, the lights actually worked. It wasn't so bad. In fact, it was rather homey. Mr Quinn strode cheerily into a large room which was painted lemon yellow. A white enamel cooker and a sink and fridge and an L-shape of white kitchen cabinets occupied one corner of the room, and in its centre was a round wooden table covered in a floral oil-cloth and four kitchen chairs. Open shelves lined with red and white checked paper housed a large collection of coloured saucepans in descending sizes. Some cans of food were arranged on the worktop: peas, sweetcorn with red and green peppers, rice pudding, pinked cushions of ravioli in tomato sauce, the bright reds and yellows of the packaging tempered by a thin film of dust. Mr Quinn was nodding at her vigorously, as if to say, 'It's an improvement, wouldn't you say?' She followed him into a child's bedroom that had orange blinds and a wall of bunk beds. Mr Quinn picked things from underfoot, pyjama tops, bouncy balls, finger puppets. Opposite the beds was a wardrobe and glued on to its doors were three swimming certificates, a hundred metres, two hundred and twenty metres, elementary survival. Martha stumbled on a miniature cherry-red lace-up boot. She picked it up and laid it gently on the window-sill. It had barely been worn. Mr Quinn turned and led her into a second bedroom, which housed a large double bed and a kidney-shaped dressing-table that wore a gathered skirt of some faded blue chintz. Bottles of scent and combs and some silver brushes were arranged neatly on the table top, and then a row of dusty brown pill bottles and tubes of ointment, some lidless and crusted cream for rubbing on sore backs. A desire to avert her eyes from all these things stole over Martha. This was private.

'All this stuff will be gone by the end of next week, the week after latest,' Mr Quinn said, making a dismissive flicking gesture with the back of his hand.

'Are they coming back for it? Were they . . . Did they have to go in a rush?'

'You could say that. It's a long story . . . won't go into it now. We better press on,' and he ushered her out of the property and was already unfastening locks and dismantling alarms and then they were inside the third flat, which was huge. The square hall led straight into an enormous sitting room that had a whole wall of uncurtained windows giving on to elegant grey stone buildings opposite. Martha went to it and peered down several flights, a large illuminated picture of stringy fan-shaped pizza slices came into view, a burger bar glistened opposite, inviting, meaty; the outline of a skinny fried-chicken portion in pink neon flickered and crackled below, next to it a record shop, a snack bar called Adieu Paris, then the side view of a department store, stony, massive, its high-ribbed columns crowned with baby palm trees. She blinked and turned to face Quinn. He stood in the shadow of a marble fireplace that was almost as tall as Martha, apologising for the floor, which was covered in roughly nailed-down heather-coloured underlay. 'The parquet should be coming at the end of the month. They've got to make a wooden subfloor first. You can't do these things by halves.'

'No, of course.' Martha nodded. In the centre of the room, where there should have been some important piece of furniture, stood a wobbly old trestle table covered with interior-decorating magazines and swatches of fabric, a yellow and white silk-striped material, a gold-coloured fabric with tiny pale grey polka dots. Then there were rows of square wood samples and little circular counters of differently coloured marble, arranged in a fan shape, overlapping. Next to these lay some bound oblongs of carpet, in the palest colours, strung together on a bobbly metal chain, the silky and luxuriously soft short pile lending a liquid appearance to the gleaming shades of bone, ivory, oyster, dove. Martha put down the samples.

'This apartment is going to be spectacular,' he said. 'Nothing but the best. Marble from Carrara. Chandeliers from Murano.'

'Oh, nice.' Her eyes fell on two brochures, one called *Salon Français*, one called *Eurostyle*. On *Eurostyle*'s cover was a huge cut-crystal, gold and onyx lamp in the shape of an eagle with vast engraved wings and a haughty demeanour. *Salon Français* boasted a Louis Quatorze-effect three-piece suite made of gold wood and sky-blue watered silk. She flicked through the pages, past the Robespierre range of white cane dressing-tables, the Madame Pompadour silver and ormolu filigree fitted bedroom systems.

'Just come and see the bathroom. We're having gold taps like swans, or is it dolphins? I could show you the brochure from the bathroom-fittings studio, if you like. Linda went crazy. She loves all that stuff.'

'Could . . . could we see my flat now, d'you think? It's just I'm slightly—' She stopped speaking.

'Of course. I've been an oaf! I'm so sorry.'

'Oh, no, it's not that *at all*. It's just that I'm slightly tired and things.'

'Of *course*.'

Mr Quinn locked up the flat and reset the alarm, humming 'Clementine' under his breath as he went along. He crossed the little lobby and held his key to the one lock on Martha's new front door. She crossed her fingers, inside the long cuffs of her jersey. He threw open the door to reveal a corridor that was linoleum-floored and tiled to waist height, like a passage on the Underground. He gestured to her, delicately, to enter the apartment first, as though he were a guest in her home now. He brushed the edge of her shoulder with his palm as she passed in front of him.

Three closed cream-painted doors, with horizontal 1930s oblong panels led off each side of the corridor or hallway. Above each door was a dust-covered internal window, which allowed a certain amount of light to filter into the hall. Mr Quinn led her into the kitchen, which was a bright room painted in pale grey shiny paint, with a large apple-green dresser (empty) set into the back wall and a square Formica-covered table into which four cream chairs were neatly tucked. Some light-coloured enamel floor and wall cabinets, speckled with rust at their hinges, were positioned between two uncurtained windows opposite the door. The adjacent wall contained a small fireplace with a jade-coloured tile surround and brief wooden mantel. Next to this stood a squat fridge, its door jammed open by the side of a cardboard box. Three cracked white spotlights hung from a plastic track over the centre of the room, one of which was working.

Not bad, Martha thought. Not bad at all.

Quinn showed her round the rest of the flat. He took her into the room next to the kitchen, a room that was completely empty apart from a washbasin and glass over-shelf set into a little cupboard and out again and into another room that also contained nothing apart from the marbled beige lino floor that seemed to extend over the whole house. Next came the bathroom. Mr Quinn said, 'I'm afraid as yet there's no hot water. But I guarantee it will be on by the end of next week latest. I'll ring in the morning and try to hurry things up.'

They crossed the hall and Martha peered into the white-painted rooms on the other side of the corridor. These boasted an extremely threadbare grey carpet that was sewn in strips; still, it was good quality. She walked into the first bed-room, which contained a large window that benefited from the glare of a strong yellow street-light. The second had an identical window and a small white wooden fireplace and a dark wood 1930s office-y chest of drawers. The third, her room, had as its centrepiece a new salmon pink satin damask double mattress, still in its plastic wrapping, a large white wooden wardrobe and a little oak desk, such as a narrow-kneed apprentice might have sat at, a trainee clerk, in some not very prosperous olde-worlde legal or accountancy set-up. She recited in her mind the opening sentence of her thesis: 'It may seem odd to speak of influence when writing on a poet whose most glaring characteristic is his singularity.'

Martha was halfway through her thesis on a little-known, post-war American poet. He hadn't been an easy person to live with. An alcoholic, manic-depressive binge drinker and sometime mental patient with a keen eye for the ladies, an adulterer, a long-limbed, grizzly, incurable romantic with a broad, waxy forehead and the jitters, the part-time Catholic son of a suicide father, he had himself come to a terrible end, his body exploding after a hundred-foot leap from a spectacular bridge. But the poems! The best ones were as good as anything.

Mr Quinn was saying something. 'New mattress arrived this morning.'

'Thanks very much.' Martha slipped off her shoes and climbed on to her bed. The soles of her feet felt exhausted, dry, hot and achy and quite at a loss. 'It's very comfortable.'

Quinn was hovering on the fringes of the doorway, massaging intently the top button of his jacket in an anti-clockwise direction. 'Now, I suspect we need to settle one or two things.'

'Yes . . . yes.' Martha clambered up, nodding in a business-like fashion, while stuffing her feet back into her plimsolls.

'We'll talk in the kitchen,' he said, and led her there, pulling out a chair for her, straightening his jacket over the back of his seat. He laid down his keys and, as he spoke, traced the flesh of his thumb with the jagged edges of the longest key until it was dotted crimson. 'Your father, I assume, outlined the sort of arrangement I had in mind?'

'I mean slightly, but—'

'Well, what I thought was this. I would like you to visit each of the flats every day or so, every other day, and as far as possible keep them in order. It's just a bit of dusting and light cleaning, really, and if you could generally tidy up after the workmen who will be calling pretty frequently then that would be marvellous. Obviously no one expects you to scrub and polish because while the building work's going on it would be a waste of your time. But if you could make sure the staircase looks cared for, and the communal areas of the building. Now and then I shall be showing people round, prospective tenants, and then sometimes you'll be letting workmen into the building, so it's important the place looks like a going concern, that it doesn't seem neglected. I've arranged for the phone to be put back on tomorrow, so the various contractors will be in touch with you that way. As far as possible I'd like you to give the building a general feel of being occupied, a sense of hustle and bustle and well . . . of life. Of course, I know I don't need to tell you that I, er, don't mean all-night parties.'

'No, of *course*.'

'You know the way unoccupied places, vacant places, however charming in themselves, however well done, never quite . . . never quite *convince*? Well, that's what I'd like your contribution to be . . . Hmm,' he added, 'and keeping squatters at bay, of course, as far as that's ever possible. Just alert me if you see anything suspicious, that's all I'm really saying. In return, there's your accommodation and let's say seventy pounds a week. How does that sound?'

But Martha wasn't listening. She was eyeing up her new surroundings, imagining mornings spent idled away privately in bed with tea and books and a rock cake, and bouts of hard study at her desk, and a gentle household routine comprised of . . . well, she knew not what, plumping up cushions, sauntering over to Adieu Paris once a week for a spot of puff pastry, spurting free scent on to the inside of her wrists from the testers in the department store of an evening. Briefly she pictured herself applying sticky scarlet to her lips as an admiring shop assistant looked on benignly amid the lilac hustle and bustle of the beauty hall. It was going to be grand! No Stacey! No Lukey! No more scurrying about like an embarrassed beetle. If she never saw them again it really would be too soon.

'Under the sink in your kitchen there's a pretty comprehensive supply of cleaning things, but if you need anything else, just keep track of what you spend and I'll settle up with you at the end of the month, if that's all right. In fact, ignore what I just said, I'll leave you some petty cash to dip into if you need anything. That seems more civilised. I know people are quite particular about their products. Linda swears by – oh what's it called? – but then the smell of that stuff makes me feel quite nauseous.'

'No, yeah, I can see it's a . . . a slightly personal thing, in a lot of ways.'

'Anyway, what do you think? Can I take it my search for a caretaker is over or . . . ?'

'Suits me, Mr Quinn,' she said, with a grin. 'Suits me just fine.'

He drew a book out of his briefcase and laid it on the table. The spine said *The Lock* by Anthony Brazil. It was her father's book. 'I'll leave this with you, no hurry. If you'd just be so kind as to ask him to do it when you see him. That would be awfully good of you. To Linda, if he wouldn't mind. Or just his name. Whatever you think.' Then he began detaching keys from the large bunch that lay in front of him. 'Five, six, seven, eight. The front door. The communal door on your landing. Your flat. Number thirteen top, middle, bottom, burglar alarm, window keys. The first flat I showed you. Number twelve. They won't be coming back, the squatters, by the way, so you needn't worry about that.'

'No? Are they? Did they?'

'And here are the keys for the other one, number eleven.'

'That's the one with the toys and things.'

'That's right.'

'And they're definitely not coming back either, or . . . ?'

'No. No, they won't, I think I can assure you. Now is there anything else you want to ask?'

'Yeah, um, do you have any idea how long it's going to be for? I mean, it would be slightly useful to know and things, but obviously . . .' Her voice trailed off.

'Well, I can't tell at this stage. We are waiting for planning permission to install the lift, and there's no point selling the flats until we've got the leases extended to at least fifty years, but the applications are in place and there's no reason to suspect hitches, although if we do decide to rent, rather than sell, once they're finished then . . . the extensions would be less of a consideration . . . so you see it's hard to predict. If I can acquire some of the other properties in the building, once we've got a return on the top floor, then this project could take quite a long time. But it's impossible to tell at this moment. All I can really say is don't get too settled.'

'Oh.'

'I'll drop off your money on the first of each month, if that suits.' He drew a wad of notes from his pocket and placed them in her hand.

'Thanks very much.' She laid the money on the table: two hundred and eighty pounds. He counted out another forty, which was to be 'petty cash'. A small fortune. It had not occurred to her that she would be paid as well as receiving her accommodation. She thought to say it was too much, too good of him, but she had been living off next to nothing for so long. She could get a week's shopping for under seven pounds — easy: two packs of economy fruited scones, two pints of milk, porridge, fourteen cheap apples, rice, four currant buns, four oranges, four small potatoes, a red and a green cabbage, two chicken drumsticks . . .

Quinn took the evening paper out of his briefcase and laid it next to the money. 'I'll leave you this as well. There's a silly interview with your Dad, the usual nonsense, but it might amuse you. Now, is there anything else?'

'Well . . .' she forced herself to speak ' . . . you know the first flat we went into, number twelve?' Mr Quinn nodded. 'Well, I um . . .' she searched for a word that would be strong enough ' . . . I really won't be cleaning that up. I am sorry but it's actually a bit dangerous. I've, er, done that kind of clearing up before and, um, I mean it's slightly something I really wouldn't want or be . . . be be prepared to do again and things. If that's OK. You'll have to get someone in. Professionals. It's a bit of a health hazard for one thing and you can't just put needles in with the rubbish—'

'Oh, I do see that. I'm so sorry. I don't know what I was thinking. You see, I was planning to get a contract firm in to see to it. I'll book it for next week. I wouldn't expect you for a moment to—'

'I think you'd find anyone would say the same.'

'Leave it with me.' He glanced at his watch and stood up, holding out his hand. 'I'll be in touch soon.

'All right, then.'

'Bye now.'

'Bye. And thanks.' They shook hands, but she could have kissed him, full on the lips, such was her gratitude. She stood, crossed-armed and grinning in the corridor, while he let himself out and she heard the torch snap on and listened as his squashy shoes descended, carefully, the stairs.

Down on the street a car door slammed, heels clopped jauntily past the front door, some young women shrieked, 'He didn't!' 'He did!' 'No!' 'On my mother's life!' There

was a roar of buses and some odd muffled whirring noises —
rotating brushes cleaning the pavements, was it? She went into
the bedroom and lay on the balding carpet with her eyes open,
staring at the dark ceiling. The floor felt dry and stale against
her back. Soon the moon would be out.

Briefly, she envisaged the flats in their new incarnation.
Spotless and dust-free, no smudges, no smears, shiny, gleaming,
sparkling clean. She'd see to it those surfaces would dazzle with
their high, spangly sheen. In no time at all the sad odour of
neglect would be banished, the whole place responding to her
keen husbandry. Within weeks the transformation would be
complete, and the building would begin to reciprocate, a little,
her care. With this kind of thing it really was a two-way street
because when you peered into those glistening worktops, those
immaculate skirting-boards, what you saw, in part, was the good
in yourself! A gleeful, childish desire stole over her quickly to
run down into the street, grab a couple of passers-by and haul
them upstairs to marvel at her great good fortune. 'Look!' she'd
cry, flinging open the door to her huge new abode. 'Isn't it
great? Isn't it grand?' She got up and peered out of the window
for a prospective candidate, a mother out shopping for presents,
say, or a gangly teen.

But she would have to wait for her best friend Stella, who
was due round in an hour or two with her belongings, which
Martha had already packed into the back of Stella's van. Stella
had been on at Martha for weeks to move. 'Come and live with
me!' she'd insisted time and time again. Stella's flat was tiny —
the kettle lived on top of the television set and the saucepans
under the bed – but it had been a lovely idea. Martha felt proud
and blessed to have a friend who made such offers.

Suddenly relief was flooding every part of her body. She was
dizzy with it. It was audible, sending little involuntary heaving
sounds out of her mouth that were ripening into giggles. She

felt relief warm the cold centres of her bones, soften the hard thudding at her heart, melting the sharp, dry ache that had thickened at the base of her throat.

Presently she ambled into the kitchen, climbed on a chair and opened all the upper cupboards. An aluminium kettle, huge and ancient, she discovered, a lovely old biscuit tin – the Queen spangled and holy on her coronation day – an iron with unravelling flex and a leather shoe-cleaning kit were revealed. Many more things: a tartan box filled with screws and keys, a red toaster with a toasted-sandwich-making attachment. A tea-caddy containing some clear and lilac-coloured strings of beads, an alarm clock, some fluted pastry-cutters in several different sizes . . . She shut the door on the treasures. She descended the chair and tucked it neatly into the table. She imagined a little family made up of four sisters sitting at the table a hundred years ago, sewing things to scrape a living, trimming hats, writing love letters for the tongue-tied to send to their sweethearts, crocheting baby garments from white cotton yarn, feeding blue ribbons through the lacy edges.

She picked up the book that Mr Quinn had left on the table. *The Lock* by Anthony Brazil, it said. (The surname was officially meant to be pronounced so that it rhymed with frazzle, but few people seemed to know or care about this.) *A terse and stylish tragedy of manners.* She started reading the blurb. *Anthony Brazil's 17th novel . . . complex . . .* blah *. . . psychological . . . chilling . . .* blah *. . . triumph* blah *. . . world view . . . humane . . . prize* blah. She let it fall open in her hands, and read a few lines of it. A man appeared to be speaking to another man, 'Of course, a civilised fellow ought to be able to dine alone happily in a restaurant without a book.'

She placed the book back on the table, face down. Her mother could not abide eating out. It was very distressing when she did make the attempt. She tried to enjoy herself, to enter into the spirit of things, but finally she thought the sums of money involved shameful; it actually made her choke on the food.

Martha tucked the book away, on the seat of one of the chairs, under the table, so it was nicely out of sight. She spoke out loud in cheerful, larky tones, swinging her arms above her head, her wrists crossing and parting again, back and forth, like a stray islander waving to a passing cargo ship. 'I am ashamed to say I've never read a single one of his books, if the truth be known, Mr Quinn, in all honesty, between you and me, but you might just keep it under your hat now.'

'Yes, dear,' she answered herself, her eyeballs rolling ceilingward, her mouth forming a wiry, caustic smile.

It was true she had successfully dodged her father's entire literary *oeuvre*, the seventeen novels, the play, the essays, the *et cetera*, *et cetera*, with a series of well-timed body swerves and deft manoeuvres – not because she wasn't interested exactly, more because, well, for some other reason that had its roots in . . . What was it? Pride?

Of course she had not been able to avoid absolutely everything. A couple of short stories glimpsed in American magazines had fallen into her lap, an extract in a Sunday newspaper, a few pages of his first novel she had leafed through at a bookstall once, patchy portions of one or two of his slimmer volumes, a chapter or two of something scanned in the draughty lavatory of a friend's house. The thing was, what she couldn't help feeling was, what he got up to in his spare time, well, it really needn't concern *her*.

Martha looked up beyond the kitchen windows, imagining Baker Street, broad and unpromising, bloated with traffic, and in her mind she hurtled down its long straight mile to her father's house, the one she had also inhabited up to the age of three or four, which lay on the west side of Regent's Park. She brought to mind the stately crescent with its vanilla façade and many long windows. It was a sort of dream world to her now, the scale of things there, the life lived. Even the doors were huge and heavy and they swung shut behind you in an instant with an enormous crashing sound, making your heart leap.

She pictured her father's elegant figure coming down the stairs in the house by the park and watched as her smooth childish frame contracted to let him pass on the landing or in the hallway, and throughout the manoeuvre, in her heart she sensed quite clearly, quite neutrally, that what he was really hoping was that she would not see him.

Now she watches him passing her again more manfully, this tight-lipped baffling presence with the beautiful clothes, and he behaves as though he is strolling in some great boulevard somewhere, anxious that someone might address him, break up the thoughts that absorb him, genuinely believing that if he turns his head away just slightly then passers-by will not recognise him and he will just melt into the crowd.

Odd bits of his various plots, skimmed, speed-read, glanced at, absorbed unwillingly through chatter, stray newspaper clippings, hearsay, radio talks, osmosis even, are embedded sharply in Martha's consciousness, like shrapnel, the different people merging and revolving in her mind's eye, asserting their characters, and all the while their foibles, their talents for brutality narrowing rapidly into one sharp central consciousness. Some bits were innocuous enough: one of the many sour men was wrangling over some prices with an antiquarian dealer who specialised in first editions.

'Is it too much for you, sir?' the vendor suggested, with a saccharine curl to his lip, a little sharp-eyed dismissive leer.

'No, it's too much for the *book*,' the man countered, grandly, with a sharp expulsion of air, regaining, instantly, his ground.

There was a woman in her forties, a cinema frequenter who, deep down, had a horror of films, the happiness inside their imaginary worlds grating against her own clotted sense of unfulfilment, while any sadnesses the films displayed instantly served to augment her own. What really distressed her, it transpired, and this was a matter of great shame and scarcely admitted even to herself, was the fact that the people in the films she went to see always ignored her, as though she was nothing; they neither addressed remarks directly to her, nor did they take her feelings or personality into account. It was as though they continually asserted that she did not exist. This incensed her, then depressed her terribly.

In a different arena two brothers, vastly successful, are still spurred on by the earliest boyhood rivalries, still compete for their mother's good opinion, even though they are now in their eighties, their mother a hundred years old.

A family gathers to celebrate the ninetieth birthday of Mrs Shipton's father, or rather what would have been his ninetieth birthday had he not died fifteen years previously.

The parents of a suicidal child who resided in a mental hospital, were conferring with the boy's doctor about all the ingenious methods for self-destruction the boy had devised. If he had put that level of energy and application to, say, thinking up an advertising campaign, the quack remarked excitedly, why, he could have successfully launched a product, nationwide!

Martha strolled out of the room into the corridor and over to the bathroom, pulling the light cord, which didn't work, and using the toilet, wiping herself with some straggly tissues she found in her pocket.

She looked at her watch and tried to calculate when Stella's arrival would be. Stella was her oldest and best friend. Just now she was at home preparing elaborate food for a birthday party the following evening. Stella ran a small catering business from her flat, which was so completely stuffed with cooking equipment that there were colanders hanging on the back of the bathroom door and mandolins and steamer baskets and gravy boats on the shelves in the wardrobe. Stellar Food, her company was called. She had star-shaped, gilt-rimmed canapé platters and star-shaped moulds and pastry-cutters and Star of David mini muffin tins (kept under the bed).

Martha washed her hands and reached for a dun-coloured towel that hung from a hook on the back of the door, but when she touched it she saw it wasn't a towel, and when she looked again carefully as she shook her hands dry in the air she saw the outline of a garment hanging in the half-light. She put a hand to it and felt the soft woollen cloth of a ladies' coat, and beneath the woollen folds, a pale, silky lining. She drew off her jacket and slipped the garment on, walking herself back into the kitchen, which was the only room where there was proper light.

She fingered the fabric's soft caramel-coloured herring-bone tweed. It was narrow-lapelled, single-breasted, soft-shouldered, with a slight hint of a kick to its skirts, which fell to the highest point of her calves – a heroine's attire. She slipped it off and examined its interior, the glossy oyster-satin lining of the highest imaginable quality. Embroidered in black on a small white satin rectangle beneath the back of the collar were the words Christian Dior. She pictured a woman dressed in it, her sharp-lashed eyes obscured by milky clouds of smoke at a railway station, her face stricken by some exquisitely painful dilemma.

In a flash a biographical note made by the poet she was study-ing came back to her: 'Bought a blue silk jacket this afternoon that made me feel instantly at least three per cent more normal.'

She put the coat back on and promenaded round the flat, surveying the string of rooms, the scarcity of fixtures and fittings. She jangled the enormous bunch of keys, and bore them over to the front door, locking herself in for comfort and snugness. She felt larky in her new surroundings and also an unexpected sense of wealth. Back in the bedroom she opened the wardrobe to reveal a narrow floor-length mirrored panel on the inside of the left-hand door. She admired the coat and herself in it. When done up, she figured, allure would ooze from the slight suggestion that, under its softly tailored folds, nothing else was worn. She lay down on the bed for a moment, the plastic sheeting warm and squeaky beneath her, and drifted off to sleep. She dreamed she had travelled back in time to a department store in the 1950s and was embarking on a shopping spree and, with her fresh and crisp pink twenty-first century grant cheque and the wad of cash Mr Quinn had dealt her, she was carousing in the haberdashery department, the beauty hall, the womenswear. White-gloved shop assistants, perfumed and leisurely, displayed luxury wares to her at next-to-nothing 1950s prices: jaunty forest-green hats, polka-dot scarves, snake-skin luggage with amber clasps and sturdy handles.

She awoke to the sound of some kind of roaring in the street, a low single-toned engine whir, punctuated by regular thudding sounds. She peered out of the window and saw a huge grey dustcart creeping up the street, its metal teeth crunching up the street waste, which men in green uniforms threw into its mouth.

Martha went back into the kitchen, filled the large kettle and lit the flame of the gas cooker. She lit the oven also for warmth, and jammed open the door with the biscuit tin. Within minutes, tears of condensation were running down the Queen's chin and dripping on to the satin bodice of her coronation gown. Martha picked up the paper and flicked through it casually. In ten minutes a film about a librarian who runs away to Rome in search of adventure was starting for those in possession of a television. She flicked ahead a few pages. A steak and kidney pudding weighing the same as three small elephants had failed to break the world record. Shame! 'Disease of the month –

alopecia' was the heading on the health page. On the fourteenth page of the paper her father's inscrutable face hovered in front of her.

'Subtle-minded' was how he was described in this particular newspaper article, and as she read it the comment stuck her as strangely realistic. Certainly her meetings with him bore this out. The way in which his personality displayed itself was so understated, so restrained, so arch that it was actually impossible to get much of an idea of it either way, if there even was one.

Next to a person of his level of subtlety, you felt 'stupid, vulgar, garish, blunt and brash', wrote the journalist. 'On his face,' she added, getting a bit carried away, Martha thought, 'a smile or a frown would appear crass, almost hysterical.' A slight intensification or loosening of the gaze was 'as far as he would go'. In his company, the interviewer wrote, she felt *intense* embarrassment for the first time in her life that she was in the habit of streaking her hair!

Martha felt a theatrically puzzled expression steal across her features, even though there was no one about to observe it. She put a hand to her own chemically untreated hair and fingered some of the strands thoughtfully. This was not an ideal way to learn about one's relations, not really. Sometimes she wished that her experience of family life might be more like that of other people, but she read on.

The subtlety was a complex thing in his writing. It suggested roomy depths of personal understanding, a brilliant mind raking, minutely, the sum of all the information that there was about the human race with delicacy and tact and truth and everything to do with high quality and clarity of vision. But in person, in the flesh, what did he really amount to? the interviewer pondered. He was absolutely a closed book, playing his cards so close to his chest. To be so intensely private! A tiny increase in the angles of the lines at the corner of the mouth, or their gradual release, was all you had to go on. Why would he not give anything away, shine, make a brilliant quip or a breathlessly nasty aside? Where was the pith and spirit he displayed so easily on the page?

With all the riches of his thoughts kept firmly behind closed doors, it was extremely tantalising, the journalist continued, as if he genuinely owed her things, as though he, personally, had amends to make for her brief journey from west to central London. There was even the sense of an affront. What necessitated the secrecy, the brief sense that things were being thought and worked upon, but all of it internal, so you went away with nothing to show for it? What was he afraid of? He had really got to her. To spend an hour with a person and not get any sense of what he was like at all! The journalist was almost up in arms. An hour! Martha rolled her eyes. How ridiculous could you get? An hour was nothing.

She stopped reading and folded the paper, running her fingernail along the crease. Some years ago it had dawned on Martha, after the most cursory and accidental acquaintance with his writing style, that people like her father found the characters of their own making so absorbing and authentic, with their nervous tics, their cigars and sharp practices, their blunt-fringed hair-cuts, their apartments that were wanting in freshness, the intricate emotional wrangles that were the territory on which marriages were lived out among important eighteenth-century furniture, or the old women, who were always of 'desiccated' appearance with their winded velvet seating and winded lives, that the need for additional figures, real ones with working hearts and minds and real blood and guts of their own, was significantly reduced. Possibly redundant even.

Another thing troubled her occasionally, at peculiar times, such as when she was dressing after a bath, threading an arm into a sleeve-hole and sometimes noticed there was still white soapy foam, sticky and sweet-smelling, among the straggly hair in her armpit. Was writing about the ins and outs of unhappiness, with *so* much elegant relish, was it just a little bit cruel? She was thinking hard just now, straining, but if you went in for other people's distress, she thought, if the very fabric of it was actually stimulating to you, were you in some way contributing to it?

A shrill intermittent bell sounded suddenly, and Martha sprang up and picked her way down the five flights to let Stella in, striking matches as she went to safeguard her journey.

'It's unbelievable! It's un-be-*liev*able!' Stella kept repeating, stamping out some smoking wood shavings as she climbed the stairs, making Martha, immediately, a gift of a small chrome lighter and confiscating her match book. 'Just think — the heart of London's West End!' she cooed. 'How many rooms have you got?'

'Six.'

'Six! Oooh. Won't Stace be livid!' She beamed. 'You'll be the envy of all our friends!'

'Here's the kitchen.' Martha took her friend round merrily. 'It's slightly . . . was just thinking you can borrow it whenever you like, for work I mean, because there's loads of preparation space. I mean, if you have a big job on. Or whenever, really.'

'Thanks a million.'

'Here's the bedroom.'

'It's perfect. What a *huge* bed, might I just say?'

They drank two glasses of red wine from a bottle Stella had brought, opening it with a corkscrew she drew out of her pocket, sipping from two polystyrene cups she fished from the bottom of her bag.

'Raven Court,' Stella said, marvelling at the bare rooms, the expanse of blank wall. 'Raven Beauty Court, more like.'

'*Merci beaucoup!*' Martha grinned. They drained their glasses.

In a little pan on the stove some plain rice was now bubbling away.

'Have you finished off all your work?'

'Yeah, the cake's done, the vegetables are all ready, the chicken's marinating. It's just a question of putting everything together in the morning. Oh, yeah, I brought a few leftovers from yesterday, just in case. There's half a trifle and some Stilton and a few other bits and bobs.' Stella laid out her goods on the kitchen table, unwrapping the little silver packages, producing paper plates and white plastic forks and spoons. And then she was smearing crumbly cheese on to oatcakes and slicing up a tomato, draining the rice through a metal sieve and fluffing it with the prongs of a fork. She set the dish on the table. Martha spooned rice into her mouth, staring vaguely into space.

Martha: You know Stacey is . . . is . . . with child? She spoke the words delicately, with awe.

Stella: Is that right?

Martha: She's only six weeks but she's already bought maybe twenty little baby outfits on her credit card. All stuffed into the back of the cupboard because I know she's worried Lukey won't take the news too well. The clothes were beautiful, but I was slightly worried she was getting into debt and things, over her head, and in the end I said, shouldn't she wait till she was a little bit further along and had told Lukey and things, and she just lashed out at me, said terrible things, that I was jealous, all dried up with envy.

Stella: That sounds awful.

Martha: It was pretty bad.

Stella: Well, you're well out of it now.

Martha: Yeah, I know. But I do hope she's OK.

Martha sometimes pictured herself settled with a family man who loved her stoically, and adored the children. In fact if they had everything, in terms of family life, that children should have, rides on their father's broad and friendly shoulders, glossy-haired cousins, bedtime, uncles who exhibited bonhomie, spry aunts with an eye for luxury goods, drawers full of French blue and white stripy underwear, ironed and neatly folded (she would make sure of this), might the whole thing put her out, for her own reasons, mightn't it lead her towards a rather grim and pinched frame of mood? It was, of course, impossible to know these things, but all you could really be sure of was that it was best not to put a toe in the territory until you had that side of things sorted out; it was the very least you could do. What an indignity it would be to live under a regime where every joy doled out to your child made you notch up a loss or a lack on your own pathetic tally. No, thank you.

Stella had found a small stash of catering-size foiled butter pats in her bag and she was stacking them up in a narrow golden tower.

Martha: I was talking to my mum a few weeks back. I said, 'Mum I've got a lot to offer someone, haven't I? I'm easy-going. I'm kind, considerate, I'm a good listener, I don't have expensive tastes, I mean compared to a lot of people I'm slightly, well . . . I'm not much bother and things . . .' and guess what she said?

Stella: What?

Martha: She said, 'And you've got big tits!'

Stella: No!

Martha: It's true.

Stella: Have you definitely pulled the plug on Dan the Man then?

Martha: Yeah, no, I don't know, really. I mean, there certainly haven't been many squeaks from those quarters lately.

Stella (brightly): That's something, I suppose.

A long pause followed.

Martha: You know there's much worse people in the world than Danny, Stella.

Stella: Well, that's always an important consideration, I suppose.

With her teeth, Martha sucked hard at the pockets of flesh that lined her mouth.

Stella thoughtfully laid the cheese to one side and began surveying the trifle, finally placing the bowl out of her own reach and nibbling another oatcake instead. She began collecting up their rubbish, stuffing plates and used cutlery and cups into a plastic carrier that she then folded over and stowed away in her bag. She wilted a paper napkin under the tap and started wiping the table, without seeming to notice what it was she was doing.

Martha: Stella?

Stella: Yes, Martha?

Martha: I mean, if you have a baby one day, I mean when you do, you won't, I don't know, completely drop me and things, will you?

Stella: Don't be crazy. I'd be much more likely to neglect the baby.

Martha (vastly impressed): Really?

Stella: Of course! You know me!

Two

Next morning Martha wakens gradually, twitching open her eyes, arching her lower back and extending her warm legs luxuriously towards the corner of the mattress that lies in the middle of the floor, a large pink quilted ship at sea in an empty room. For several seconds she wonders where she is, but the doubt is pleasant, exhilarating.

With a deep sigh and a theatrical grimace she covers her eyes with her hands. Don't say she had . . . she hadn't, had she? . . . woken up in some sort of hideous . . . *situation*? 'Oh, please don't let it be that,' she mouths the silent prayer, scouting about the room for signs.

At the foot of the bed, askew on the bald grey carpet, lie ripped-up shreds of polythene and the discarded tissue paper that wrapped Martha's sheets for their journey from Stacey's flat. Gradually, as she regards the delicate swirls and mounds of unfurled white leaves, her precise location dawns on her. It reaches her like news of the best kind, relief flooding her heart and mind. Of course! She savours the particulars of her new abode as she stretches and turns in her half-sleep, counting up the rooms, calling to mind all the vast empty spaces.

Almost immediately she comes up against something that limits the outward motion of her limbs. Another pair of legs that are bony, boiling hot and thickly matted with hair are stretched out on her sheets. Their outline, hard calves and narrow ankles, is familiar to her when she traces them tentatively with her toes. Her room is night-dark apart from a thin strip of dawn light that spills in at the top of the window where a red blanket is pinned to the window-frame, its centre sagging slightly. Martha rolls over and takes in a man's ashen face, crowned by a little coronet of glossy chestnut curls. Danny? He sleeps with a smooth, angelic smile on his mouth, his arms wrapped tightly round a pillow, as if it is his child.

In the street outside she hears a couple quarrelling good-naturedly, they stop beneath her window, and then a spluttering, heaving sound wafts up, a stream of liquid, thin and lumpen, hitting the pavement and more coughing and retching and spitting noises. The sound is drowned suddenly by the juddering roar of a night-bus, stopping and starting up again, the wham of the electric doors flinging shut and then quiet.

Martha examines the head on the pillow that looks so peaceful and makes her think of lullabies. Where had it sprung from? Her mother occasionally sang her a lullaby about three sailors from Bristol City, who ran out of food and had to eat each other. It was terrifying.

'Danny,' Martha whispers, almost soundlessly. He does not stir. 'Danny?' she tries again, although this time the sound of her lips opening and closing and the crackle of some spittle in the back of her mouth is the only noise she makes. His expression alters, his smile slackens slightly and then returns to his mouth, even more brilliantly. What she had seen before, on the other nights, at tender moments, is nothing compared to this.

She revisited the twelve nights she and Dan had spent together, at large intervals, over the past eighteen months, all their sweetness and futility magnified so that they seemed to her the richest moments of her life and also the most humiliating.

Lying in bed, happiness swelling in her body, overwhelmed with strong, delicate feelings for someone – she considered the way his particular eyelashes, elegant and spidery when he fell asleep, would be thick and matted at the time of his waking – the fierce hot longing, on her part, for a kind word or a bit of admiration, nothing spectacular, just to be thought a bit funny, a little bit pretty. And sometimes this sort of comment came through, although often his amorous pronouncements were of a more general nature. 'This is what it's all about,' he'd say, trailing his fingers on the smooth slope of skin that ran from her neck to her underarm to her waist. 'There's nothing better in the world than this.' But she didn't trust herself to reply. He spoke of a generic contentment, whereas hers was of a more specific order.

She never quite saw any of it with him, but she had the vague feeling that he liked the high life. For him what could be nicer after some delicious food in a restaurant, drinks in a bar, dancing at a party, boisterous and romantic in drink, perhaps a little unsteady from its after-effects, than calling in on a girl. Carrying on the festivities into the small hours. The soft warmth of a girl's body supplying the perfect foil to the sense of an ending.

But to her each night spent might have marked something more ambitious: the striking up of something delicate, the arrival at an understanding, at the very least some kind of embarkment.

He was always perfectly pleasant in the morning, he never sloped off in the night leaving her to face the day and the strangulated sheets alone, instead he often took her out to breakfast in a local café, their eating of eggs or sausage or rock cakes, their slurping of tea having a holiday feel to it. They had running jokes like a normal couple, pretending to mishear each other so that 'Extraordinary!' became

'Strawberry' or 'Sean Connery' over the brown Formica café table top.

One thing she sometimes wondered, did the fact that she took the precaution of not quite having sexual intercourse with him stop their romance from really 'taking'?

At their last meeting they had talked for nearly two hours about concerns he had for his sister, that she had fallen in with a nasty crowd whom he feared depended too readily on drugs, and that he didn't know how to get through to her without being heavy-handed. Between them they evolved a strategy for his dealings with her that was kind but would not make him feel he had colluded with the more negative aspects of her behaviour.

Martha had experience in this department herself. Her brother had been estranged from the family for years now. His life had become so extreme, his demands so huge and impossible, his angers and resentments towards the family on such a dizzying scale, so dearly hoarded and tended, so hot and fuming in their separate, careful compartments — he was quite systematic about it, they were the only things in his life that defined him in a way he understood, it seemed — that having a conversation with him was actually shocking. He exploded with accusations from seventeen years ago and cheerful, vicious boasts about his hepatitis scare or his gangrenous toe. The latest inflammation or infection. You could not mentally process his complaints, they were so violent and bizarre. Finally, if the language he used to express his fury and despair to you was one of needles sinking into his skin, many many times a day and also at night, what was there left for you to say to his wiry frame, his white, sullen face? How did you counter the 'I'll live!' he barked at you, threateningly, when you asked him how he was.

Danny had seemed indebted to Martha's fellow feeling.

There was something between them now, something truly intricate and emotional, a more authentic kind of nudity than the other sort, which to him was evidently second nature. They had said they might speak again soon on the matter of their wayward siblings, they had even discussed attending a meeting for people who were in the same boat as they were, but still no call came. 'You've got to stop treating your heart like a hotel,' was what Stella said. Her other friends said things that were worse.

Martha lies half dreaming half sleeping until morning comes. Again she cannot imagine where she is. For a moment she thinks she must be at the man's house, this strange, empty room with nothing in it, no traces of personality. Then she remembers. She creeps out of bed and slips on the tweed coat over her nightdress. It is a hugely glamorous garment, considering it is just an old foundling. There is something deeply female in the suggestive cut of its lapels, the darts and gathers of its skirt, its narrow-waistedness. Noiselessly she stuffs her bare feet into her plimsolls and ducks out of her front door, sprinting recklessly down five flights of stairs, leaping the last few into the large square of rough, dusty concrete that serves as an entrance hall to her building.

Sometimes, after she spends the night with Dan, little spikes of regret gather in a pink rash on her neck and at the top of her back as, after a visit to the hairdresser's, short, cut hairs, escaping the pile of locks being swept away by the junior, itch and prickle sharply under your clothing.

Out in the warm breeze the pavements heave with Saturday-morning shoppers, and Martha moves against the general flow, which takes some negotiating, but she finds herself liking the crowds, you can lose yourself in them, become anonymous. Increasingly as she weaves in and out of the people, it comes to her that setting up home on a street that everybody knows, where hordes of gorgeous people flock on a daily basis from all over the country, well, it is actually making her feel like a success. The World of London shop next to her building is doing a roaring trade this morning, thimbles embossed with sharp-nosed royal princesses and Union Jack water-wings all seem to be flying out of the store. There is a constant buzz of people rotating the plastic postcard carousels that flank the entrance way: the Queen smiling, the Queen frowning and waving, the Queen in lemon looking as though she's about to sneeze.

As she blinks and smudges the clumps of sleepy-dust from her eyelids it seems to Martha that there is something extra bright about the morning light and her surroundings, which glow crisper and more colourful with each moment. She marvels at the gleaming shop-fronts with their elegant arrangements of merchandise, the mannequins in the shop windows dressed in seven or eight garments, red roses embroidered on a turquoise lacy bodice and skirt, a cardigan, boots, hosiery. Even the piles of lilac and black rubbish sacks that lie in clusters at the kerbside and the discarded polystyrene hamburger boxes, orange and hinged in the gutter, seem beautifully coloured and expertly made. How can this be the street where she has woken up, where she lives? She ponders the question with the utmost cheer.

The fresh morning on her face is lively and bracing. The scent of chips and reddened chicken quarters fills her nostrils from a streetside heated cabinet that borders the Adieu Paris awning. She blinks. All the familiar objects around her, the great stores, the little shoppers' landmarks, seem to have a sheerness to them that makes them more alive, her own. She might become a connoisseur. 'Oh, no! You don't want to get your chips there! They only change the fat every eight weeks. Like eating ash. You mustn't buy chestnuts off him, he uses an inferior Spanish brand, they'll be half rotten, as often as not. Oh, yeah, that man there will do you ten tulips for one fifty, if you pick your moment.' When she peers down at it even the back of her hand seems pinker, seems bluer and more fleshy – the nails especially oval, hyper-real, hard, semi-opaque and coral-coloured with milky-hued tips.

It begins to rain, warm slanty drips falling against her knees and ears. The year is slipping forward, and there is an idea of autumn in the air, she hears people complain of it, although the weather is really very mild, the leaves only just beginning to crisp and colour. Martha perseveres through the crowds. It is the tail end of the sale season and it is difficult to weave the wrong way through the walls of sturdy, tenacious, last-chance bargain-hunters. They will not leave the West End until they find items of such consummate good value that their friends at home cry out with envy and admiration. Martha is confused about bargains. Her mother bought things because they were the cheapest available – bent tins, seconds, off-cuts, misshapes, flood-damage sale-stock – and her father, reassured by a hefty price tag, was instantly drawn to what was most expensive.

The two households, her mother's and her father's, were so different that to try to find similarities, to try to link the two operations even in the slightest way was actually impossible. It gave you huge headaches. To have a foot firmly in each camp would have actually made you a freak.

A gaggle of young girls surge towards her, glamorous in the extreme, out on a spree in strappy dresses and pointy, clacking shoes, the whole circle heaving, rocking from side to side with extravagant mirth. Martha glimpses the sophisticated black lacy undergarments that peep out from the edges of their glad-rags, bold and old-fashioned against their milky and rosy skin. She takes in their elaborate make-up and brilliant hair – so dazzling that they look like the colour and brightener have been turned up as high as they can go. Stopping to admire them, she tries to get the measure of their blithe tenacity, wondering whether it is something she has or could acquire, finally following them through the heavy glass doors of the nearest department store, her corner shop!

The shop itself seems to be undergoing some kind of brutal renovations. There are hoardings throughout the store behind which new escalators are under construction. You can hardly hear yourself shop with the thud of change, the angry sounds of sawing, and the drilling and the workmen, all in Sta-prest navy overalls with gleaming silver buttons and shiny black leather boots, cackling and swearing to one another good humouredly. When you think about it, the place is practically a building-site. Placards in store depict the smart new central atrium that is being constructed, the overhaul of the easy-flo escalator system, the new little pockets and corners for refreshments and recreation that are springing up on every floor. The men behind the fish counter in the food hall seem to have been kitted out in dazzling navy and white striped coats with sharp lapels. She wonders if this is a recent innovation. On their heads perch jaunty, bleached-straw boaters, on their feet calf-high, white wellington boots. Looking at them standing in line, framing neatly the shoals of red talapia, golden haddock fillets, tuna steaks, whiting, mackerel and salmon portions, they seem on the verge of breaking into song.

In her father's house that faced the park there was a long narrow basement room, a store in which large quantities of goods were kept: packaged foodstuffs, tins, bottles and jars, boxes of tea, sacks of rice and potatoes, bottles of whisky, cleaning products, matches, stationery items, and also household tools, tennis rackets, Thermos flasks and a large wicker hamper filled with red plastic picnic ware. This room with its white walls and blue-black marbled linoleum was known as The Shop. It had been one of Martha's favourite haunts: you could sit tightly wedged between the spare fridge and some sacks of flour, the air dry and cool, and no one would disturb you for hours.

Unable to resist a quick tour, a sort of personal stock-taking, Martha dashes up the escalators, breathless and excitable, just absorbing the array of goods, familiarising herself with the fine items she surveys. Like news of the best kind, it dawns on her that with just one concentrated lunge from her front door she can be at the heart of plenty whenever she likes: evening dresses, white ceramic soufflé dishes in descending sizes, board games in brightly coloured boxes, sets of soap in hinged wooden cases that are shaped like lemons, flower-patterned tins of crisp Italian biscuits. She fingers the powdery white pile of some jumbo bath towels on the fourth floor, thinking of the future.

In the children's department two black nuns are out shopping for baby clothes. One holds up a little pink dress, with ladybirds embroidered on it and a scalloped hem and neckline, the colour shocking against her dark skin, her black and white clothes. She makes some thoughtful measuring movements with her hands, trying to conjure up the size of the child they are shopping for. The other nun, a younger, softer-looking woman, nods enthusiastically at the garment, but her heart isn't in it. Martha looks at them clumsily searching for the price tag, checking the dress's make and washing instructions. Then, with horror, she sees that the younger nun's eyes are glossy with tears. She is having some sort of collapse, her mouth gaping open as if she is emitting screams, but no sounds come. They put the dress down, the older woman feeding a comforting arm round the other's shoulders. They scuttle across Childrenswear and Shoes and

Toys to the escalator and rapidly make their way out of the store.

Back in the food hall Martha balances her purchases in her arms against her body. Bacon, eggs, tomatoes, a loaf of brown bread, milk, orange juice. It will cost a fortune, but there are things to celebrate now, and she can almost hear her wages thick and crackly in the soft pocket of the coat.

She puts down her shopping, just as she is about to drop it all, on the counter by an unmanned till and, with almost no warning, the tail end of the evening comes back to her. The doorbell had rung at ten to three, and she had raced out of bed and down the stairs and into the hall, still largely asleep, and through the letter-box had come a low voice, drunk and full of the promise of romance. 'It's Danny,' came the hoarse whisper. 'Stacey gave me your address. You're not sleeping, are you? I was just passing the end of your road,' he said. 'Can I come and see you for a second? I won't stay long. I wanted to ask you something.' Within minutes of his arrival, his eyes filmy and sensuality-bent, he mumbled, 'I do love you and everything,' and then, with his hand in Martha's, he had promptly passed out in a kitchen chair, still buttoned into his coat. For a while, long, low, comedy croaks were emitted from his mouth at regular intervals, only it wasn't quite funny, then he went quiet.

Martha squirms as she recalls her gentle and then quite strident attempts to wake him; how her systematic pushing, tugging and shaking of him, half an hour later, then another half an hour later when she herself went to bed, proved unsuccessful. It was ridiculous, really, she thought, as she retreated singly to her bed again after each vain attempt, it wasn't as though she hadn't slept alone almost every night of her life. And yet she had woken beside him.

She runs back home with a spring in her step and a strong

longing to reconfirm the fact of the many white rooms, rooms she can just about call her own. She races up the stairs, depositing her shopping in the kitchen.

Her flat is spectacular in the morning light: in the hall the marble pattern on the dusty lino looks rich and complex and the tiles on the wall are sparkling. Peering through the open doors, she looks kindly on each separate room. That the absence of other people could feel like such complete luxury amazes her. No Stacey! No Lukey! She blinks proudly at the wealth of space, beams at the idea of this exhausted building poised on the threshold of promise, just about to come into its own. It is the sort of place where anything might happen. The large empty space is a setting for whatever she wants now. It comes to her suddenly that the feelings she is harbouring for it are actually ones of love. But it brings with it responsibilities, the plenty, that expectant little desk. Even the sounds of other people's vomit – well, it was *real*.

Just then she hears Danny rummaging about in the bathroom. She remembers with regret that there is no hot water. She had forgotten all about him, but she listens to the sounds he makes peeing and washing with a largely open mind. Proceeding quite merrily, she hangs up the herringbone coat on the point of her bedroom door; sliding off her shoes and straightening the sheets and blankets, she clambers back into bed. Almost immediately she drifts back to sleep. Some moments later, when the brightest imaginable rays of sun are flooding in over the top of the red blanket she has pinned up as a temporary curtain, and the street noises grow louder and more lively, the thick roar of buses, the rumble and squawk of taxis – it's a bit like being in bed in the middle of the street – she vaguely senses someone, a Danny person, stumble into her bed, kissing wetly her shoulders, and then he begins rubbing himself against her eagerly, with clumsy gusto, like a little dog. Before she knows where she is, what day it is, whether she is asleep or waking and who it is she is dealing with, she feels someone's limbs thrashing about next to her, and suddenly, quite unexpectedly, hot semen spurts against the back of her leg.

Awake now, wide awake, Martha remains absolutely still, biting the pockets of flesh that line her mouth until they go numb. Then she draws herself calmly out of bed and wanders into the bathroom. The bathroom floor is damp, and she steps into the bath, turning on the taps. Gathering up the sticky hem of her nightdress she draws it carefully up her body so that it does not make any contact with her skin. She fills her mouth with air, in order to avoid any smells that may linger as she pulls the garment over her head, crushing it into a ball and flinging it into the waste-paper basket. She turns on the taps and sits down in a shallow puddle of freezing water, shivering as the bath fills around her, dabbing at herself gingerly and then with a thoroughness, scrubbing both her legs and her arms until the skin is pink with tender red patches, stung with cold.

She works away at herself, taking thick controlled breaths, fury rising off her like smoke. She whips up mounds of icy white lather, which she spreads, like a foamy second skin, across her stomach and the tops of her legs. Something needs to be frozen out, that's all she knows. Ridiculous large tears droop warmly against her nose, which is now crimson with cold, dribbling down her cheeks, as she reaches for her toothbrush, squeezes a thick sausage of paste on to it, dips it into the bath water, and sets about cleaning her teeth. She brushes each tooth carefully, on the front and at the back, beginning with small fast circular motions at the gum line, and then lighter, slower, sweeping strokes up the flush front of each tooth, as the dentist had shown her, even though her teeth are chattering away. After a while she raises her body to its full height in the bath, steps out of it, crams the nightdress into the rubbish bin and wraps herself in a towel. It is a dim source of pride to Martha that she hasn't minded in any serious or detrimental way anything that has happened to her for a considerable number of years and she is not about to begin now. She drapes her coat over her shoulders, loosely buttoning the woollen garment over the damp cotton towelling, shocked at the sudden weight of the soft wool that smells of kindling. She slips her wrists into the armholes, cool ancient satin against her elbows. Tiptoeing to the kitchen, the long bath-sheet trailing out below the hemline like a little train, she sits herself down on the chill lino, cross-legged, next to the fridge, feeling its soft, low hum against her back, her body making little nervous heaving movements, her eyes and nose streaming into her collar.

After a while Danny's footsteps sound, hollow against the lino. He lingers semi-clad in the doorway. 'I'll make some tea,' he says. But she waves at him, jerkily, to sit down again, and she spoons tea-leaves into a teapot and they both listen for what seems like an age to the sound of the kettle's convulsive boiling and the water pouring. All her movements are carried out with extreme caution. She fetches two thin china cups from one of her boxes in the hall, unwraps them and places them, saucerless and unrinsed on the table. She bought him a present recently, a mug with the words and music to the song 'Danny Boy' printed on it, the lettering in green, lyre-style Irish Tourist Board characters, the musical notation in black. Both verses. She saw it staring at her from one of the boxes. 'But come you back when summer's in the meadow,' she reads. 'Or when the hills are husht and white with snow.' That's her favourite line. In a mildly self-reproving spirit that involved blushes and one or two semi-stern expressions, Martha often picked up little trinkets for him that bore his name, a pen, a pink stick of rock from

Brighton pier that spelled DANNY in ruby letters, all the way down to the end, but somehow these things never found their way into his possession.

She can tell from his face, from the way his body is crunched over and the constant fidgeting of his hands with one of the buttons on his shirt, that he would rather be anywhere else in the world than where he is now.

'Cheers for the tea.'

'That's OK.'

He puts down his cup and stands up, drawing a small brown vial of pills from his inside coat pocket. 'Have one of these,' he says, handing her the bottle of yellow pills.

'What is it?'

'It's diazepam – Valium. Only five mils. Have a couple if you like.'

'Oh, OK.' Martha swallows the pills and Dan takes two himself. They wash them down with giant swigs of tea. His need, his distress as great as hers, on the other side of the table. Once or twice she thinks of extending an arm towards him, touching a toe against the back of his knee, even smoothing down one of the curls that spring across his forehead, but she holds back. She does not want to presume on his feelings.

Through the bedroom window she watches as he climbs singly into a taxi. The cab shudders in limbo as the driver turns to question his passenger. Martha looks at the top of Danny's head, raised for conversation, through the cab's back window where, on the back ledge, a square pastel-coloured box of tissues and a stack of magazines lie. She feel her legs surge forward and, like a passenger in someone else's vehicle, finds herself speeding wildly down the corridor out of her front door, down the stairs, across the hall, vaulting buckets and abandoned packets of sugar and the discs for a sanding machine, and out of the door on to the street, rushing towards the taxi, which is still throbbing and gurgling opposite the entrance to her building. 'Dan,' she cries out, 'Dan, wait a minute,' but he is suspended in another world, separated from her by glass and steel and diesel oil. 'Dan, wait.' She stops in the middle of the road, calling to him from just a couple of yards away, willing him to turn round, to haul her into the cab with him, as he has done playfully after parties once or twice. But he doesn't seem aware of her. She thinks of climbing in beside him now, but something prevents her and then the car, black and shiny and muscular, rumbles noisily to clear the road of jay-walkers and stray shoppers, and speeds away. Once she knows it will be impossible for him to hear she calls his name at the top of her voice.

'Danneeeeeeeeeeeeeeeeeee.' Heads turn sharply to stare at Martha. A mother with a double pushchair collides with her, sharply, scraping a patch of skin from her ankle, which bleeds thick drips into her shoes. 'Why don't you fucking look where you're going?' The twin children start to wail and kick their legs. But she hardly hears the woman or her infants. She just gazes after the taxi, which is almost out of sight now, weaving in and out of the bus lane, disappearing round the back of Marble Arch, now at the mouth of Bayswater Road. It is all she can do not to wave. Still, she nods to herself as she slowly mounts the endless cold stone steps, Come on now, she searches for a way of putting it neatly, Look, you don't inhabit so starved a state that the last few hours can be seen to constitute romance.

In her flat the only remaining sign of him, apart from a lingering smell, which is a bit like roast lamb, is the bottle of pills that lies, unlidded, on the kitchen table. She sits down and tips them into her hand. There are twenty-six altogether. Is he trying to kill her on top of everything? You could significantly reduce the female population with stunts like that, whittling away at their confidence and conveniently leaving them the means to whisk themselves out the picture, in case they became bothersome. She shrugs her shoulders and makes a tutting sound with her tongue against the roof of her mouth. The lengths these men would go to to eject you from their lives. As if she had ever even telephoned him!

Two days before Martha's thirteenth birthday, when the days in the house by the park with its private air-blue curtains and its thick panelled doors were firmly rooted in the past, she had locked herself in the bathroom of her mother's home, shivering in her underwear with a headache of such intensity that it gripped at the tendons in her neck and severely impaired her vision. She lay down on the floor, reeling as a thick barrage of feelings came at her, with such violence and speed, that her young, bewildered heart was entirely unequal to them. She felt as though her skin had been scraped back and all her nerves, the huge network of interdependent wires and junctions, were exposed, raw and loose-strung for anyone to pluck at and grab. Her head rang and smarted with all sorts of sharp threats, and a lurking, throbbing sense that mad things had been assumed, by herself as much as anyone else, about her age, about her strength of character. She heaved herself up, staggering and dizzy-headed, and dragged herself over to the large mirrored cabinet above the sink. Dimly, she wished she wasn't such a one for taking things to heart.

Flinging open the cupboard door she rooted about until she found some metal strips of pills. She depressed the small foil-covered indents, scraping free the little chalky tablets with her thumbnail, and lined them up, forty-two, on the cloudy lip of the basin. She cupped them in her palm, held her hand under the tap so that the white dots bobbed about on a pink pool of water then lapped up liquid and medication in five brief slurps. Mistakes, grave and careless, that had been made with her crashed into her consciousness, one after another, layer upon layer assaulting a second time her shaky, heavily breathing frame. The light around her seemed harsh and excluding, ice blue like the shadows given off by a television set when you looked in through an uncurtained window and saw a family, pallid and luminous, spreadeagled on sofas with bowls of snacks and slippers and blankets. She went to the front of the house and peered out towards the crossroads. On each corner of the intersection she saw one or two girls, mainly dressed in black, shivering, waiting.

The street into which Martha and her mother moved when they left the house by the park was named after a famous anti-slavery campaigner. It was a busy road, full of solid, four-storey, plain brick houses with broad bay windows and sitting rooms with marble fireplaces. About half of the houses in the road were divided into flats and there were some large seedy-looking brick and clapboard hotels in the parallel streets. There was a lot of pavement life, teenage girls roaming up and down the kerbside in groups of two or three chatting and cursing and shrieking with laughter at the crossroads, by the narrow patch of pavement by the off-licence, at the turning into Brownswood Road. They always looked lively and businesslike, but also they often appeared to be cold, dressed in clothes that never seemed to provide adequate protection from the elements: skimpy skirts and bone-white legs in winter; short sleeves revealing arms riddled with goose-bumps, and particularly blue veins, the hairs standing on end. Martha walked past them every day, foolish in school uniform, name-taped blazer and scarves and jumpers and vests, and sometimes they'd nod to her, 'All right?' as she passed them, shy and awkward. 'Hello!' she'd pipe back at them, with a smile.

Martha looked on anxiously as the smallest of the girls climbed into a green car, following some speedy negotiations, a girl not much older than herself. The distant tinkle of an ice-cream van floated in and out of hearing. 'Frozen marge', her mother called it, after which it had never quite tasted the same. Before that she'd liked the oyster, a rounded double wafer lined with mallow, filled with ice-cream, dipped in chocolate-flavour coating and desiccated coconut flakes then trickled with chocolate sauce, but it was much too expensive. Everyone said she had a sweet tooth and it was true. She retraced her steps to the bathroom. The floor under her feet was like ice now. She lay down on it and huddled herself in her arms. She wrapped her feet in an old T-shirt, stroking them, tracing the outline of the five smooth white toes as if they belonged to someone else, to a child.

All this had followed one bitterly cold winter's night when a man had come to her mother's house at two o'clock in the morning, ringing and ringing on the bell, shouting out into the night, pounding his fists against the front door, running up to it with all his weight and heaving himself at the entrance, his hard boots crashing against the wood, his strange low screams echoing through the house. Martha's mother burst into her room, her long, muscular arms tensed, her eyes darting and alert, her entire physique, even her shaggy red hair, braced for action, for success. Calmly she instructed her daughter to call the police. 'Then close your door and get back into bed.'

While Martha dialled, her mother locked herself in the bathroom with Cathy, a friend who had been staying in their house for some time, the wife of Pete, the man hurling himself against the front door. The police called, Martha hovered outside the bathroom, emitting tiny sounds until the women realised she was there and hauled her into the small cold room that was situated on the landing between the hallway and the first floor. They set her father's large crimson velvet chair against the door, and next to that they placed the lidless wicker washing basket, which was trailing clothes. The bathroom door was thin, with narrow, semi-opaque etched-glass panels in it through which they listened to the leering threats that came soaring through the doorway, crude and vicious, and worst of all the dull repeated thud of Pete's thick body flinging itself against the front door. The lino on the bathroom floor was freezing on her bare feet and badly cracked at the edges. By the bath and the stem of the toilet there were signs of discolouration. Cathy used the toilet, peeling back her jeans and lacy pants and drawing them down, almost to her knees. Her pubic hair looked like giant spiders. A ripe, adult smell rose up. Then a new sound came from below. Pete was striking at the door with some kind of implement. And then there was a sharp, muffled crash and Pete was in the house. He had dragged a broken step-ladder from a nearby skip and had used it to smash the door in, his body fierce and swift on the stairs. Through the glass panels Martha saw the outline of the door hanging eerily half off its frame as Pete raced up past the bathroom to the floor above. Not one of them moved. They scarcely breathed as they listened to the sound of Pete's boots moving stealthily around the upper rooms of the house. Then, they heard him begin his descent, the muffled low rumble growing to a thunderous galloping crash of feet on wood. In a flash Martha's mother shoved her daughter into the bath, throwing some towels over her, then emptying out the dirty washing from the basket on her head. Martha reeled from this assault, but she lay there completely still, trying to tense her body against the freezing enamel so that the little shivers and silent heaving shudders it was emitting would not stir the laundry.

Within seconds Pete's huge fists were through the glass in the bathroom door and his fingers reached stealthily to throw the bolt from its catch, flinging over the chair and in an instant he came upon the two women and the child. Cathy, her trousers and pants round her knees was still sitting on the oval plastic seat, paralysed with fear, her hands fixed tightly to the lip of the toilet bowl. Martha heard shouting and then the dull, hard sound of Pete's arm making contact with Cathy's head, with her hair, the rough crash of her body colliding noisily with the cupboard above the basin, which broke and smashed down on to the floor. Bottles cracked and splintered and in the bits of silence you could hear the slow glugging and seeping of lotions out of their bottles on to the lino. Martha, eyes closed and buried, imagined the white walls spattered with blood.

Finally, when things had been still and silent for three or four minutes she ventured to peep out through some old black jersey that stank of cigarettes and alcohol. She saw her mother sitting noiselessly in one corner of the room, looking out of the window at the night sky, and in the other corner, there was Cathy rocking Pete gently to and fro, to and fro, in her arms. All three had faces wet with tears. Pete's hand bled and there were shards of glass everywhere. Cathy's shirt was torn and her eye was swelling up red and purple, like a plum. A narrow gash above her left eyebrow was drying to a deep wine colour. Pete was crying softly, and under her breath Cathy began singing to him what sounded like a lullaby. In the front doorway some neighbours gathered to inspect the carry-on.

During the past months that Cathy had been their guest, she had been astonishingly accident prone. Martha had returned from school one day to see her arm in plaster. 'Bloody cyclists, they don't look where they're going.' At other times she'd had a black eye or a yellow and purple arm, a lip crunchy with dried blood and scabs. She'd relay the incidents, the brawl at the pub that had taken her into it, although she'd only been crossing the room, in the wrong place at the wrong time. She was always very philosophical about it, though, humorous and cheerful under the bruises, through the plaster-of-paris. Cowering under the week's laundry in the icy bathtub, listening to Pete's fleshy punch hit Cathy's white-blonde head, Martha guessed that Pete had been responsible for all the other wounds too. How could she have been such a fool? Cyclists! Walking into doors!

Her mother's house, now and then, was a place of refuge for people who were out of sorts, and on several occasions during Martha's life there had been an addition to the family. They would make up the narrow bed in the spare room for troubled souls who found themselves in need of her mother's assistance for two weeks or two years, you could never be sure when they arrived. Cathy, their witty and masochistic on-off lodger, had been preceded by Sarah, who had been more withdrawn and timid, both women trying, or playing at trying, to escape their nasty husbands. There had been a troubled, spiky adolescent, called Sheila, who had shared Martha's room for a couple of months at one time, during the summer holidays. She had arrived sulky and fresh-faced, but after ten days or so in their house her face broke out into violent, weeping acne which extended down the side of the neck to the narrow backs of her shoulders. The girl was horrified at her new self, at the berry red swellings with sore creamy heads, but they suited her, allowed her to sink into herself. As well as wounds, these marks were a form of armour. Martha, at nine, barely knew where to put her peachy-faced complexion at this time. It seemed to her an assault to Sheila even to walk into a room, her own clear skin tactlessly glowing and smooth-cheeked. But her mother had worked wonders with the girl. She had grown in confidence, gone back to sixth-form college, passed exams and had begun to study to be a nurse.

Once a newly bereaved mother appeared in the kitchen, slumped against the table, staring hopelessly into the ivy-leaf pattern of a mug of some other person's abandoned tea. Mary Hodgson had spent almost six months with them, for the most part holed up in her room, unreachable inside her sharp vacuum of grief. Wild with loss for her daughter, a girl a year or two older than Martha, she paced the landing at night clutching her ribs and repeating over and over the name of her child, which was Lucy. Martha pictured the child, who had fine red-gold hair and wore a green uniform against the mottled sky-blue background of her school photograph. Sometimes she went to Mary, and stood with her in the passage, her thin arms wrapped round the older woman's waist, stroking the small of Mary's back as she choked and heaved back her sobs. Once or twice when the bereaved mother had seemed inconsolable Martha had climbed into bed with her and the two had fallen asleep together, the smaller pair of knees slotting easily into the space defined by the larger pair, Mary's arms wrapped hot and clammy round Martha's as Martha lay listening to the older woman's breaths.

One night she overheard Mary saying to her mother, 'The terrible thing is, I know it's not her fault, but every time I see Martha I feel furious that it's not Lucy.' After this Martha steered herself out of the way as much as possible. Now when she heard Mary crying for Lucy, she kept to her own bed and just cried with her, silently, on the other side of the party wall.

Another time a woman who had a young child and was trying to come off drugs came to stay, although in the end that had turned into an enormous disaster. When she finally left she took with her some of their things to sell, including Martha's school coat.

Martha's mother was at home with harsh things. It was

something Martha had noticed in her, later in life. Rough dealings, sharp practice, savage persons, threats, police stations and fluorescent-lit prison visiting centres, the muffled, waxy atmosphere of funeral parlours, hospital wards . . . in these environments her mother was in her element. She actually found them soothing. It was the smoothness of things that terrified her, living the numb life of a dead person.

To get into prisons these days it was not unusual to have your clothes and shoes fed through X-ray equipment, babies were stripped down to their nappies, you were led past ferocious-looking drug dogs, had your body felt up and down by huge women with severe facial expressions who would order you to to loll your tongue around your mouth, up a bit, down a bit, to the side now. They'd pry open your toes sometimes. Martha's mother was a heroine in such places, for there was located in her exactly the right kind of dynamic, nervous cheer. She'd fixed up the son of a friend with a window-cleaning round, after he had served two years at the young offenders' institute at Felton for seventeen shoplifting convictions, and now he was firmly on the straight and narrow and the round was a booming business and he had seven full-time employees. Having read in the newspapers that one in three men in prison under twenty have children on the outside, she had joined a scheme that sent women into prisons to teach basic parenting techniques to these youths, how to change nappies and make up formula. This scheme demanded a lot of props, dolls, squares of muslin, bottles, thermometers, baby baths, and all the methods of contraception, prevention being better than cure. She was instructed in how to talk to prisoners about the disciplining of children, the importance of household budgeting, of encouraging their offspring with their schooling. She had found a solicitor for one young man whose ex-wife had stopped bringing in the children to see him, so that a court order could be won which would guarantee at least some level of contact. Another man serving life had shown her the letter he was writing to the son he had never seen, for his fifth birthday. 'Son, even though I am away from home never ever think that I don't love you that I don't think about you every day. You are the only good thing I ever done.'

Martha's mother visited regularly a lifers' wing at a local prison and had at her fingertips all sorts of knowledge regarding standard prison procedures such as the structure and thinking behind the sex offenders' treatment programme that all paedophiles and rapists and some murderers had to complete in order to get their parole. She could talk freely about the six stages of the classic abuser's offending cycle: the trigger fantasy, the personal permission-giving, the targeting of the victim, the creating of the opportunity, the overcoming of the victim's resistance and, finally, the offence itself.

But her leanings towards the troubles of others, amazingly, were not voracious or unseemly. She was hardly a coarse person. It was a careful thing. Although she was clumsy and could not wash a lettuce without soaking her sleeves right up to the elbows, she did have a delicacy to her. It pleased her enormously that teenagers who refused to speak to any adults unbuttoned their agonies in her company. That one or two persons on the far brink of despair allowed themselves to be hauled back in by her. She dashed off long and feeling letters to prison inmates, who said she was the only reason they got through the day. She had a talent for helping people, for making them feel her strength in the midst of their own prolonged weaknesses. The amazing thing was she actually got results. Men and women arrived at the house, walking wrecks, bruised, nervous shadows of themselves, emerging not many months later with jobs and cheery bedsits to go to, enrolment forms for college courses and evening classes in Cuban dancing, one time! They came round to show their holiday snaps, these people who formerly could not walk for grief or on account of their self-destructive tendencies, those who had resolved never to trust anyone again and proved this to themselves by slicing daily into different portions of their anatomy, yet now they played volleyball once a week and spoke cheerily of the old woman who lived above them, or the nice man in the newsagent's who had called them back into the shop because he had realised he hadn't given them enough change. You had to admire the particularly robust kind of femininity that she had.

The morning after Martha took the pills, curled up in her grey-covered hospital bed, her arms hugging her guts, her head fuzzy and empty next to a barred window, a hospital orderly sidled up to her and posed a shocking question in an embarrassing theatrical whisper, 'When did you have the unprotected sex, dear?'

It was too much. Her head ached fiercely, and tears spiked the underside of her eyes. Her throat was parched. She was itchy all around her hairline, which she'd been scratching earlier, flaky pieces of scalp accumulating on her pillow and tiny smears of blood colouring her fingernails. Gradually it became clear what had happened. The fourty-two pills she had taken were birth-control pills. The shame! They thought she'd been trying to give herself an abortion!

The pills did no real harm. She was sick on and off for thirty-six hours, but that was all. During this time, her head hung low over the lavatory pan, which her mother had scoured for her with bleach brought from home, she worried briefly that she might not be able to have a baby when she was older, but it wasn't something she had set her heart on, so when the doctor gave her the all-clear, straight away, in that respect, she was only slightly relieved.

Cathy had tried to come and visit her in hospital, but it was in Martha's mind that she might have brought Pete and the sight of the two of them, in each other's arms and at each other's throats, would have been more than she could bear. They had been Cathy's pills, that was something she was almost sure of. If Cathy should have a child because of the lack of them, because of her? A child with Pete. She imagined the child a long bloody sausage after Pete had laid into it for crying, for making gentle baby sounds. This was insupportable. She woke up in the night screaming. '*No!*' she cried out. '*No!*' Suddenly her breaths started to come uneasily, shallow and fast, or not at all and then she felt as though she were choking on them. Her pulse was racing. The neighbouring patient called for the nurse, who was afraid that some ill-effects of the pills were setting in. The next day Martha confided her fears to her mother. 'I'll take the matter up with Cathy,' her mother said, reasonably.

Seven days later Martha had a mammoth period, her first, waking with a thick, gelatinous mass of black blood between her legs. All day long the blood ran down from inside her, thick and trickly. She did not know what to do so she lay in it, fearing to stand, because each time she shifted in her bed more blood came. Finally she pulled off the sheet and formed a kind of nappy out of it. She waddled towards the telephone and rang the hospital. After an hour of waiting a nurse rang back and told her this was not a surprising outcome of the overdose of oestrogen. When, the following month, only a modest amount of blood appeared she was relieved almost to the point of hysteria.

Martha tips Dan's pills back into the jar, screws the cap back on and places them on the shelf above the sink where they are the only item. Presently she gets up again and investigates the stash of cleaning things under her sink. The brooms and bits of linen rag, the sloping metal dustpans, the woolly mops, the rainbow-coloured comedy feather duster, the galvanised roughly moulded tin pail, the collection of brushes, long, short, smooth, transparent and nylon and the harsher wiry metal ones – they feel to her, suddenly, like instruments of safety. She loads a plastic bucket full of the various detergents and drapes it, red and heavy, over her forearm.

In the harsh morning sunlight the flats seem alien, the long series of rooms ghostly and abandoned. Stale smells of neglect hang fetid in the air, ancient fried food odours, cigarette smoke, sour milk, bitter arguments. Martha makes little observations as she plots her cleaning campaign, flinging open all the windows as she continues her inspection. Number fourteen is even larger than she remembered. She imagines the forty-foot room as it will be, decked out in white marble or rose-hued parquet, gilt furniture, thick silk curtains, hulking great ornamental pieces in gold and crystal, gorgeous and hideous all at once. In one of the bedrooms she discovers a blue damask sofa which is shaped like a galleon ship from the Armada, with curved, voluptuous ends. It is completely encircled by many layers of bubble wrap secured with cream-coloured masking tape. A label proclaims that it comes from Eurostyle on the Edgware Road. Martha sits on it, listening to the small exploding noises that come from beneath her. The marble will be a delight to sweep, and once a week she can wash it down with a warm mixture of washing-up liquid and water, ten parts to one, or however she is instructed. She pictures a pair of voluminous silk lampshades supported by life-size golden birds of prey mid-flight, an enormous crystal coffee table edged with silver. As she traipses round with cloth or brush Martha imagines sliding about on the cool, slippery surface in her socks, brandishing the broom, rounding up dust vigorously into neat little piles, cornering it; sometimes there is almost a hint of ambush. She addresses it sharply, in a way she imagines a sheep-dog addresses its charges, or a sheriff tracking down pesky wise-guy villains and other tough and slippery customers: 'Hey, don't you think you're getting away. Oh, no. Not so fast.' She muses on the pale carpets intended for the five bedrooms. The soft pristine cut pile will feel almost liquid to the touch, as you bend down to it. She conjures up its future inhabitants, eating their exotic takeaway dinners off golden plates, sipping from goblets, graceful liveried attendants standing by, all courtesy and epaulettes. Their potential glittering splendour she will safeguard keenly for the handing-over point. They will reap the benefits of her keen husbandry.

The second apartment she cannot quite face today, but she pokes her nose round the open door anyway. Someone ought to at tend to it. Worse than anything, worse even than the needles and the odour of decomposing cat-shit and cigarette butts and the crusted sofa that crawls with dirt, are the tortured-looking sheets, reeking at the window.

The lumber in the third flat seems unfailingly sad this morning. Martha shakes her head at the signs of broken life. Where were they, these people, now, who no longer had need of their effects? Is it too much to hope that they are safe?

Martha lingers in the child's room complete with books and toys and bunk beds with greyish-white crocheted matching coverlets. In the centre of the room is a child-sized table with three rush-seated mini wooden chairs tucked into it. On the table is a pile of books and a round floral head-dress, a little wreath of red and pink and white silk and wax flowers, with a transparent plastic comb attached to the back to keep it in place, like those worn by brides-maids. A small bottle-green bobbly duffel coat with pale wooden fastenings hangs, singly, from the bedpost of the top bunk. In the pockets are sweet papers and a notice about a school trip to the zoo, which has the word infinitesimal in it.

The sun goes in behind a cloud and the pale rectangle of light on the bedroom carpet narrows and elongates, then fades altogether. This room is like the room of a dead child that its grief-stricken parents like to leave untouched, an odd mourning capsule, all the signs of life fraying and curling and yellowing with the passage of time. A pile of purple foil and gossamer sweet wrappers catches Martha's eye. They have been kept for making something, she guesses, some kind of picture: the skirts of an old-fashioned lady in a collage. An Easter bonnet. She studies the swimming certificates, their browning edges marked with thumbprints. When her brother Matt had vanished from home for the first time, aged fourteen, his room at home had taken on something of this character.

Martha is jolted out of this reverie by the sound of the telephone ringing in her own flat. She races in to answer it. At the other end of the receiver Stella is requesting a meeting at their favourite café, the Dear Friends.

As Martha hovers at the steamy mouth of the café she notices something very appealing in the curve of Stella's neck; with the crown of her newspaper dipping and rising she seems to Martha feminine in the extreme. It is not the first time it has occurred to Martha that whereas she herself is frank by nature, Stella is open. It is a far more graceful attitude, neutral and easy, and it doesn't cause alarm.

Once, on one of their rare Sunday excursions to feed the ducks in the park when she was ten or so, Martha's father had dismissed the face of a beautiful woman Martha admired as having a forced intensity and it had struck her that his words had carried his opinion of herself also. Generally, though, their talk was of ducks: their habits, their mad colouring and jerky natures. The types of bread they preferred. They tried out different sorts. 'It's cake they like most!' Martha said triumphantly. 'Look!' she almost screamed at the duck nibbling small pieces of cherry scone with the scarlet cherries picked out. It seemed to her then that her father was fascinated by ducks, that with him 'ducks' was almost an obsession. At Christmas she bought him a book, *Enjoying Ducks*, and some duck ornaments. She almost bought some duck pâté, but she did not know whether this would be a welcome gift to a duck lover or not, and decided against. She cringed to think a year or two later of the duck tie, the ceramic duck toothpaste holder, the nylon duck-sack wash bag. He hadn't been obsessed with ducks at all, no more than she was. All this duck-fancying had been convenience. Something to draw on. They pointed at ducks as they walked. 'Look at that one there! Oh, my goodness, look at that one there, Dad! What does it think it looks like!'

She had always tried to be light-hearted in his presence, not to cause disturbance with any sudden outbursts, or unexpectednesses. Once when they all lived together a million years ago, she had spotted him in the kitchen and asked him for a drink and before she had realised what she had done his hands had flown to his head and he had muttered something under his breath then scuttled away, as though she had disturbed him in some quite ruinous way.

Stella rises to greet her friend, folding her newspaper neatly and laying it on the table top next to the sauce-encrusted plump red plastic tomato-shaped ketchup dispenser.

'Hi there.' Stella's face is highly animated, a strong smile flickering across her lips, her eyes shiny, but the features seem unhappy with their show of feeling, twitchy at their own stray quivers of lip and mouth, which look strange, look comic, but they aren't unbecoming.

'You OK?' Martha asks, peering quizzically at her friend.

'Sorry, yeah, I'm fine. How are you, though?' Stella's mouth is doing funny things again. 'I've got a bit of news.' Stella's face is serious now, composed, but you could detect a trace of something working uneasily in it. 'I'm not quite sure how to put it but . . .

'It's a bit embarrassing,' Martha hears her friend say. The note of awkward formality that has been introduced into Stella's usually dexterous manner does not quite ring true. Martha's gaze wanders. Next to the counter, above the chilled cabinet where the refrigerated sandwich fillings lie in rectangular, thick-lipped, stainless-steel dishes, yellow and pink, fawn and green, a notice has been affixed. 'BACON NEWS,' it reads. 'Until further notice, due to unforeseen sharp increases in bacon pricing, all bacon orders will incur an extra surcharge levy of 20 pence. Sorry for any inconvenience. The Management.'

'Let's get some tea first, shall we? Then you must tell me all about it.' Martha takes charge of the situation.

'OK.'

'Don't look so worried.'

'All right. Thanks, Mar.'

How bad could it be? A new waitress approaches them, a girl in her late teens who is painfully thin, an embarrassment of skin and bone showing slack and pointy from under her loose clothes, her head enormous, ghostly on her tiny frame.

'D'you want anything to eat?'

'Er . . . I don't think so.'

'Sure?'

'Just two teas, please.' The waitress goes away, and Martha and Stella follow her with sad, staring eyes.

'Don't think she'll be very good for business,' Stella says.

'Poor thing.' The teas arrive almost instantly, accompanied by a large Eccles cake on a saucer. Stella makes to send it back but Martha feels strangely protective of the waitress and she picks it up and nibbles on it absently for a few seconds to spare her feelings.

'So how are you doing?' Martha asks.

Stella takes a theatrically deep breath. 'We-ell,' she says, 'I looked in at this party on my way home last night, just some old customers of mine, it was on my way home and . . . Well, I got talking to this one guy, Martin, a friend of Jenny's, and we talked pretty well all night, and I know it sounds mad after five minutes, but he seems pretty keen on me and I feel a bit . . . I sort of feel like I could really fall for him.'

'I've never heard you say that before, about anyone.'

'I know.'

'Shit!'

'I know. I feel a bit in shock, I haven't quite taken it all in yet.'

Martha gives her a small, playful shove. Her voice rings out with delight for her friend for two or three minutes, virtually uninterrupted. 'It's so nice to hear a bit of good news, once in a blue moon . . . I was just looking at you through the window and thinking how beautiful you looked. He's obviously good for you. Tell me more about him. Are you seeing him later?' As her voice rattles on she looks at the reflection of them in the plate glass, their personalities blurred by the steam. She examines again the stick-thin waitress, staring into her face, as the girl stands hunched behind the counter, the bags under her eyes glowing grey and violet as she picks at the red skin round her nails with her teeth.

'He seemed like a really, really good person,' Stella is saying. 'He's an art teacher in a school, but he does his own stuff as well.'

'Great!'

'It was amazing because all the time I was talking to him

I felt he was listening really closely to what I was saying, as if my words were really, I don't know, valuable to him or something.'

'That sounds great.' Martha's stomach tenses. She visualises the small of her back, as though there is some call from it to the rest of her person to gather there. She continues talking in little excited swoops and peaks of merriment, admiration, wonder, gentle teases, delight. The softish glances of her friend rise, brimming with pleasure as Martha speaks. Once she can see this happening everything feels more coherent.

At another table she hears a plump black teenager telling her friend, 'When I was a kid, the only thing I would eat was soup. It was soup soup soup every meal. My mum was always at the cooker with a big ladle. Then when I got to eight I thought, Enough, enough of all this soup business – I haven't touched a drop since. I can't even take a hot drink, tea, coffee, nothing!'

And suddenly there at the mouth of the café is an unremarkable-looking man, shortish, mousy, and at the sight of him Stella's face glimmers with light and her hair bounces on her shoulders and the man approaches and she climbs up and kisses him and there are introductions and everywhere little courteous flourishes of hand and lip.

Martha peers at the new arrival, detecting in the man's pale smile a *wealth* of enthusiasms, pet likes, curious little ways, established habits, positive, lively interests, a healthy appetite and a thirst for home embellishments, all underwritten by a certain sportiness of outlook. 'Work hard, play hard,' she imagines him saying lustily. It is an expression she loathes.

Three

A week later Martha completes the very last of her unpacking. The final two boxes contain her paternal grandmother's dinner service, which has been stacked neatly in shredded newspaper for almost five years now and it pleases her enormously that it will finally see the light of day. As she frees each plate and bowl, each gravy boat from its paper casing and rinses it, glancing briefly at the strips of the past, the ribbon cruelties and sentimentalities unfurling from the powdery newsprint, wiping and arranging each item, singly, on the dresser, she casts her mind back to the long string of sorry rooms these dishes have inhabited, all the while cooped up in their boxes. She pictures the ten-by-ten sterile college bedsits on the outskirts of London, the grim, overcrowded flatshare with her friend Mary above a Chinese takeaway on a street that was so forlorn it struck Martha even then as a little ostentatious, its sorry location dividing a concrete graveyard from a red-brick prison. The windowless bedrooms. Well, she has a treat in store for them now!

It means a great deal to Martha that she has always been entirely self-supporting, just as — she had often supposed — it meant a great deal to her mother to accept, after the purchase of the large bay-windowed house situated on the fringes of a busyish red-light district, nothing further from Anthony Brazil Esquire.

Martha takes a short stack of china and climbs on a chair, reaching out a hand to the back of the dresser to steady herself, arranging the dishes as best she can, their gleaming scalloped edges overlapping against the apple green shelves, before descending the chair and beginning the process again with another armful. Under the open shelves of the dresser, in the cupboard below the drawers, which are lined with waxy yellow and white checked paper, she arranges more china: rows of lidded vegetable dishes, which stand on fancy turquoise and golden feet, great domed soup tureens with removable interiors so that hot water can be inserted in the cavity between to keep the food hot; there are sauceboats and sauceboat saucers, rectangular platters with rounded corners, three each in seven different sizes, side plates, soup plates with lids, gold-handled bread and butter dishes, a cake stand. She stands back to admire her handiwork. She could actually open up a hotel!

She takes out three saucepans and some cups, a willow-pattern tea caddy (full) and a blue enamel bread bin with a lift-off lid and white curly lettering, and arranges and wipes and dusts until the broad low-ceilinged room almost convinces as a kitchen.

Extremely casually, from the seat of the kitchen chair where she tucked it away last week, she reaches for *The Lock* by Anthony Brazil and turns it round several times in her hands. For seven days she has held out against its neat little edges, its proud, sober skin, but its cover has penetrated her dreams and flickered into her thoughts at the oddest of moments. This morning, when she was dry and dressing speedily after a bath (four steaming kettles plus two inches of cold bath water) and halfway into a garment with the neck-hole stretching across the crown of her head and her damp wrist delving into a sleeve, she realised that the unread book had taken up a position in the forefront of her mind.

Martha lets the book fall open in her hands. And the way it falls, the ease and momentum with which the pages lie flat and unfolded in front of her eyes, it really does seem that in many ways it is a great deal more interested in her than the other way round.

Taking short, ill-formulated breaths she skims a few paragraphs on unconsecutive pages, puts down the book and gets on with more unpacking. Nothing catches her interest. She sighs deeply and composes herself. She introduces some cushions on to the floor in the room she has designated the sitting room, and puts a rose-patterned cup and saucer on a wicker tray, placing the tray on the floor next to the bank of pale cushions. She adjusts the angle of the props, imagining how they would appear to a third party. Gazing out of the window she spots a small sign etched on the glass of a fast-food outlet: TURKISH DELIGHT KEBABS. 'Urggh,' she says, imagining the taste of lamb fat and rose-coloured gelatine combined.

She returns to the kitchen for a duster and reads, standing up, a few more lines of the book, a quarter of a page near the end, a half-page near the beginning, peering at the words through narrowed eyes, as though regarding through a microscope an ungainly specimen in a science laboratory, some kind of extra-straggly insect with furry legs, or the skin of a pickled amphibian reeking with formaldehyde. It is a small stretch, a bit of a leap to tolerate it lying there, but it is in no way beyond her – this is what it occurs to her, she feels. She wrinkles her nose. There seems to be a man, quite a nasty piece of work, cocksure but full of ill-concealed self-loathing, although you don't get a very strong sense of his personality, his leanings.

The words mean nothing to her, but the physical effect of

the book Martha cannot deny: just feeling the spine in her hands and flicking the pages is unsettling her deeply. Her heart beats with muscular, bullish thuds and even the parts of herself she views as passive have been cranked up to a far higher pitch so that their ordinary activity is concentrated and racing: her veins seem to her enlarged, elastic, extra-receptive, her blood hot and thick. This reading is exhausting! She puts the meat of her palm to her forehead for a moment and traces a circle all the way round the edge of her face with it, blinking, breathing deeply.

Just then the doorbell sounds twice and Martha makes her way downstairs to let in a man who has come round to reconnect, service, repair and/or possibly replace the hot-water tank. She leads him up, offering him tea, a towel for his rain-flecked curly black hair as she shows him round the flats. She is in the middle of making garbled excuses for the mess the squatters have made, when she pushes open the door of number twelve and sees that the room has been completely cleared. Even the stench has gone and in its place there lingers the smug odour of hygiene.

The electrician/plumber gets out his tools and unpacks some equipment he has brought in a series of grey cardboard boxes. He flips open his tool-box: gleaming spanners, wrenches, thirty screw-drivers. He gestures knowingly at the pipes and ducts that line the ceiling of the boiler room. His verdict on the tank is that 'These old models can be a bit spiteful.' Martha leaves him to make the tea.

When she returns with a mug, a saucer of biscuits, almost immediately he tells her he is having trouble with his daughter. 'She's sixteen and she wanted to leave home. Well, I was against it from the outset, I knew she'd find it hard getting into school if she was sharing a flat with older girls. Anyway, she was determined, but I couldn't afford to pay the rent, even if I'd wanted. Course I slip her the odd tenner now and then, although my wife gets angry and says she'll never move back in with us if I keep subbing her. But I like to give her what she wants. It's part of being a good dad. Anyway, she went to apply for housing benefit and the lady at the DSS says she can't get any benefit unless there's a reason she can't stay at home.'

'What kind of reason?' Martha asks.

'You know, trouble.'

'Trouble?'

'Violence, abuse, you know the score. Next minute she's asking me to sign a piece of paper saying that she can't live with me because I've got a terrible temper I'm not able to control. I said, "It's a lot to ask." I mean, as I say, I don't even want her to move out. Anyway, she went on and on at me about it so much, I just want her to be happy, so in the end I wrote the letter saying that for her own good she has to live away from home, away from her dad. And now I've got a letter back from a social worker asking if I can come in for an interview. I know I've been stupid. I couldn't tell my wife what I did but she found out. Hit the roof. "What if we have another kid?" she says. "It'll get taken into care. They'll keep that record on file for ever. If there's a little girl attacked in the flats, you'll be the one they come to. And don't think Mel — that's my daughter's name — is going to respect you for this. She's just making a fool out of you."'

'What a mess.'

'I know. That's life, though, isn't it? You've got do what you can for your kids. But I must say, I had tears in my eyes when I filled in that form, saying she wasn't safe in the house with me. It cost me a lot to write that, you know. It's changed me. I can't explain.'

Don't get so involved, Martha chides herself, as she lets the man into number fifteen and number fourteen and then her own flat, and then finally when she is seeing him out into the street and off into his van in search of 'parts', which reside on the other side of town, she hears herself say — it's the least she can do, 'Well, however she chooses to play things, she's lucky to have a great dad like you.'

Back in her flat, *The Lock* is calling to her again. Its eyes follow her around the kitchen. Its edges needle and cajole her all at once until she feels she is not really her own person. She covers it with a cushion but to no avail. Moments later, her body slanted uncomfortably against the wall, like someone embarking on the most provisional kind of activity, she reads a few more odd sentences from the middle and a few more from the last couple of pages. Finally admitting defeat, she takes a seat at the table and relaxes, slightly, her suspicious gaze. She lets the book fall open in her hands.

On page thirty there is a description of a man and the mess he has made of the affairs of his heart. It is his fiftieth birthday party. He is downstairs in the basement bathroom, three-quarters drunk and maudlin, fetching champagne bottles from a bath filled with ice, trying to reattach the labels that are swimming on the surface of the water, wishing, as he fails, that he'd purchased a cheaper brand after all, if no one was even going to see.

His mind turns to three or four of the women upstairs with whom he's had romantic entanglements, one of them hideous now, another half barking. Literally. She actually barks. Then he conjures up the face of his wife, his first wife. Suddenly he is cataloguing all the romances he has embarked on, every single one, from his early teens up to that very night. He examines the variety of hats and hairstyles, the night clothes, the style of talk most likely to result in the woman staying with him, through the night. He brings to mind the soft and trusting girls who've adored him, believing him to be much more than he was and then the flinty-hearted ones who've tried to break him, to re-create him in their own mould, the lace on their underwear, the jewels at their throats as scratchy and deceiving as fish hooks.

In his mind he divides these liaisons into two distinct portions, those that took place before the death of his beloved nine-year-old daughter and those that followed it: empty and compulsive. His daughter's blonde, severe face haunts him still, even a decade after her death. Once, in the early hours of the morning, he had seen himself in her eyes, caught red-handed at the thrust of some shady deal, and he has never quite recovered from the harsh judgement of his character, of his soul, that had flown from her small pyjama'd frame.

Those thin grey eyes that saw everything in the most honest light followed him round to this day. They were in the bathroom with him now, faithless and searing, as he busied himself with the relabelling of champagne bottles so that his friends could note the moderately expensive brand, reckon up the generosity involved.

Martha lets the book close in her hands. In her mind she re-examines the description of the little girl, the eyes the mouth, the hair.

At his daughter's funeral the man had started a bitter quarrel with his wife, the memory of which caused him to this day regular welts of shame: actual long red hives would spring up on the skin of his arms and legs and itch and take hours to go away. At the funeral, his wife had taken control of all the arrangements; it was she who had gone to the undertaker's, to the mortuary, to the inquest, to the police station, to the hospital. He was unable to do these things. He couldn't speak. He just remained at home, slumped in a chair, swallowing whisky, smoking cigarettes, a puff a swig a puff a swig, till huge piles of bottles and packets lay empty at his feet and he had to try to find ways of summoning more supplies. He couldn't move himself. Occasionally, he recalled, he had eaten slices of strong cheese.

At the suggestion of the funeral director, his wife, who did not wish to be awkward in any way, had agreed to a white coffin and unbeknownst to her that particular model came with some complementary pink and yellow transfers of flowers and toys on either side of the brass handles. It was a coffin intended to benefit the siblings of the child that had Gone, to make the whole affair less frightening, less traumatic, less horrible. The child had no siblings but she had a father who was appalled by what he saw. Those floral transfers seemed to him an insult of the worst kind. They reminded him of the unfailingly nasty timbre of his own mother's voice, which in his childhood had said vicious, spiteful things to him in the smoothest and kindest of tones. Those transfers were out to humiliate him, with their sunshine yellows, their baby pinks, their rocking horses and their paltry daisy clusters. At the very moment that the dwarf coffin came into view, towering high on the tall shoulders of four Irish funeral-parlour workers, the small crowd hushing, taking steps to let the men with the casket through, he turned to his wife, spitting words at her, bitter and vindictive: 'It's the most disgusting thing I've ever seen,' he lashed, screwing up his face with deep hatred pangs, at the very point when she needed his surest support. Marriage was the hardest thing in the world, unless you had a peculiar talent for it, it occurred to him now, in the bathroom on his fiftieth birthday.

At the funeral people turned to stare, absolutely astonished at his display. His wife, composure itself, looked at him as he ranted, tears of incomprehension in her eyes. When she tried to take his hand, to soothe whatever hideous feelings had stolen over him, he flinched and shoved her away. She cried out and fell towards the freshly dug pit, and only the stiff arm of a helpful bystander prevented her from plunging into the muddy brown grave hole, there and then. The man tried to change, to temper his rage, but each sight of those pink and yellow flowers on the white coffin was more than he could bear. 'I'll never forgive you,' he hissed, as he turned away. 'Never.'

At this point his wife's usually timid mother trotted up to him and slapped his face hard, right in front of everyone, at the grave-mouth. 'You think of no one but yourself. Be a man,' the elderly lady in the black two-piece demanded. At this he had sunk back from the crowd, taken himself off to kick at the leaves that lay some twenty feet from the proceedings, cheeks stinging, rage crackling in his knuckles. After a while his wife (why had she?) came to get him. The actual burial was starting. 'I'm so sorry about the coffin,' she murmured. 'I know it's horrible. But come and stand with me. Let's try to keep each other going. I know it's the hardest thing we've ever done. I feel exactly the same as you.' She kissed him tenderly on the cheek, and he allowed her to take his hand like a child, let her lead him back into the heart of things and then, as the first dark shovelful of earth landed splat on the coffin top, he threaded his hand round her waist and bellowed like a baby into her shoulder.

What his wife had done at that juncture, his then wife, well, the wealth of kindness involved in the gesture would stand up against any huge and famous act of humanity. It was breathtaking, heartbreaking, well, it was holy, really, he decided, fishing out the last of the bottles, the last of the labels from the bathtub; perhaps he should have stayed with her after all.

At lunch-time Martha wanders out to meet Stella at the Dear Friends. The skinny waitress lingers at the chilled cabinet, eavesdropping Stella's squeals of delight in relation to her new romance. Martha looks on as the little smiles and soft glances that drop from Stella's moony features strike the waitress as a kind of assault. 'He's so thoughtful! When he stayed, the first time, he noticed that I was running out of face cream and turned up the next night with a huge new bottle, exactly the kind I like, without even saying anything.'

The waitress makes a sick face. When you were that slender, there was no buffer between you and the world, so that the world's miseries were your own miseries and the world's joys — well, although they were constantly dangled in front of your eyes, they were so exotic and out of reach, they might as well be on Mars.

On the way home the bus shoots erratically through the brightly lit streets that are glossy with rainfall, lurching forward, swerving past cars, a clumsy wall of red racing onwards at high speed, now and then performing shocking emergency stops, as if it is only a vague afterthought at the back of the driver's mind that people might want to board or dismount his vehicle. He is in a world of his own. The conductress, a thin, sprightly grey-haired woman, seems to regard the antics of her colleague with a degree of amusement, as though he is her high-spirited child. She might even be proud as she smiles and shrugs and bites her lip good-humouredly. What speed! What tight corners he makes!

After a few moments of her own company on the balding claret-plaid bus seat, Martha is joined by a large woman, whose face is thickly caked with orange make-up that sits in greasy wedges on her creased skin. She wears a thin, black 1960s-style raincoat, with broad, pointy button-down epaulettes. Her hair is a stiff, shiny, copper-coloured beacon. 'It's turning cold, isn't it?' she says, as she slowly lowers herself, with grace, on to the seat. She rustles some silver paper inside her handbag and in seconds Martha smells the sugar heat of spearmint wafting from her seat mate. The woman offers a strip of chewing-gum to Martha.

'Thanks very much.'

'It'll be Christmas before you know it.' She confides this as if it is a warning. 'It's my sister, you see,' the woman offers. Then, bending in towards Martha, she makes some small circular motions in the air with her index finger, pointing it in the general direction of her brain, and lowers her voice; 'She's not very well.'

'Oh, no!'

'I try to take her round a bit, just to take her out of herself. She likes to go to the big hotels in the West End, so I take her once a week for afternoon tea. You know, finger sandwiches, scones, fruit cake, French pastries. She's always gone in for that kind of thing. Doilies and silver trays. It's quite dear but you know . . .'

Martha nods. There are tiny almost invisible spikes of dark hair peeping through the patch of skin above the lady's top lip, where balls of sweat are also gathering.

'But the thing is, now she wants to go all the time. In the middle of the night, even.' The woman folds up her bus ticket neatly and pops it into her purse for safe-keeping. She moistens her lips. A lone scrawny teenage boy gets on and starts scratching at his groin, snapping the low band of his underpants in his fingers . . . Martha stifles a giggle. 'Dear oh dear!' says the woman, giving Martha a friendly nudge; then she bites her lower lip theatrically and rolls her eyes towards the roof of the bus.

'Anyway, some of the hotels up west *will* serve you tea and a cake in the lounge at eleven o'clock. She likes us to get dressed up in suits, bit of jewellery, you know the kind of thing. But the thing is,' she leaned in so close to Martha this time that there wasn't quite air enough for them both to breathe, 'I'm a bit worried what people might think. Two girls out alone at night. Hanging round hotels in their gladrags.'

'Well, I suppose you do want to be slightly careful.'

'I mean, well, for a start she likes to wear tight clothes to show off her figure. She got the looks when they were handing them out, you see. She's got my mother's figure, whereas I'm more like our dad. Anyway, last time I took her up to Park Lane, she was wearing this red outfit with gold sequins, Lycra, fringes, you name it. She said she picked it up in the market, for a few quid. Well, I didn't like to say, "It shows", but, well, you know what I mean. I like a more sophisticated, tailored look, Jaeger, Spectrum, you know, for something dressy. Anyway, you should have seen the skirt.' Her smiling eyes narrowed and she shook her head from side to side at the memory of it. 'Figure or no figure, she's not getting any younger either.'

'Few of us are,' Martha interposes.

'Quite right. You're young yet, though, love, you don't have to worry about any of that for a good twenty years at least.'

'Thanks very much!'

'Anyway, I thought, I've got to do something, haven't I? Women get chucked out of hotels for less if you see what I mean. So I turned round and said, "Look, I'm not trying to be funny, Bet, but people might get the wrong idea, if you make so much effort when you come out." I thought that was the kindest way to put it. I'd given it some thought. I don't like to go around upsetting people. "The wrong idea?" she says. "About the two of us?" she says.'

Just at that moment the bus careers round a corner at such a fierce speed that both women are violently pitched sideways, Martha's head flung into her companion's full, creamy bosom, and it is only the extremely tight grip of their hands on the rail of the seat in front that stops them from shooting out of their seats, there and then flat on their backs, up the aisle. Before they can even catch a breath both women are slapped back hard against the side of the bus and each other and the backs of their seats as the bus completes its circular manoeuvre. Someone shouts out in protest, but the conductress ignores the complaint.

The woman dusts herself down, with her gloved hand, regaining her composure in a deliberate and graceful manner. 'Goodness me!' she says.

'I know,' Martha agrees. They both take deep breaths for a few seconds. Then Martha turns to her. 'You were saying you told your sister that people might get the wrong idea or something?'

'Hold on.' She takes smooth shallow breaths and runs a handkerchief across her brow. She returns it to her bag, although it is now streaked with dark pink oily marks. 'Let me just get my breath back.' She raises, slightly, her right hand, then lets it fall again. 'That's right, dear. Where was I? That's it. Yes. "The wrong idea?" she says. "The wrong idea?" She repeats this about ten times, bleating it out like a little lost sheep. Then it seems to click with her. "Oh, you're worried that they'll think we're, that we're,"' and here the woman lowers her voice further, '"that we're LESBIANS!" I didn't know where to put myself. We were walking through Reception at the Dorchester Hotel at the time and she shouts the word out at the top of her voice. I didn't know where to put myself. Dear oh dear! There wasn't a head in the foyer that didn't swing round. I said to my husband, I said, "Ron, there's never a dull moment with that one, manic depression or no manic depression."' At this she begins to giggle and the giggle rounds into a tinkly laugh, and then into deep, throaty gurgles of pleasure. 'Oh dear!' she said. 'I shouldn't laugh. I don't mean to be unkind.'

'She's lucky to have a nice sister like you.'

'Oh, well, there but for the grace of God . . .' The woman draws out the handkerchief again and dabs at the tears that sparkle on her under-eye area. 'Any mental illness in your family, love?'

'I'm getting off here,' Martha says, smilingly. 'It's my stop.'

'Ah, well, a pleasure talking to you.'

'And you.'

'Bye now.'

'God bless,' Martha says, without quite knowing what she means. The last time she had wandered into a church, a year or so ago, at a low ebb and completely at a loss as to the correct procedures, she had found herself, when faced with a statue of Jesus on the cross, feeling so unexpectedly moved and so lacking in the means to express this that she had stiffened the four fingers of her right hand and raised them gently to her bowed forehead in a military-style salute.

Martha gets off the bus, smiling as it speeds away into the evening gloom. She hopes she may meet the woman again. She feels as though they are friends now. Throughout their entire conversation she had been delicate in the extreme.

On the way home Martha looks in at the department store. She surveys the individual tear-shape blackcurrant mousses decorated with red berries and blackberries and *fraises des bois* in the chilled patisserie unit, thinking how pretty they would look in her kitchen, all of them, the whole cabinet, the entire bakery section. The nine different types of bagel, the soda farls. 'Shall we slice that for you?' the female servers chime politely with each sale. She glances at the rich people dining on seafood and white wine at the oyster bar, in the corner of the food hall, watching a slender lady in camel-coloured clothes nibbling a lobster claw, holding an asparagus spear through forked fingers like a cigarette. Martha admires the seafood canapés laid out on silver trays, eyes up a row of Prawn Délices, a cone-shaped confection of salmon and prawn mousse resting on a bed of watercress, priced at £4.70. An impossibly grand, extremely elderly lady hobbles over in a black suit that drips with diamonds: brooches, necklaces, bracelets. On her gnarled fingers are several thickly jewelled rings. 'Oh!' she exclaims, in some kind of ecstasy. 'Oh, how elegant! Just think of the time they'd save, if one were giving a supper party!'

Martha has taken to making regular trips to the department store, vaguely in the name of research, morning or last thing, sometimes both. The renovations are growing more and more brutal by the day, a friendly assistant informs her, in order that the store can be brought up to date. Words like 'reassuring' and 'quaint' it wants banished from the shop floor. Distressed gentlefolk buying one each of four different vegetables – a thing of the past. 'A lot of the staff . . .' she pauses and drags her index finger across her throat '. . . the chop!' she says merrily, with much grimacing. It's all very hush-hush but the new-look store is to be dynamic and forward-thinking and its wealthy young clientele will mirror this. On each visit Martha notices the latest innovations. Very occasionally, if she has a friend coming, she picks up a little fish: 'Could I just have six ounces of cod, please?'

'Of course.'

'Last of the big spenders, eh?' Martha offers by way of apology.

'At these prices, pet, who could blame you?'

The men at the fish counter always look sheepish as the digital scale tots up the price of your purchase, and prints it out on a sticky label, which is swiftly attached to your package. One assistant, a young man with sandy hair, sometimes colours and pulls odd faces, transferring his weight uneasily from one leg to another at these moments. He'll throw in a bit extra: a handful of shrimps, some monkfish tail, a bit of salmon-pink cod's roe to make it up to you.

Martha likes to reckon up, at dusk, the number and range of the new products on sale. Any shifts in the display strategy or alterations in the distribution of merchandise throughout the departments she notes. The placing of things she finds fascinating. It cheers her also, giving her a great sense of reserves.

That she can rarely afford to buy anything for herself scarcely impinges on her enjoyment; nor does it augment her desires, for what she likes best is to monitor the ebb and flow of product to customer, to observe supplies being shifted, reordered, restacked and redesired, all this life going on happily adjacent to her home.

Last week a set of saucepans, eight-piece in navy vitreous enamel endorsed by a famous TV personality, was given prominent display on a large table positioned to the right of the cash tills; posters, mounted on board, of the saucepans at work accompanied the display; written testimonials by the TV personality, endorsing the efficacy and durability of the cookware, lay in a pile printed out on pink slips of paper to be read and taken away by prospective customers. Then, three days later with no ceremony, the pans seemed to have been diverted to a side table with thirty per cent deducted from the price. They have fallen utterly, and for an unknown reason, from grace. This is the sort of episode Martha ponders at length.

She wanders home, swinging her carrier-bag of modest purchases in her hand. She has asked the builders to leave all their materials neatly in a little cordoned-off area of the downstairs hall and the steps she herself has cleared of the accumulated debris. A sweep and a polish has brought them up nicely. She likes cleaning. She even likes the atmosphere of improvements that pervades her building. In some dim and abstract region of herself, she feels it is good for her to be living in a place where the bywords are renovation and repair.

She makes it her business now to keep the three flats in her charge as spotless as they can be, and the making of them clean and sparkly, with speckless floors, sheeny and streak-free, between the areas of rubble, the areas of fuzzy underlay and provisional surfacing, seems to her immensely soothing, like some strange sort of insurance.

Back in her flat, and without meaning to, she thinks of taking up her father's book again, bringing to the task a brand of sour humour. She blinks, snatching up the volume with a little shrug, a tiny, defeated half-sigh.

The man, in a drunken flurry of self-disgust, is musing about his daughter's babyhood. That part of his life belongs in a very particular compartment that he seldom visits. Where had this bewildering streak of sentimentality come from, he wonders? Was it a legacy from his own father, that weak, ineffectual, foolish hysteric prone to tears? To summon his baby daughter's face, the light grey eyes, the complexion of warmth and repose is something, on a daily basis, that he fights. He doesn't know what to do with the appeal that that visage holds for him now, the shy, surprising flickers of dark and light that used to fall over her features when, tiny as she was, she was understanding something in him, perhaps more deeply than it ever intended being understood. The precise details of their co-habitation as she grew older, he also tries not to recall. His oafish, bungled attempts to mirror something of her delicacy with his own behaviour had convinced no one, least of all himself. How could he live up to what she wanted, this pink and white, golden-headed bundle, who smiled and cooed, but later on was possibly the most exacting person he had ever had dealings with in his life?

Had there been an aspect to his relation with his daughter

that had been purer, more whole than any other that had come his way, before or since? Wasn't there a high, moral quality to her that had been absent from any of his wives? It was not something he could describe or put a name to. The lack wasn't quite tangible, it was all mood and nuance and glances, but he had definitely harboured feelings for her that were stronger than any others he had known, and it had been something wholly involuntary, something that, in part, he had even tried to resist.

Martha closed the book at the end of the first chapter, bemused, intrigued. What a strange creature her father was. She conjured up a picture of the straight-backed, grey-suited man writing down the words, in silence, with his do-not-disturb brain in his do-not-disturb office.

Occasionally she wondered if her father felt happiness in the highly controlled environment in which he existed. She did hope there were people he loved and trusted in a way that suited him, and them, because there was a certain strand of ordinary experience from which she knew he was excluded, holed up in his study day and night, communications only arriving by the near-silent fax machine, behind a closed door.

She wondered, now and then, did this not feel like loss? She felt he took risks living his life in this way, that anyone like him did. Absenting himself from the ordinary civilian wear and tear of life must in some way be an error, because the wear and tear brought with it, as well as the major pains and aches, good things, unexpected bolts of feeling, experience, riches. To shy away from these things, from the colours and lights of life, only to re-create it all, in your own terms, in minute detail on the page – this was at best eccentric and at worst, well, wasn't it a little bit, well . . . insane?

Sometimes she worried for him. What if there was no one in the world with whom he came first, for whom he counted more than anyone else? That was fine when you were young, well, it wasn't fine exactly, but you certainly didn't want it to be the case when you were getting on. A line that had made her uneasy in *The Lock* was haunting her slightly. The 'hero' in a blaze of alcohol was speaking, in his trademark morose swagger, to his wife's spectacular twenty-two-year-old niece: 'You know I don't know that I've ever really believed in love.' Of course, she knew from her American poet, she knew from every quarter of life how much less texts yielded when you chased after an autobiographical angle all the time, but even still. How would her mother feel on reading that? How would her brother?

She pictured her brother, sullen and vacant, his lips slack, cheeks hollow and sunken, ape-like, his tiny pupils swimming almost imperceptibly in his loosely focused eyes.

A conversation from years ago, when he was less adept about such things than he was now, floated back into her memory. He had a girlfriend who had a daughter and the daughter had a birthday and no presents, he explained. His voice was apologetic, exhilarating, seductive. Did Martha have a bit of spare cash? 'There's a doll she wants very much that's nineteen ninety-nine. She saw it on television. Talks and does a pee or something. Liked it straight away. Talked about it all the time ever since. A little child at Christmas,' he said, 'with no presents!' (It was June.)

'How old is she? What's her name?'

'Her name? Her name? The doll's name?'

'No, the little girl's.'

'It's . . . it's . . . it's . . . I'll call you back.'

There was something spectacular about the trouble he made for himself. When she was fourteen and he was eighteen or so, living in a basement with a cheery red-haired girlfriend who baked her own bread and worked in a clothes shop, he had staged a break-in at her mother's house one night, smashing the glass in the back window, leaving large muddy boot prints in the kitchen with a boot borrowed from his girlfriend's dad and stealing nearly all the household's books, most of which had belonged to Martha's father. Then he'd jumped on a bus and taken his spoils in a suitcase to a shop on the Charing Cross Road.

Once she'd visited Matt in prison, with her mother, where he seemed estranged even from himself. He'd grown a bushy moustache. His hands were twitchy, and his head made spiky, frail, jolting movements now and then, darting behind or straining forward suddenly, like a man in dread of being followed. He wore baggy royal blue tracksuit trousers that were loose and saggy in the bottom and grey supermarket running shoes, he who used to boast such a sense of style. Against the livid yellow lights and the harsh din of scraping chairs and officers' reprimands and jokes and shouts and babies' wailing and the continual heavy, echoey thud of the tinned-drinks machine, Matt bragged about his new friends and the extremely violent crimes they'd committed, the people they'd murdered, hacked up, even, at dawn. He made a circle with thumb and forefinger to indicate the size of the pieces. He was grinning, his ghostly skin streaked with large violet shadows. He'd made friends. He was a success. He was the prison table-tennis champion. 'The King of Ping?' Martha offered. He'd nodded enthusiastically. His eyes looked like they were half on fire and half, well, dead.

Suddenly, out of nowhere a burly officer appeared, hauling Matt out of his chair without a word, and escorting him speedily out of the visiting room. Martha and her mother were appalled.

'What's going on, Mum?'

'I don't know, darling.'

The two women sat in the enormous echoey pale yellow hall that was so hot it was almost tropical. Martha shuffled in her chair, arranging her knees neatly under the strange shiny yellow wooden table that had a small clear plastic partition separating inmate from visitor built into it, dividing the table top into two brief, uncomfortable shelf-like ledges. It was an odd piece of furniture, severe and a bit kinky. Martha imagined a company that produced such specialist pieces, and wondered about their other lines: confessional boxes, isolation booths for quiz programmes, strange one-sided glass cabinets for peep-shows. She looked around. It was nearly the end of the visit and all around them couples were embracing hungrily over the plastic partitions.

'He's putting on a brave face for us,' Martha's mother said. 'He's very thoughtful.'

After more than five minutes, Matt traipsed back and took up his seat at the table again. 'They thought one of you might have slipped me something.'

'Finish off now, please,' a guard boomed at them. As he said this, a man three tables away was taken off by the same officer, while his wife, cradling a small child, sat nervously staring damp-eyed in the opposite direction, chewing her lip.

Matt was murmuring something. 'That's a real shame. He *was* expecting something today.'

When it was over they drank tea and ate vast amounts of biscuits in the visitors' centre. Martha's mother lit a cigarette, her first in years, her fingers stumbling blindly over the match and the matchbox, the introduction of flame to cigarette tip taking almost half a minute to get right. 'Well, I'm very impressed. He's managing to stay cheerful. He made an effort for us. I know they've got a very good drugs unit here, it's one of the best in the country, so, you know, with a bit of luck . . .'

Martha stuffed a custard cream into her mouth to prevent herself speaking. But what she felt was: 'If he's off drugs, I really am a Chinaman.'

A few years later Martha had kept him company, all night, with her mother in the visitors' room at the intensive care ward when his girlfriend was dying in hospital, the life force extinguishing and rekindling in her on and off for almost five days so that no one, not even the doctors, could tell what was happening. The little scene being played out was absolutely horrific: it was the end, there was no chance at all, nothing, then suddenly an unexpected flicker came, it seemed there might be the tiniest possibility of a chance, although what her life would be now, well, it might be worse than . . . Then there was no question of there being a chance, and yet was that another flicker? A new kind of sigh . . . Then just No. No. No. No. No. Matt's despair and sorrow reached many great swooping peaks throughout this blank, unhurried time. At intervals he'd slope off to the gents' and come back calmer, happier, smiling weakly, his face slack and red-eyed with pinprick pupils. There were several other families in the small grievers' cubicle. A television mounted high on the far wall, controls out of reach, blared out the bizarre Open University programmes of the small hours. Three long fluorescent lighting bars attached to the ceiling brought out the greens and blues in everyone's faces, so that all the room looked ill with the same complaint. There were tears everywhere and half-hearted attempts at cheer and jokes, and many extended arms. There were always at least two people locked in an embrace of sorts. The room was boiling, and as there was only space for about half the visitors to sit down, there was endless shuffling along the corridors, to the drinks machine, to the lift, to the toilets. Dizzy with grief and sweating profusely under the heat and lights, members of the different families, over time, even turned to each other, unsure who their own were any more. By then it hardly mattered, what with the thick, lurching sob noises, and the sharp inward cries of pain. Every quarter of an hour or so a couple of visitors would dress up in the plastic surgical apron and gloves and mask and go into the intensive-care ward, where it seemed that almost everyone was dying. Martha had donned this uniform and accompanied her brother to his friend's bedside. It had become obvious that he loved her, that she was the most important thing in his life, when he took her hand, looking out across her beautiful dark eyes and slender features covered by a mass of white tubing, his head shaking slowly from side to side.

A week later Martha had tried to shoulder his demands as best she could. 'I've found a hotel, for the reception, can I give them your credit card? We're having a coach and black horses. It's eight hundred pounds. Can you lend me the money until Wednesday?' He was sobbing on the telephone. 'I need the money by two o'clock this afternoon. Please, Martha.' He went silent and then his voice trickled off into the background. Martha imagined the sound of a needle going in. Was that a sound? Could he have eight hundred pounds cash? Martha was eighteen years old, living off the wages of a Saturday job in a lingerie shop. Did she have any savings? Could she bring him thirty pounds by six o'clock tonight as a deposit for the hotel? Could she get in touch with Dad for the money? Fifteen? Ten pounds then, could she leave ten pounds under the doormat by six o'clock?

Finally the funeral party was held in her mother's house. It had seemed more suitable, the room in the hotel being a windowless grey conference suite on the eighth floor. Martha rapidly buttered bread for sandwiches, sliced up fruit-cake, arranged jewel-coloured jam tarts on plates. The people who came!

Every eighteen months or so, when he went into treatment, or said he was going to, or managed to get hold of some money somehow (don't ask) to do a so-called travelling cure, Martha's mother would springclean his flat from top to bottom, once working round a stray man who just lay silently on the floor, occasionally breathing. Martha had helped when she was younger, although she would not do it now. Even her mother, who was the opposite of squeamish, put on gloves to do the task, scrubbing down the walls with disinfectant, throwing away the rug on the floor and replacing it, bagging up the sheets in black rubbish sacks and bringing clean ones in from home. You could only make it less nasty. The fridge was marbled with grey-green fungal growth. Martha's mother held her breath and gouged it out with the back of a spoon. The toilet was a sick joke.

Martha had a horror of needles. Her mother gathered them up and put them in a huge padded envelope, wrapped that in newspaper then placed it in three thick bin-liners. 'I'm so sorry about the smell,' she'd say to Matt on his return, with reference to the sharp, dry, bleachy odour that emanated from all the surfaces. Four weeks off drugs, in theory, Matt cast his eye about the place. A basket of washed and folded clothes caught his eye. 'No ironing, I see.' He smirked.

Martha looked away, darting her gaze into the kitchen, surveying her handiwork. The sink gleamed, there was a tea-towel neatly folded over the bar of the oven door. She'd even resuscitated the grill-pan, which had had an inch of putrid bacon fat in it that could have been a year old. His voice filtered in and out of hearing. Would he really boast and glower over his gangrenous toe like that if he was taking to heart the principles of Narcotics Anonymous? How could you tell?

Once, when his flat was gone and he was sleeping on the floor of a building in King's Cross that doubled up as a safe-house for people who had connections with the IRA, his mother had come round and insisted that he come back home with her, practically dragged him. He had sores that wept pus and blood, in fact he seemed to get blood everywhere at that time, in the butter, even. It was awful, but you couldn't look at that blood without thinking of his hepatitis, of his septicaemia. An ordinary funeral parlour wouldn't even embalm you if you had septicaemia, Martha had heard, and that was after you were dead!

Martha had not even been able to sit down at her mother's house with such a strong sense of disease in the atmosphere. In the swing-bin in the kitchen under a pile of potato peelings she could clearly make out the metal point of a needle. Did her mother know he was taking drugs on the premises? 'He's a walking health hazard,' Martha whispered to her mother as she left. 'He shouldn't really stay here, unless he's going to be more careful. He's putting you at risk.'

'Oh, I don't really mind. There's a only a small chance of anything nasty happening. And he does so need my support.'

Slowly, almost theatrically, Martha counted to ten, inside her brain. Then she said, 'Imagine how ashamed he'd feel if he made you ill in any way.'

Her mother spoke lightly. 'Oh, it wouldn't bother him.'

Martha could not think of anything else to say.

'Anyway, it's OK, darling. Look.' She pointed to a box that contained three bottles of bleach and four bottles of disinfectant.

Matt was thirty now and had no idea what to do with himself. Not in terms of his desires or his ambition. It was not his lack of prosperity or prospects that worried Martha, it was just that he literally did not know what to do with himself. He had no idea how to shunt himself from one side of the day to the other. He had collapsed inwards so thoroughly, and so long ago, that he was actually unable to arrange his life in any other way. At other times, she thought, if he did not have the getting hold of drugs to live for, he'd give up the ghost once and for all.

That week the hot water finally came on. Mr Quinn happened to call round just as the plumber was performing his final tests on the boiler, so the three of them, gathered round her bathtub, performed a little switching-on ceremony. 'We ought to have a star to do the switch-on, like the Oxford Street lights,' the plumber suggested. Quinn gestured towards Martha in a courtly fashion indicating that, in his book, she was the match of any star.

Martha bent forward, clasping her hair out of her face with her hand, gingerly dislodging the hot tap until a tiny brownish trickle appeared. They waited. The trickle grew stronger and the colour of the liquid gradually turned clear. Martha bent and turned the tap up until a thick stream of water was coursing out of it. All of a sudden she felt some large words were in order, but she could not think which ones. She dangled her hand over the rim of the bath so that it just caught the edge of the water. Rapidly she withdrew her fingers, which were pink.

'Hot?'

'I'll say!' She beamed. The men aped her smiles and Quinn gave her back some small, nervous pats.

Every day now many, many workmen called. Mr Quinn telephoned her. 'We've got to get our skates on,' he announced. She said she would leap into action. The marble floor went down at number twelve. It was beautiful. Like an ice palace. And she'd made great strides with her flat too. The kitchen was coming along nicely. She'd bought a cherry-red plastic bucket with a white handle and a matching washing-up brush and two red and white checked linen dish cloths, which were almost too good to use. An offcut of fabric that was printed with pink cherries on lush green stalks she ran up into some very basic kitchen curtains with a needle and thread.

Her work had taken an interesting turn also. She had found inspiration in a peculiar corner. In a rare work of criticism a certain literary journalist had illustrated his article on her American poet with five short extracts from one of his more difficult long poems. Then, towards the end of the essay, the critic had revealed that the last verses of the poetry he had quoted he had actually made up himself. In three minutes flat! He seemed so proud about it. Bumptious. As if it proved anything. 'I rattled off these verses that are as good as his,' the critic complained, 'and they aren't any good at all,' he crowed. 'Ha!' But these cobbled-together lines hadn't fooled Martha. Oh, no! Apart from the fact that they were deliberately mystifying, something her poet would never stoop to, they proposed emotions that were *so* clearly inauthentic as to render them utterly worthless. They didn't even sound as though they meant what they said. And then, this . . . this *amateur* critic had gone and committed foolish errors in his use of diction such as writing 'and' in places when her poet would certainly have used an ampersand.

At nights she often found herself wandering up and down Oxford Street, in the last of the light. Certain things happened at regular times she was beginning to notice. The huge, industrial grey dustcarts came roaring down three or four times throughout the night, and men steered space-age-looking white street-cleaning machines with large green rotating brushes up and down, up and down, pretty well round the clock. Sometimes she'd sit quietly on the pavement, knees folded under her, coat wrapped round her legs like a tent, just watching things, watching the life that was going on. Late night was delivery time and massive gleaming crates on wheels were trundled out of lorries and slammed into the supermarket by night workers. In the dark early hours of morning, you could see men and women buttoned into sturdy coats accumulating outside the fast-food restaurants. They clutched polystyrene cups and if you were careful you could make out the little circular whorls of steam that rose up, melting their features under the romantic street-light.

How odd, how full her flat felt at night when she could hear people's intimate conversations, drifting up, word for word, through her closed window, into her bedroom, as though they were up there with her, arguing their arguments, screeching out their obscenities, wolf-whistling her building and bellowing their declarations of love. How the roar of the buses and the sound of foot and mouth and taxi brakes and creaking delivery lorries with their metal cages on wheels that shunted along the pavements, and the giant, growling dustcarts dominated her night thoughts, soothing and ominous, like the sea's noises. It occurred to her one night that while all that was going on directly underneath her resting body, it was impossible, really, to feel in any way alone.

One night about this time when she is returning home from one of her regular evening sorties and the sky is just a thick brown smudge that hangs heavy with a trillion particles of dirt, all London's flaked-off dead skin, exhaust fumes, bad breath, bad faith, she sees her brother leaning on the thick glass of the souvenir shop next to her block of flats, his figure framed by a whole wall of round commemorative ashtrays and coaster sets emblazoned with glossy, dazzling holograms of Sherlock Holmes, complete with pipe and deer-stalker and, in some of them, the violin.

'Hi there!' he says.

'Hello.' She is amazingly pleased to see him. She has not seen him for almost a year, only spoken to him on the phone once or twice, but she does not feel put out by the sight of him now, nor does she feel particularly surprised. She gives him a little excitable punch on the shoulder, which he endures good-humouredly.

'Coming in?' she asks, turning the key in the lock.

'Go on, then.'

She gives him a brief look up and down. His jeans are cleanish. He wears a filthy floor-length light-coloured leather coat that is too large for him and a bit feminine-looking and badly stained and too hot for the time of year. She chews her lip for a second, thinking that it is completely different from any other garment she has ever seen him in. He doesn't quite look himself in it, but it seems festive, fancy dress, light-hearted. He has plimsolls on his feet and sports a greying sweatshirt, worn inside out. It's a look, she judges. She examines him more closely. His fine mousy-coloured hair and thin-featured, angular face seem more reduced than she remembers them, his whole figure, drawn and wiry, beneath the skirts of his coat, his cheeks sunken in.

Martha leads him up to the flat. Halfway up the stairs, when he is stumbling a flight below her, she stops and swings her head round to face him through the banisters. 'How are you doing?'

'Oh, I'll live,' he says, in a tone that is fairly mild, almost philosophical really. Of course. She walks up a few more stairs.

She stops again. 'How's the drug-taking going?'

'Oh, everything's under control.'

'What does that mean?' They carry on walking up. 'What does that mean, Matt, eh?' she repeats gently, more kindly, looking back at him over her shoulder.

'Moderation in all things,' he says. She turns to look at him again, and sees him affecting the expression of some-one bashful. His face has coloured slightly, he is trying not to smile.

'So you're still on the gear, then?'

He looks agitated now. 'I've been staying at Mum's for a couple of weeks. Doing this detox thing.'

'Really?'

'Yeah.'

'With some pills from the doctor?'

'Yeah.'

The very first time Matt had requested a home detox at her mother's house many, many years ago her mother had telephoned through regular progress reports. 'I've been a real Florence Nightingale, running about, getting everything sorted out,' she said, her voice ringing with pride 'There were quite a lot of medical problems. We got some great pills from the doctor.'

'D'you know what they are?' Martha's mother wasn't sure. When the large clear bottle was examined it transpired they were morphine.

But isn't heroin a morphine substitute? Martha wondered silently.

She and Matt are sitting in her kitchen. 'Nice flat,' he says admiringly.

'It's only temporary. Just looking after it for someone for a little bit.'

'Any chance of a sandwich?' he asks.

'What? Yeah. Course. What d'you want in it?'

'Got any bacon?'

'I have, actually.' Martha takes some slimy rashers of Danny's bacon out of the fridge and arranges them under the grill. She puts two slices of bread in the toaster. They both liked the bread to be cooked on only one side. She halves a small tomato and places that under the grill also.

'Just go to the loo,' Matt says.

'OK. Food won't be long.'

When he doesn't come back for five minutes, she goes to see if he is all right. The bathroom door is closed and she calls to him, 'Matt, food's ready.' Inside the room nobody stirs and Martha taps it lightly with her hand, 'Matt! Matt! It'll go cold.' And then, 'Is everything OK?' Worry strikes her and she bangs on the door panel. 'Open the door, please. Open the door,' she says, but still no reply comes back and then it occurs to her that the door may not be locked and she tries the door-knob and it gives but before she enters she says, 'I'm coming in now, OK?' and she turns the handle and then she is face to face with him perched there on the lip of her bath, smiling weakly, his tight features slack and rounded, eyes watery and half-closed. There is a spoon and some tin-foil and a small yellow bottle of citric acid on the floor. Under his shoe, she can see the gleaming metal point of a needle.

'Time to go,' she says.

'Wh-what?'

'Off you go. Let's be having you.'

'Shhh,' he murmurs, and reaches a hand to her cheek.

Martha puts her arms round him, heaves him away from the side of the bath, pulls him on to his feet, guides him towards her front door, bearing half his weight, and carefully walks him down five flights of stairs, her arms supporting both of his elbows, their bodies knocking into each other, his hands warm, his neck pink and sweating, his feet leaden and uncoordinated. 'That's it, nearly there,' she says to herself by way of encouragement. She is beginning to buckle under the weight of him, but there are only a few more steps. She pauses at the door to her building, staggering slightly as her brother sags in her arms. 'Matt?'

He opens his eyes a little wider and looks up at her. Speedily she rehearses her words in her head.

'Matt, I'm chucking you out, because I don't want to make my home available to you for taking drugs. It's not that I don't love you dearly.'

He nods, weakly.

'D'you understand?' She turns the latch of the front door, holds it open for him with her shoulder, and waits for a lull in the density of pedestrians before giving him a little shove on to the street.

Back in her kitchen Martha switches off the grill. The bacon is perfectly cooked. She puts it on a plate and breaks off a triangle of the dark red and white meat and pops it into her mouth. The taste of salt and grease floods the back of her throat. She cannot quite tell if it pleases her or if it is disgusting, the sharp, salty animal fat that clings to the inside of her mouth, to her gums, to the spaces in between her teeth, or perhaps it is delicious, luxuriously savoury, full-flavoured, crisp. How can she not know, she wonders. Why is she not more awake to the world of her feelings?

She puts the bacon in the fridge, knowing she won't eat it, but will throw it away tomorrow when it has greyed and softened a little. Bacon makes her think of men.

She decides to phone her mother.

'How're things?'

'Oh, all right,' her mother says.

'Any news?'

'Well, I've got Matt here doing a detox. He's asleep upstairs.' Martha takes a deep breath. She notices her hand is shaking; she tightens her grip on the receiver. 'He's doing so well. He's really beginning to open up. He talked about going to see a therapist last night. He's making a real effort.'

'Great,' she says, but her voice is flat.

'I'm trying not to get my hopes up, or at least . . . No, it's good to have hopes, it's expectations you have to watch.'

'Oh, right.'

'I just wish I had more wisdom so that I could give him better advice. I mean, we're doing really well, but it's hard to think of ways of keeping him going. He hasn't had anything for ten days now. He's really full of despair, Martha. When he begins to talk, he terrifies himself and has to stop. It's terrible what comes out. So bleak. It breaks my heart. I don't know what to do for him.'

'I do wish he would talk to a professional.'

'He says he'll think about it. I'm trying to make things as pleasant as possible for him here. I've cleared the decks a bit so I can spend a bit of time with him. We had lamb chops last night. He's very shivery so we've got the heating on full. It's lovely and warm.'

'Great.'

'I'm so proud of all the effort he's putting in. He's doing marvellously, if you think about it.'

Martha speaks slowly five sentences she has been trying to frame for a number of years now. 'I know, but I mean he's had these problems for more than fifteen years. I mean, my worry is they're not just going to go away. Even, as you say, if he hasn't had anything for ten days, I don't think it's possible, if he's feeling all that despair that he'll be able not to slip back. He'll only be able to stop if he devotes every single second of every day to the act of not taking drugs. I hate to be negative, but I can't help feeling we're totally out of our depth.' The words expelled through her lips, Martha's stomach makes a series of thick, painful lurches.

'Why are you being so pessimistic?'

'Well,' Martha reaches for the most gentle tone available to her, 'I just don't think that we're the best people to help him.'

There is a long, agonising pause. She feels her mother trying to make huge, dizzy, mechanical shifts. 'I do hear what you say,' there is a hint of tears in the voice, 'I know there's sense in what you say, but I . . . I . . . I can only work with what I've got, can't I? I do have to try and be accepting of that.'

'I know. I know. You're doing brilliantly, really.'

'Anyway, darling, how are you?'

'Me? Oh, you know. Just chugging along nicely.'

'How's the work going?'

'All right, I think, there are one or two pretty nice bits.'

'You're so hard-working and good.'

Suddenly there is nothing else to say.

'Lots of love, then, Mum.'

'Lots of love.'

She wonders what the time is and goes into the bathroom to get her watch, which she had not replaced since her morning wash. It isn't in the small enamel bowl where she is certain she left it. It isn't by her bed either, or on the gleaming white rim of the bath, or in the kitchen. She notices that a saucer full of change in her bedroom has been relieved of all the larger silver coins. She looks in the bathroom again and sees the syringe floating on top of some cotton wool on top of the waste-paper bin. She doesn't want it in her house.

Martha exhales and goes out into the night again, snug in her coat. It is ten o'clock, the huge clock that chimes above the department store tells her. She crosses the road and walks to the edge of the park and follows it for half a mile until she sees a small row of shops on the opposite side of the road. A café filled with orange light beckons. She enters, relieved, and takes a seat at the table nearest the door. It is a long, narrow room, its black and white tiled floor and pale blue walls spotlessly clean. She counts out all the coins in her coat pocket and orders a hot chocolate. She peruses the menu; she is not hungry and has no more funds but it's nice to hear about the different combinations.

In the far corner of the café a couple sit, the tall man with his back to Martha, leaning forward urgently to kiss the other person, a girl, across the width of the table top. The back of the man's head looks oddly familiar. Martha knows that neck. She has stood facing those small ears. Who is it? She wipes her eyes with the edge of her sleeve. The man's jacket she has seen before also and recently. It is someone quite important. Who is it? Who was it? It's Martin, Stella's new . . . friend! All she can see of the girl, who is obscured by the large man's back, is a baggy damson-coloured jumper sleeve, a bottle-green gloved hand. Stella owns no such garments, nor is she likely to. Anxiety gathers thickly at the base of Martha's skull.

Martin, up to tricks? This is insupportable. To be party to something so injurious brings with it responsibilities she cannot run to just now. She imagines facing Stella with this news, over her kitchen table with the sound of night traffic dragging blandly in the background.

Martha freezes, ducking her chin into her chest. She has to get away without being seen. She stands up rapidly to make her escape, but in her hurry she catches the edge of the saucer with her coat sleeve, and cup and half-drunk drink fly across the room, spraying the walls with dark brown droplets and landing with a loud clatter on the black and white tiled floor. Martin swings round to reveal his kissing companion. It is Stella after all.

'Martha!' Stella calls, getting out of her seat and crossing the room. 'What are you doing here? Is everything OK?'

She knows she must look shaky and she feels pink blushes stinging on her cheeks. The waiter kindly clears away the mess and brings her a fresh drink, on the house. She fancies he sees she is troubled but, nevertheless, Martha is hugely grateful for his lack of harsh words.

Martin insists she drink her new drink at their table.

She sits down weakly opposite Stella and arranges her legs under the table in the small triangle of space that is free, determined not to brush her limbs or heels or any part of her against anyone else's body, especially not Martin's. Martin's trousers are made of thick fabric and he wears boots and thin, delicately ribbed, dark socks. Martha takes a slow, careful sip from her warm drink, as though it is boiling hot, raising both saucer and cup up to her chin, in separate hands, then while her face is part obscured by the crockery, she affects a kind of muscular compression with the result that a sort of smile is rigged up on her face. She determinedly turns up the brightness further, clenching something, hard, in her mouth, in her neck and her eyes and she lowers her drink to face her friends with this manufactured brilliant cheer. The awkwardness of their expressions immediately betrays the fact that they have witnessed all these procedures, the cranking-up, the good show.

Stella shuffles her chair away from Martin's so that she is seated opposite her friend. She stretches her torso across the table towards Martha, taking up one of her hands, enclosing it in her own, squeezing it, and then, with a half-smile and a shorter, briefer squeeze, she lets it go. Martha does not know where to look, but she opens her mouth to speak because she knows someone must, although her levels of embarrassment are already excruciatingly high, near breaking-point.

'You're in disguise,' Martha suggests, indicating Stella's uncharacteristic attire.

'I was cold, so Martin lent me his jersey and his gloves,' she says.

'Oh, right. Of course.'

'So,' Martin announces, benevolently.

'It's great to see you,' Stella adds, her voice coated in kindness, her head attentively inclined, her mouth friendly in the extreme, her hand stroking her friend's sleeve.

'Can I get anyone another drink?' Martin asks, eyeing the room for the waiter.

'I'm fine.'

'No, thanks.'

'So,' Martin says again grandly and he says the word as if it denotes, for him, some measure of success. No one says anything back.

'And how is your marvellous little café, Martha?'

Martha replies evenly, 'We went there today. I mean, it's nothing amazing, but it's pretty nice.'

'I feel we should go back there soon to see how that new girl is doing. D'you think she's all right?' Stella asks.

'No-oh, not really,' Martha is loath to admit that anyone anywhere in the world isn't all right at this moment, but she wants to be fair to the waitress.

'And how long have you been frequenting the place?'

'Oh, I don't know. Ages, probably. Years.'

'It is somewhere we like to go, isn't it, Mar?'

'Of course,' Martin says, making a sort of coy reverential expression with his features, with his forearms as if to say, please, *please* do not think I ever mean to intrude on any of your sweet little gatherings. Martha sees something dismissive of their meetings in his gestures also. The man is a huge pig.

She takes another sip of her chocolate, although this time she just holds the warm china between her lips, inhaling the sweet, bitter fumes. She doesn't want it to run out before she is ready to move on. When she raises her eyes again she sees what looks like the end of some silent communication between Stella and Martin; Stella's head is bobbing upward as though at the tail end of an encouraging nod, she is egging him on, eager, permissive. He is meant to proceed now, somehow, along some path, with some newly forged plan.

Martin has started speaking, 'We were wondering, weren't we, if you'd like to, well, we're going to a party in a moment and wondered if you'd like to accompany us, which we'd very much like?'

'Oh, thanks, that's very kind, but I am a bit on the weary side. Normally I'd love to, though.'

Stella is smiling approvingly at them.

For a moment Martha turns dully away. In truth she is finding their behaviour a little hard to take. She imagines them planning how they will handle her, how best to arrange themselves to spare her feelings. A little scheme fleshed out for their not wounding her with their togetherness. If this is something they have discussed Martha feels only horror. It shines on her brightly, at full wattage, how clumsy their behaviour is. They have got the balance wrong, arranging themselves so acutely.

Then, in a sudden flash, it occurs to her what it is she wants, what it is she really needs, and the news breaks through to her, to every inch of her flesh, and the feeling rises, warming her veins and her skin and her heart and is crowned by a huge smile that she feels launching itself spectacularly, dazzlingly on her lips. Now that the water is on *she can go home and have a long hot bath*. She might have had a better idea but she can't think when! She springs up and, with a show of utmost cheer and one or two deft apologies and a rather stylish flourish of her left hand, she makes her goodbyes.

Four

The next evening in the department store there is a huge extravaganza going on: bagpipe players cruise the food halls in full regalia, right down to their shaggy white-fur sporrans. Slow strains of 'Amazing Grace' fill the air, throbbing, emotional, so loud they actually assault the ear. Customers are deserting the food hall in droves even though some other men in tartan are handing out little parcels of smoked salmon speared with wooden cocktail sticks. Clear plastic thimbles full of whisky are being presented from a silver tray by a man in a kilt. The bare backs of his knees are a pale yellowish ochre, as if stained by tobacco. An elderly, brightly dressed man, who has wandered in from the street looking a little the worse for wear, has downed six or seven whiskies in the space of a minute before a hand is put on his shoulder and he is encouraged out of the store. The alcohol glistens orange on his whiskers. Martha grins at him and makes a dismissive movement with her hand in the other direction, as if to say 'They really think they're it, these people with their fruits-of-the-world promotion.' He seems to appreciate her gestures.

She takes a wander through the confectionery hall to clear the mind, allowing the scent of chocolate, thick, sweet and deep, to linger in her nostrils. She walks blindly forward, in some kind of heightened sugar trance. A central display table is covered in large silver-filigree pedestal baskets filled with coloured chocolates, several hundred of them, each unit beautifully wrapped in pink and pale green crenellated foil, and next to them lies a large china dish printed inside and out with old-fashioned pink roses and filled to the brim with chocolate hearts wrapped in red paper, and then there is a sort of wicker ark filled with thirty pairs of chocolate animals, chicks, hens, rabbits, cows, sheep, giraffes, the whole thing presented in a crisp balloon of Cellophane, secured with huge pale green and lilac petersham ribbon. The entire display holds her transfixed for several moments. She spies a huge white stork, whose middle section is hollowed to contain many, many lace-wrapped clusters of pink and white sugared almonds to be dispatched to guests at a christening, she presumes. Next to it stands a four-foot solid white-chocolate doll, bigger than many of the store's most fervent confectionery customers.

Some of the items cost more than a hundred pounds. If she were a rich man with children she rarely saw, wouldn't she dispatch such a gift to each of them? Wouldn't it make them indebted to her for the rest of their lives?

In the confectionery hall, it seemed to Martha that chocolate, that life was a thing very much worth celebrating, always. How did people – the buyers, the manufacturers, the store designers – have the energy to make those sorts of displays, she wondered. She actually found it a little bit moving.

That night Martha sat up until four finishing *The Lock*, propped up with pillows, nervously flapping over the pages, pausing every now and then for gulps of cold tea or a nibble of a doughy fruited bun, guiltily racing towards each fresh word, each fresh paragraph. Only now that the initial hunger and thirst for the words had subsided, had shrivelled a little, it struck her squarely that none of it *was* fresh. It was all stale and jaded,

this highly controlled examination of the systematic shirking
of responsibilities, this lengthy sojourn into the various dis-
tortions, evasions, equivocal responses, bad reasoning, flawed
psychology, ridiculously intricate justifications that were the
hero's stock-in-trade. Everything was sacrificed in order that
his coal black actions might appear for one or two moments
white as snow, in his own eyes at least. Throughout the
narrative the hero developed his own branch of psychology,
a sort of sliding scale of maxims and home-grown wisdom
derived from personal observations custom-designed to beat
down all forms of opposition. Some of it was commonplace
and banal: 'Children are blunt unfeeling creatures, who notice
nothing.' Other portions were more contrived-sounding: 'She
made a colossal row about my not wanting to spend Christmas
Day with her and the children, and it suddenly dawned on me
how hypocritical this was, when they none of them even believe
in God!'

It occurred to her, with the mildest touch of disdain, that
it was quite possible she had thought better of the author, in
the abstract, *before* she had read this book. She could see she
was not exactly impartial, but she'd hoped for something more
imaginative, something more truly fictional such as . . . such as
what? A novel about a community of pirates cavorting wildly
on the high seas in the last years of the eighteenth century?
No, that wasn't quite it, something free and wild, a modern,
backward community in a southern American state, privately
reinstating the drowning of witches, the local cops turning a
collective blind eye. (But you loathe those kind of books! she
told herself. I know. I know. But . . . but . . .)

If she had had to describe in a sentence the kind of book
she would have expected her father to write — a heartless,
intricate cautionary tale about the frantic circles inhabited by
squalid persons of low moral energy — she might even have

come up with the plot of *The Lock* herself. If it wasn't true you'd have had to make it up, the terse and nasty little tragedy of manners. The decline into moral lawlessness of the central character, the basic premise that life was worthless – the book wasn't without power, she didn't go as far as that, it wasn't *not* good, but the universe it painted was so horrible, the days lived out so bleak and useless. One thing was clear: its author had a mighty dim view of the species. The lack of dignity involved in this stance, well, it couldn't be the whole story, could it? Could it?

The next morning Martha staggered home from the college library, lugging two large carrier-bags full of books, stopping at intervals to rest the crooks of her fingers, which were scored red by the overstretched, sinewy plastic handles. Now and then she looked over her shoulder to make sure no one was following her. It was hardly likely, but you couldn't be too careful. The corners of the many volumes scratched and bit the flesh of her calves or bumped her shins when someone passed her at speed, but she persevered.

She thought of her life as a thirteen-year-old schoolgirl, conscientious beyond, even, the desire of the teaching staff. At this point homework filled her entire evening, that and the heaving about of leaden textbooks, seven or eight a night, so many that they actually looked like luggage. Soon the webbed acrylic strap of her schoolbag began to show signs of fraying, then threatened to wear right through as she dragged home the thick, dense-leaved volumes night after night, and the chain of small round bruises that ran from the back of her shoulder to the tip of her breastbone matured from grey to ink-blue, fading to purple, to yellow, and back again. The numbness of her arm, when she put the bag down, the back pain, the freezing and damp dark winter evenings walking home from the bus stop with the kerb crawlers pulling up every five seconds, it seemed to Martha like yesterday.

How civilised the teachers were, next to the heart=struck inhabitants of her mother's house, the pallid, jittery men fresh from prison who started with shock and affront when someone even said, 'Hello'; the blank-faced women in shock; the raucous girls who jostled at the corners of her street. One time, a lifer released on licence into their care had complained every night for a week that he had not slept a wink. His face grew drawn and his shoulders shrank and he lost his appetite and almost stopped talking, all through tiredness. Everything was tried, a special pillow, a different room, a psychologist, until after ten days it transpired that it was nothing more sinister than his bedroom light that was keeping him awake. It had not occurred to him to switch it off, all the bulbs in prison being operated centrally by the wing officers.

Also, there was privacy at school. It was possible to drop your guard. You could have sadness and misfortunes without someone who was much worse off colliding with you at the threshold of the bathroom. Using up all the water!

Back home Martha laid out her secret cargo on the kitchen table. The library had stocked every single one of her father's books. She had paid the surcharge that entitled her to double her lending power and withdrawn them all. Arranging them chronologically on the Formica surface, face up, she opened one or two, noting the typeface, the paper, the acknowledgements, the changes in publishers, odd little mistakes such as 'The right of Anthony Brazil to be identified as the author of this work has been asserted by *her* in accordance with the Copyrights, Designs and Patents Act.'

She surveyed the four rows of unjacketed books: the peacock blues, the sky blues, the faded reds and yellows, chocolate browns, a mid-green, all arrayed like counters or cards in some kind of memory game. She shuffled them round on the table, inhaling the ancient, woody smell of the library, parched leather and dust. Not all of the books had dedications. The ones that did generally just used initials, anonymous, discreet. For RW. To DWC. There were certainly no With Loves, With Gratitude, or For Evers. There was not even an In Memoriam. She examined the title page of each book for words that meant something to her. MOC: Mean Old Cow. SFB: Stupid Fat Bitch. She looked at the date stamps to see which books proved the most popular with the lenders.

One book had been taken out nineteen times that year alone. It had the best title, which was *My Then Wife*. The book had been published in 1979. She would have been six then, Mathew ten. Those three years between leaving the house by the park and 1979, they had not seen their father once. She had often suspected this might well have been her mother's wish. She needed to get back on her feet, reinvent herself, find her sea-legs. You couldn't do that with the past looking over its shoulder, coughing or clearing its throat, just at the moment you were about to make your embarkment. Besides, her father could never have set foot in their new house. His elegant clothing, upright bearing, the clear, cool eyes — how could he have been expected to negotiate the high turnover of guests, the night-time wailing, the jam smears in the butter, the jumpy ex-cons? That would have been more than any of them could have borne.

My Then Wife opened with a blazing row between not a man and his wife but a man and his mother. All sorts of accusations from years ago were flying through the air. This mother had been a spectacularly bad example of the genre, leaving her two children for years in the sole charge of a nanny in a dingy Pimlico flat. As the argument progressed it became clear that the man was not as young as his words suggested, that in fact he was seventy and his mother was eighty-eight. The son remembered clearly his mother's twenty-first birthday party, the dress she had worn, the shoes, the music he had overheard from the nursery wing; that was before the trouble had come, eight months before to be exact.

'You see, dear, I've always been able to put things behind me, quite easily, let go of them then move on, but you seem to have such an obstinate kind of personality, determined to cling on to every little upset. It's such bad luck for you, dear.'

Martha put the book down for a moment. She peered at the smooth author photograph wondering: Was there something artificial in his stiffness, some absence of texture to his skin that rendered him rather less than a person should be?

The author of the book gradually fading from her mind, Martha brought out her own work. Her poet needed her attention, and she pored over his collected poems for the next four hours scarcely noticing the time at all. The agonies of life he put himself through, it was more than extreme, the words themselves seeming to stem from the unravelling of the very fibres of his person, the sharp hurling of his skull against the hardness of his world, his skin thinning increasingly in the face of the colossal hurts and wounds that were for him as everyday as bread, and all the while death dangling, like an old friend, in the back of his mind. Of course he did bad things, couldn't stay faithful, showed disloyalty to his friends and wives, let people down all over the place, after all for much of his life he was an ill man, but he always kept faith with what was really important. He was always most fully himself. There was no doubt at all that he was absolutely the real thing.

At five Martha took a bus to the Dear Friends, sitting next to an earnest young Japanese woman who was hunched over a textbook. Martha tried to make out some of the exercises from the corner of her eye. There was a series of questions.

'Are greedy people good at sharing?' she read. What was this realm of study? Psychology for beginners, a portion-control manual for catering college?'

Stella was in good spirits, although Martha noticed that she did not mention Martin's name once. Was it some curious kind of delicacy?

Back home Martha stooped to gather the sprawling pile of mail that lay at the foot of the front door to her building. Absentmindedly she sifted through the various letters, separating out the envelopes between her cold-stiffened thumb and fingers: bills, furnishing samples, council circulars, pizza money-off coupons, two for one. An advertisement for a place called the Shyness Clinic on Devonshire Place caught her eye. A large see-through packet contained a security-equipment brochure. She flicked it open. A glossy double-page spread showed a security man's bedroom attached to the presidential suite of a Milanese hotel. Opposite a slim four-postered bed with floral canopy was a bank of twelve television screens that provided views of the surrounding area, short-range, medium-range, and long-range with up to a 500-metre radius (aerial views). These sorts of systems started at forty-two thousand dollars.

There were two brief notes from friends. One was a postcard suggesting a trip to a new play from a red-headed slightly hysterical girl Martha had met at college who sold theatre programmes and ice-creams at weekends, and could get complimentary tickets. The other, from a person Martha had known since junior school, a stiff notelet with an autumnal woodland scene, ended, 'Have missed you, Love Laura.' She folded the cards into her bag, only they were too bulky and she took them out again and placed them on the floor in the corner by the front door, vaguely intending to see to them later.

Martha's eyes alighted on the bottom stair where some plans had been left, a large sheet of pale green graph paper with heavy fold-marks depicting the architect's design for the reception/lobby area. She stooped to examine the artist's impression of the glossy black and white diamond-checked marble floor, the velvet curtains hanging over a wall in which there was no window. There appeared to be a tiny gold desk with some kind of filigreed cage surround and a black, liveried porter sitting at it, half obscured by an urn stuffed with tall flowers in this space that is barely twelve foot square. Mr Quinn's decorating ideas, it had to be said, were getting a bit out of control. Were they limitless, his funds? Were there not loans to be repaid, targets to be met, margins, projections, feasibility to be taken into account? To make everything high quality, built to last, top-of-the-range was one thing. But what would be next? Fountains and aquaria, a concierge arranging outings on pleasure boats, a linen department, room service? And if he was unable to acquire the rest of the building?

At the bottom of the pile of letters, Martha noticed a large thick envelope addressed to her. She slid a finger under the flap, pushing it along to break the seal, but the paper was sharp and she sustained a long, sleek cut. She sucked the slitted skin with her lips and tried not to drip blood on the envelope's contents. It was an old-fashioned, formal wedding invitation, the card thick and white, the lettering raised, black, curly script so fancy that it was hard, at first, to make sense of the letters. Not Stella and Martin already! Yet she knew these cards took several weeks to print and really close as they were . . . She read the card, every single word, even the Reply By Fax and the fax number. Then she read it again. And again. Some people with long Italian names invited her to the wedding of their daughter Stephania. She knew no one of that name. Where the groom's name should be all there was was the name of her father, Anthony James Brazil. She tried to work it out, but all the combinations she lead herself towards baffled her completely. So if the groom was her father, she tried to clear the fog in her head, if her father was the groom, but wasn't it some kind of mistake, some muddle over generations? So the Italian-sounding person, she must be . . . No, that couldn't be right! For a moment she was unsure whether her father's middle name really was James. Wasn't it Michael? She was almost certain of this. Could it be a cousin of his who was to be wed? A young man, starting out in life, her brother's age. She sat down for a moment. The fax number she recognised as her father's.

She inclined her head to the opposite side from the side that she usually inclined it towards when thinking. She had not minded, not in any giant or detrimental way, anything that had happened to her or round her for nearly eighteen months and she wasn't about to start now. You see you have to look at this in another way, she urged herself, in order to get the required thoughts. Sometimes, she reminded herself sternly, if you're honest, you do worry about him getting lonely, cutting himself off, entering a narrower and narrower sphere of his own making, while the real world carries on, pretty much unregarded.

Martha slips into her coat and goes out into Oxford Street again. It is quieter than usual, she doesn't know why, and she walks determinedly, taking quick steps and keeping her body as close as possible to the slick plate-glass windows of the shop-fronts, only veering towards the centre of the pavement when someone else, walking in the same fashion, refuses to move out of her way. The sky looks bruised with clouds, the filthy grey smudges clotted deposits of all the city's smoke and grime. She peers down at her legs, walking her along, her arms swaying slightly, her pace steady and loose-limbed. She feels a strange thick fog spreading in her body, bearing down on her, an extension of the gloom above and then a sense of remove grows around her as though thin needles of invisible screening lie between her and her surroundings, dimming her reflexes and her references, cordoning her off from the world that other people go about in. Her ears are clogged and blocked, and she sees herself lagging behind her body; even her vision is a little blurred. But her limbs keep going, orderly, brisk, rational.

As the dark clouds above the tube station begin to clear a little and sharp threads of brilliant sunshine pierce the street, bathing the tops of shoppers with such a soft golden light that you cannot see their heads, she sees what she is looking for: a large stationer's with a phone and fax bureau in the basement. She borrows a single piece of paper and a pen from the baby-faced man with no hair who sits behind the counter. She leans against a book and writes in small neat letters, 'Many congratulations and every happiness to you both. Wouldn't miss it for the world. With love, Martha.'

The bald man behind the desk nods approvingly and sends off her fax transmission. He is all smiles. Martha thinks to stop and talk to him, searching her brain for something interesting to say. 'Isn't it a lovely day?' she mumbles, but ridiculously she can feel a tear running down her cheek and she turns her face away and scuttles back towards home.

It is a turbulent and terrifying street scene that greets her when she emerges from the bowels of the shop. She has never seen so many desperate buses and choked cars, horns sounding, people swarming red and angry and it seems that this time the teeming, roaring, grinding, screaming street before her has really gone too far.

She ferries herself to the department store and rides the escalator shakily to the top floor. In the bed and bath department she positions herself next to a huge bale of baby blue towels and inhales their odour, dry powdery cleanliness in her nostrils, in the air around her. She reaches out a finger and strokes the short, soft-looped pile.

Back home, she bashes open the door to a deafening clamour: drilling, banging, hammering, low, growly suction noises, sharp-edges flinty sounds, and they seem to be coming from all levels of the building.

The works on her building are gathering speed now. Nearly every day a different team of men with their own particular sphere of expertise arrives: a new architect has been employed, after a dispute with the old one, a Danish man, good-looking and soft-spoken; there were parquet fitters, upright and gentle-manly, who warned her about the dust and the noise. In the luxury flat they were installing a kind of flooring in which solid blocks of wood were arranged in large squares each framing a rounded configuration of chevrons, which formed a flower-like pattern. This type of effect was called Versailles. It was one of the most expensive kinds of flooring in the world, costing nearly two hundred pounds a metre, the men said. When finished the floor's rich and smooth dark-honey-coloured patina would look beautiful, deep and glossy like a mysterious lake against the cool white of the walls. Martha slid on it in her socks and that was pleasant enough, but dancing was what it was really for, surely. Then Italian marble specialists rolled up, cursing under the weight of slabs of rose marble for the bathrooms ('An inch thick, not four mil,' Quinn had said, 'it really does makes all the difference') and long and broad pale grey lengths for the worktops in the kitchen. There was a taciturn, bearded carpenter who was copying some kitchen cabinets from an eighteenth-century design to support the marble, and a carpeting expert who was dyeing all the bedroom carpets especially to match some fabric samples he had been given, the palest dove grey, the most delicate duck egg blue and deepest midnight navy. He was jovial, in fact he was overfriendly, and gave her snippets of information she would rather have been spared, such as the history of his indigestion, which he linked to a particularly heavy Indian meal eaten at top speed the night before. Then there were the painters, who were the men she liked best. They called her in sometimes to see their handiwork, standing back and shuffling paint-pots out of her way. They asked her advice about one or two of the colours. 'Is it to your taste?' they asked her. 'Would you have chosen a bolder colour scheme?' The smell of fresh paint and polish and new underlay Martha adored, she often popped into the flats to take a sniff, but it had its poignant side, the odour bringing with it, unfailingly, the sense of endings: overfamiliar, inevitable, sad.

Martha wanders up the stairs, greeting the men she passes and smiling, addressing brief, low-key remarks on salty subjects. On her landing she peers through the door of the family flat which has been left open. 'Hello?' she calls out, as she pokes her head round the door; 'Hello?' as she wanders over to the children's bedroom. In the family flat things have changed almost beyond recognition. All items pertaining to the family have been stuffed into the children's bedroom, which is now a ragged jumble of bedding and cans of food, dressing-tables, bunk beds and chairs, saucepans and towels. In the kitchen the fitted cabinets have been ripped out, and the old cooker and the fridge stand forlornly trailing the wires and pipes that have been rudely gouged from their sockets, still sporting the grease-marks and bits of dried dinner and wear and tear of family life. Next to these discarded goods there are some glossy new appliances: a double oven, a six-ring steel chef's gas hob, a dishwasher and a washing-machine, all with stainless-steel fronts standing gleaming in the centre of the room, waiting for connection. Martha shakes her head at these changes.

The family seem further and further away, their difficulties hardening into some sort of irrevocable permanent reality.

She gathers an armful of the children's clothes that have been slung unceremoniously into a crumpled pile on the floor and begins to fold them carefully, matching up the little bobbly sleeves of jerseys, the corduroy legs of mini trousers, buttoning buttons and smoothing down creases. She nips back into her flat for a moment and returns with a bag full of paper and ribbons she keeps for wrapping birthday presents. As she folds she inserts white tissue-paper leaves between the jumpers and the vests, layering each item neatly in one of the spare packing boxes, tying the parcels with red or blue satin braid. It is the least she can do. She peers into a black bin-bag in the corner of the room and tears it open, revealing the scent bottles and silver brushes and combs from the dressing-table mixed up with leaky shampoo and some opened packets of dry food. Carefully she removes the precious items and covers them in the bubble wrap that has been left by the door, arranging the goods carefully in two of her best old shoe boxes, labelling clearly the lids of the boxes, SPECIAL THINGS.

The harsh strains of morning light are flooding the room, whitening the skin on her arm as she does the packing; picking up a child's shoe here, tripping on a yellow rubber duck and stowing it away neatly there, putting all the stray pieces back into a jigsaw-puzzle's box. It is a saddening task, this tidying and arranging. But it feels to her respectful, and it is because of this she perseveres.

She thinks of the baths she shared with her brother when they were young and perfect: him bright and lanky aged eight, her rounded and curly at four. What a hero she had held him then, turning cartwheels down the length of the street, clasping her hand firmly in the face of traffic or danger or thunderstorms, bringing her breakfast in bed when she was ill once, with toast cut into fingers, and on the fingers, in red and yellow jams, he had painted faces and little waistcoats and buttons. She pictured him showing off his prowess on the skateboard, *so* elegant, or launching huge bunches of daffodils at their mother, still dripping dew and trailing mud, from the local park. This was before he had become morose and masochistic. When he was little he had not been exacting in the least, not flailing about and slumping in turn with his crazy demands: two eyes for an eye, four teeth for a tooth, five, six, even. Even with whole mouthfuls, if he took aim and struck a blow to each of them, her, their mother, their father, and if the cull of teeth lay dead and white, their bloody roots tangled like dark plug-wires on the floor, would it be enough? 'Would anything ever be?' She said the words quietly into the still, silent room.

She wondered where her brother was now. Martha dimly wished him things, for his safety, and then she wished that if he wasn't safe that he might be with old friends, and be warm and clothed and sheltered, even enjoying himself, actually having times. At other moments her hopes for him are of a different character, more austere, more astute. Then she longs for the day when his life becomes so terrible, so intolerable on every separate level that he would be cornered into a workable plan of recovery, because it would seem easier and nicer than carrying on as he was.

She hoped he wasn't back at her mother's house, lapping up her hospitality, skinning her nerves with his unmeetable promises, forcing her into agonising paroxysms of love. And then the sad thing was he had been known to use these little sojourns of comfort and fine treatment at her house as little rest cures. In their mother's home he recuperated, ate chops from her vegetarian plates and rested up on soft pillows until he saw a return in his energy. Then, when he had accrued enough strength, off he'd go, fitter and fatter, more able to meet the physical demands which the getting and taking of drugs tended to make on him.

In 1994 the number of deaths that came from heroin were numbered at about five hundred. She had all the figures at her fingertips. This was nothing compared to the two hundred thousand fatalities that cigarettes and alcohol directly cause, but as a portion of all serious and dedicated, intravenous, long-term career addicts it still numbered almost three per cent. She had leaflets and reports from the X Trust, the Y Campaign, the Z Foundation, the W Project. She was on all the mailing lists, had all the support-group numbers. All agencies seemed to agree on one thing: don't let the addict become your primary focus, but lead your life as happily and decently as you can because that was what would help the addict most.

She imagined Matt picturing in his mind his own funeral, furnishing the graveyard with mourners, stricken and bedraggled. Sharp grey rain would be shooting down. She was sure this was something that he did, conjure up this scene as some sort of daydream, a chance to deliver that last filthy reproach to all. 'After what you've done to me,' he would be saying, 'this was the only possible outcome. Look at how bad I feel, look how miserable I am. I cannot countenance a life without drugs. I would rather be a dead person. Now will you feel for me?' This was something she had to be prepared for. 'Now will you recognise what a terrible start in life I had?'

If he should father a child and the little baby was born shaking and heaving, fighting for its life, screaming with painful withdrawal cravings, feeling from its very beginnings that something essential to its well-being was absent and being denied — that was what you'd call a bad start in life. That was a poor, ruinous funeral to picture in your mind's eye, the dwarf coffin, light as feathers.

She had heard of elderly women who gave up half their pensions to buy dope for their fifty-year-old sons, spitting the resin into a cup of tea during a prison visit, watching their golden boys stuff the brown lump under the elasticated waistband of their tracksuit trousers, and straight up their anuses, keeping it safe and warm for later. Or grandmothers who scored heroin in pubs for their granddaughters or great-grandsons whom they considered ill, in the belief that heroin was the best medicine for them. These women accepted eagerly the sacrifices they had to make for their youngsters' life-styles. The pain their boys caused them, their girls, well, it was the same as if your child required a kidney, you couldn't turn your back, not when you were really needed. 'You see, I love him to bits,' they'd say. But they'd got the whole thing the wrong way round! The true sacrifice, the equivalent of the kidney pain, that would be saying, 'Sorry I can't make this drug-taking easier for you by showing it any friendliness,' then showing them the door. That would be agony and huge wrenches, that would be truly going against your own nature, for another's good, not all this topsy-turvy rushing about with pills and ten-pound notes.

Almost anything you did for an addict just helped the illness along. That was the problem. In her mind the rules chimed: *If in doubt do NOTHING. Do NOT cover up for the user, do NOT give their habit support of any kind. Let the addicts FEEL the CONSEQUENCE of their actions. Do NOT try to lessen their difficulties because it is the difficulties the addicts face which may lead them into recovery.*

Sometimes she wondered if she could know Matt casually, run into him now and then, for a drink or some food, regard his drug-taking as a life choice, an expensive, dangerous hobby like parachuting or hang-gliding. But there was nothing that did not have to do with drugs that caught his interest. Besides, she wanted her brother back, the humorous, thoughtful, velvet-skinned child in the bath, the kind and nervy twelve-year-old who read her bedtime stories about a friendly bus. The thirteen-year-old swerving round the corner on his green-wheeled skateboard purchased with the proceeds of his Saturday job at the fishmonger's, so suave! The man about the house.

One day when she was fifteen or so Martha came home from school to find a languid-looking man with crumpled hair and an old-fashioned collarless shirt sitting at the kitchen table. Half shaven, with a floppy bone-coloured jacket slung casually over the back of his chair, as if to mark out, beyond doubt, that it *was* his chair, he sat reading a newspaper Martha did not recognise. Round his neck was a gents' second hand evening scarf with greasy-looking fringes. He did not look up when Martha entered the room, although he could not have been oblivious to her presence. Martha peered at him closely. 'Hello?' she said.

'Oh, hi there,' he answered. There was something about him, his loosely crossed legs, his clammy-looking face, his overall mien, which she could only really describe as shaky-looking. With an odd little expression that suggested he knew his behaviour was a little ridiculous-seeming, that he himself found it so, he stood up and extended his arm in order to shake her hand, so she had crossed the room obligingly and it was only then that the thick wave of stale-alcohol smells hit her. She took a deep breath. 'Mum's at the shops. She'll be back in a mo,' he informed her.

Mum! Her mouth hung open, and she peered at him through narrowing eyes.

'Yeah, hink so.'

He said 'hink so' and 'mo' with a little boyish gleam in his eye and a vocal flourish as if to say to her, 'I have beguiling ways once you get to know me.' His 'hink so', he seemed to suggest, had melted hearts in the past. But Martha had no desire to get to know him. 'Bye then,' she said, and went up to her room, spreading out her books, sharpening up all her pencils at both ends.

But the next morning he was eating slivers of toast and lime marmalade in the kitchen, quite ensconced. 'Mr Tambourine Man' was playing. It was a song she loathed. Once, much later when a friend had asked her what world record she would like to break, if she could choose any, she had said 'Mr Tambourine Man'.

After that he was always about, and it seemed to Martha he was always either fetching or draining or rinsing out the thick brown cider bottles that bore the Woodpecker insignia. He saved up the empties to take back to the shop, lining them up outside the back door. The deposits on fourteen bottles equalled a new bottle, on the house so to speak. At night Martha heard the strange arrhythmical squawking of bed-springs. Then one morning she had come down and there he was splayed out in a chair in the sitting room. Martha heard small comedy frog-like noises and wondered where they were coming from until she realised that the man was croaking in his sleep. Low, long belches, every ten seconds or so, half a snore, half a hiccup. This kind of drunkenness she had only witnessed in cartoons. Still the fringes of his silk scarf dandled the lap of his trousers where the fabric looked darker than on the knees, on the legs. Martha closed her eyes and opened them again as another low gravelly croak slipped out of his mouth. They were not without scent these noises, they smelt a little like farts, or farts crossed with something sharper, less ripe and more acidic – vomit, that was it.

Martha's mother emerged, brisk, cheerful. She cleared away the bottles that circled his seat, raising her eyes to the ceiling good-humouredly. 'I don't know,' she said, almost unconscious of the fact that she was not alone. 'What are we going to do with you?' Her words were fond, she went to the man and laid a light hand on his shoulder. She straightened the folds in his scarf, laying it flat across his chest for warmth, her face brimming with soft feelings.

The months wore on. Martha kept more and more to her room. The man was all right drunk, but sober! His friends visited and chastised her mother for her bourgeois ways, the yellow paint in the sitting room, the wealth of books, a legacy of her father. The man was a book-dealer by trade and occasionally made Martha a gift of something rare and battered; she felt compromised by these gifts. They seemed like bargains. The early editions of Shelley stiffly bound in calfskin with tooled gold lettering but no backs. Gradually his business seemed to decline. Then Martha noticed he, too, began selling some of her mother's books, exchanging them for cider. His scarf grew greyer and greyer, the silk fringes lank and ratty, specked with tiny morsels of food until finally he laundered it, afterwards, with great care and performance, ironing in a large brown mitre-shaped singe, because he got distracted, head in the clouds, lips clamped round a cider bottle. Still the bed-springs jangled appallingly at night. The croaks made regular appearances at dawn. In fact the high and low notes marked out the different times of day. Time passed. Martha stopped acknowledging the remarks the man addressed to her. Her mother, furious, chastised her: 'You think of no one but yourself.' Martha said nothing. About this time her brother decided to move back in and that spring he lurked moody and bleary-eyed on the top floor, while the man drank steadily in the basement kitchen. Her mother moved between the floors of the house clearing and clucking over her boys.

The day of the wedding approached and Martha was calm now. She sat on her chair in her kitchen writing her thesis and was quite calm. When she walked out into Oxford Street to pick up a scone or a fruited bun, or to observe the bilious traffic raging and spewing up fumes, it seemed to her she was the calmest individual in an atmosphere that actually invited frenzy and aggression. She woke up calm. She ate a calm supper at night. She conversed calmly with the people she met who did not seem to her calm at all. One lady on a bus complained to Martha at length about her awful dental problems. Yanking her index finger against the corner of her mouth she revealed the offending rotting gums. 'I had to go private in the end. Twelve hundred pounds he charged me, and for making it worse! I'm a lady, I don't like to use words, but the things I could call him!' Her gums were almost black and the teeth thickly caked with chalky yellow plaque, particles of which fell out on to her hand as she spoke, falling like Day-Glo dandruff on to her black trousers. And the smell! It had taken Martha's breath away. Even when she was climbing off the bus, the woman was calling out after her, 'Let that be a lesson to you, d'you hear, young lady?' That wasn't calm at all.

Her poet wasn't given to calmness. He ranted and raged wildly, once firing off a letter to an esteemed critic who had disliked his latest offering, which bore only three straggly words 'YOU HURT ME.' Calmly she tried to think of all the ways that people hurt people. Her poet wounded his first wife by writing a long sonnet sequence about an obsession he had with another woman, although, to give him credit, he didn't publish it until the marriage was long dead.

One morning, during this time, it occurred to Martha, perfectly calmly, that if she ever tried in any serious and really efficient way to hurt her parents, she ran the very severe risk that they actually might not notice. This thought led to other, darker lines of inquiry that pitched themselves against the insides of her scalp or flashed into her brain, sheer and dazzling. If it transpired that you were actually incapable of inspiring tenderness in others, did that mean huge frightening things about the rest of your life, about your powers, your chances?

On the day of the wedding Martha fusses at the mouth of the church unbuttoning her herringbone coat then doing it up again, picking at a hangnail on her little finger, giving the briefest of smiles to the thirty or so guests as they arrive. They do not even know who she is, these men in suits, austere, sharp and straight-backed, the smartly dressed women who looked intelligent and artistic in a disciplined sort of way. Martha puts a hand to her head to restrain her hair, which is blowing wild and straggly in the wind. Her thin, pale scarf billows in her eyes and tiny drops of rain are flecking the back of her neck. The church is vast, dark, strange-smelling and cool. The assembled guests barely fill a pew, yet they arrange themselves in ones and twos and threes over the first four rows of seating. Three priests walk in through a side door dressed in yellow and white robes with sashes trimmed with gold and fringed with emerald green. They each make a stiff bow to the altar, and walk up the shallow steps and each one bends to kiss the altar cloth. If there was one thing Martha's mother and her father shared, it was a distaste for Christianity. If there was one area where they agreed it was that religion was a crutch.

Everyone stumbles to their feet. The bride wears a simple short-sleeved ivory silk high-waisted dress that makes her look a funny shape, narrow in places, broad in others, but you can see from her face when she turns to examine the select congregation that she is beautiful. Her eyes fix on Martha and her mouth breaks into an enormous, delicate smile. She looks shy. Her night-dark hair is glossy and slightly wavy down her back and her eyes are huge, full of soft feelings. The bride turns again and crosses herself in front of the priest, colours a little and lowers her head. She is in her own world. She isn't obviously younger than Martha, possibly she is slightly older, and this is a relief. Martha's father stands stiffly by the woman's side.

The strange ceremony proceeds and an ancient, shrivelled Italian woman in neat dark suit with bosoms worn low climbs up to the lectern to read a passage from the Bible in Italian. Then suddenly all the Italians sink to their knees and bury their heads. Martha joins them, clumsy, self-conscious. She imagines their prayers, their sorrys, their thank-yous. Her father has arranged himself, his features, so they are unopen to scrutiny, but his fingers betray something, shuffling his large bunch of keys from hand to hand and back again, the clinking metal resonating loudly in the arched gilt roof of the church. The bride carries a large bunch of greenish-white roses and he bends to sniff them, burying his head in the blooms. Above him hangs a large bronze crucifix and the Christ figure in agony. Martha focuses on the nails beaten into his hands, into his feet, tries to imagine the pain, the ripped skin, the open flesh, the chipped bone, the pressure of a body suspended by these sharp wounds.

Her father does not seem to be speaking the words of any of the prayers, but he looks thoughtful. What could make someone who thought religion the worse kind of cooked-up nonsense embark on this kind of an adventure? The only possible answer came back at her instantly, clear and true: love.

Afterwards they have lunch, the twenty-eight or thirty people, in the pink and gold private dining room of a grand hotel adjacent to the church. The chief priest accompanies them and Martha takes the seat next to him. He speaks animatedly about his love for his nephews whom he rarely sees, offering

Martha his pudding because he lacks a sweet tooth. Always has. The bride sits on Martha's left, in wedding-dress and lacy cream shawl, making speedy inroads into her food.

'I'm so sorry Matthew couldn't make it,' her father's new wife begins. 'I did send out an invitation to him. At your mother's house. I don't know if he received it.'

'You see, he's not at all well,' Martha explains.

The woman nods. She knows. 'He's in my prayers,' she says. Her face has delicate little lines around the pale brown lips indicating big-heartedness and her soft eyes to Martha seem infinitely kind. 'I want to say if there's anything you think I could do, not to help him, because obviously that would be to presume . . . but anything I could do and I don't even know what that means, not really, I do hope very, very much that you would always say to me, count on me as a friend.'

'Thank you. Thank you.' A waiter comes and refills Martha's glass. The bride's glass is still full, but she places her hand over it, nevertheless.

'Will you be living in the same place, or or d'you think you'll set up home again somewhere else or . . . ?'

'I have a flat not a very long distance from A — from your daddy, so I imagine I'll come back and forth between the two. I need solitude for my own work, and obviously Anthony does and—'

'Can I ask what your work is?'

'I'm a violinist.'

'Oh, really?'

'When I meet your father and tell him what I do he said, "I'm so unmusical I can barely play the gramophone." And I fear it's true.'

'It is?'

'Well, obviously there are different ways . . .'

'And so you'll do the practising in your flat, use it like a rehearsal place, an office and then . . . at the house . . .'

'Yes, I'll visit at the house. Perhaps not every day I'll come there . . . We'll see how it gets along.' The bride sighs and flaps her hands slightly.

The priest chats to Martha about a convent at Marble Arch where there are nuns praying twenty-four hours a day for all the people in London, because city life is so hard. 'I'm very glad to know that,' Martha says. She is.

She peers across the table and there is her father's face smiling and the smile is wonky, tentative, a nervous thing. Something important is happening for him. He looks, as she fixes him with her gaze, slightly at a loss, dwarfed, swamped, at sea in this new and strange territory. She looks again. Something in his face has opened up. She has never seen it like this ever. It is still a private face, but it has altered unquestionably. There is more living in it. The things that are happening on the inside of the scalp seem to be having a bearing on the things that are happening on the outside. She has never seen anything like it. She cannot take her eyes off him. What will he do next? She bends to take a spoonful of the priest's pudding, which he has passed to her, a little chocolate and strawberry confection fashioned to resemble a swan, and when she looks up she sees to her amazement that, as a result of some kind of teasing from a fellow guest, her father is actually blushing. There are roses in his cheeks, roses of mirth and shyness and embarrassment mingled. Martha drops her spoon, which falls with a clatter to the floor. She thinks back to the article in the paper she recently read about him: 'To say that his face is inscrutable seems like a waste of words, like saying a book isn't swimmable or a guitar shouldn't be eaten.' Or whatever it was. If you could see him now, though, Martha thinks, if you could see him now. And the funny thing was, this slight show of feeling, it hadn't shattered anything, not at all, it was actually enhancing the other things, the elegance, the intelligent bearing, the acutely defined interior sense of self.

As she stares at him Martha feels an onset of her own feelings, unfamiliar ones, rose-coloured, limitless, askew ones, ones with a kind of speed and momentum to them that take her entirely by surprise, and for a second as she feels them soaring she realises she ought to do something important, historic, make some kind of monumental presentation or declaration, do some high-handed, formal thing, a speech or some sort of composition or unveiling, at the very least she ought to tell a spectacularly funny joke. She scours her mind for something: thinking, thinking.

She shovels a bit of chocolate swan's wing into her mouth, mashing a strawberry against the rim of her plate with the back of her spoon, for inspiration. The strawberry tastes odd to her, powdery, saccharine, as though strawberry-flavoured pulp has been injected into a delicate super-fine crimson casing. When she catches his eye again he is still looking at her. Martha takes her courage in her hands and shuffles round to where he is sitting, squeezing into a chair vacated by someone whose early departure was necessitated by the pressures of work.

'Everything all right there?' she says, instantly regretting her tone, which has come out a bit nursy and patronising; it had a slight, 'And how are we this morning?' slant to it. All her father does is nod, but it's in no way unfriendly.

Emboldened by something – possibly the brace of chocolate swans that are swimming inside her (chocolate wings, meringue feathers, choux-pastry heads), or is it the wine? – she takes the conversation on. 'Slightly makes me feel like getting married.'

'Well . . . I rather think it might suit you.'

'Do you?' That he could have considered what she might like is a crazy idea, stimulating, jaunty. 'Do you really?'

'Well, of course I can't really say with any sort of certainty, but since you mention it . . .'

'Well, you may well be on to something.'

He nods courteously, respectfully, she feels.

'Any news of the dope fiend at all, or not really?'

'Well . . . business as usual, I think, with him.'

Her father nods and takes a brief sigh. 'He writes to me now and then, mainly things to do with money. And he puts these hare-brained schemes to me. He says what he'd really like is to become a mini-cab driver and could I get him a car. But I can't. I really can't. If it's just a question of him driving drugs round for other people . . .'

'And I suppose you have to think of the public as well.'

'Of course, the poor unsuspecting public! And then he sends me these crazy photographs.'

'Photographs?'

'Well, there'll be a picture of him sprawled in some hospital bed with an enormous bandage on his big toe, the bandage itself a foot high. Or a photograph of his arm with a huge hole in it. Literally a hole. His exhibitionistic streak is . . . well . . . well, it's so odd.'

'Yeah, but he absolutely doesn't do it to try to make you feel bad. I'm certain of that. I mean, him sending you those pictures, it's not meant to be unfriendly in any way. It's just him keeping in touch. It's the equivalent of other people sending out . . . I don't know . . . snaps of their new baby or something.'

Her father laughs. 'That's exactly what it is. And he is his new baby, practically every day!'

He pauses. In the pause Martha thinks, Aren't we getting on well, though!

Her father has started talking again, only now his voice is less animated than when describing her brother's cheerful postcards from hell. 'Speaking of which . . .'

'Speaking of what?'

'Well, we'll have to arrange things extremely carefully ourselves.'

'Carefully?'

'In order to accommodate everyone, in the best way, without too many . . . disturbances. I don't know if Stephania mentioned to you that she is expecting a child . . .'

Martha closes off her hearing. A baby! She nods swiftly, up and down, up and down, too much, she realises as she performs the motion, but she didn't have the first clue about how to stop. 'Of course, yeah,' her voice was saying. 'Yeah. The baby and everything. That's right. That might just need a slight bit of accommodating, somewhere along the line.'

She pictures an unattended pale-faced baby shut away in a low dark basement room, its limp cries piercing her heart like needles.

'Well, quite,' her father replies.

Martha's heart sinks, in tight uncoordinated lurches; in fact her entire body slumps against her chair, and she doesn't see it coming but suddenly it dawns on her that her chin is almost level with her father's coffee-cup. She makes to stand up, but trying to manoeuvre her legs into some sort of platform for her body is impossible. Words are flying out of her mouth and she feels bits of undigested swan's beak gnawing at her insides. 'You know, I . . . um . . . the thing . . . You see, the thing is . . .' She is on her feet now and leaning casually back against her chair, only the chair is not leaning against anything and it falls over and she almost goes down with it. 'Goodness!' she says. A flurry of waiters leap over to rescue the chair. One goes to fetch her coat. Martha straightens herself, smoothing down her dress, tugging at the hem, raising a flattening hand to her unruly hair. 'I've got a bit of work that I have to finish by this evening, I wouldn't generally mention it, it's nothing much, but if I don't get it done, while the iron's hot, I mean, it'll makes things slightly awkward if I . . . so thanks enormously, it's been really . . .'

Just then she sees something moving beneath her father's mild expression: a dry, humorous note which for a second seems to imply he is finding her little, shocked display, on his wedding day, faintly amusing. It is a loathsome expression he holds, superior, arch and deathly cold. She takes a deep breath and one or two steps back because suddenly she feels some low, icy rage stirring in her and breaking its chains and seeping and soaring through her guts flooding freely her heart and lungs. Her father is speaking: 'Sort of wouldn't mind looking over something myself,' he says, glancing at his watch,' but I don't suppose, no, perhaps not today . . .'

If she doesn't get out soon — well. The fury creeps up further. Her face and head are boiling hot now, pneumatic, crimson, with steam flying out of her mouth. Her hand is trembling round the glass it clasps and she imagines the heavy crystal flute smashed hard against his cool face, grinding in the jagged shards.

Just then the waiter arrives smoothly with her coat and eases the glass out of her hand in order to feed her arm into one of the silky caramel-coloured sleeves. And in seconds her voice says goodbye (politely) and thank you and good luck (foolishly) and she is wandering homewards but she is pretty sure her father saw the look on her face, the sharp, bitter eyes that flashed violently with some kind of freakish, murderous intent. The last time she had seen that look was four years ago when she had opened her eyes during sexual intercourse to gaze into her frenzied bedmate's face and his eyes were two thin, cruel slits, and he was actually cringing! She had avoided it since then.

How she got home she did not know, because a peculiar kind

of grief stole over her, and it was so physical that her feet stopped walking in their accustomed way and her mouth let out these strange sounds, low animal noises, and her hands kept springing up, making tangled, thrashing movements, as though trying to rearrange items on a narrow, low shelf. 'What is it?' she kept asking. 'Nothing has really changed,' she said. 'Everything is absolutely all right.' But in her heart the small counters of sense that kept her brave had all been played and there just weren't any more left. She howled in the street, marching blindly on, her body swinging wildly from one side of the pavement to the other, knocking into people, she couldn't even tell if they were men or women, falling down kerbs, once actually thudding against the bonnet of a car that crawled along in a traffic jam adjacent to her building.

Over the next few days Martha took a remote view of things, avoiding herself carefully, moving about with stealth in relation to the sharp little jolts and stabs that circled her, withdrawing scrupulously when it was required, taking pains not to press for any reactions or impressions or ideas. During this time she countered anything difficult that arose with a thick, blank wad of refusal. It seemed like the kindest and the safest thing. If she wasn't actually there, if she denied and dismissed wherever possible, then of course nothing could get at her. She tiptoed around the scenes she encountered. It was behaviour that seemed to her, wherever she had got to, gentle and respectful, like that which a child might show to a relative who was ill or nervous or very elderly, or one who housed a furious temper.

Starved of thoughts, her head clung on to aches. These were spectacular, coursing wildly from the dome of her scalp to the pinched and knitted tips of her shoulder-blades. Seams of pain shot down her arms. It was a great strain simply supporting her neck, which felt full of something weighty and poisonous. To keep it from sagging, stooping, buckling over took concentration.

When she blinks now, it takes seconds for the darkness to clear, and it is only very gradually that her blurry vision, ringed with black circles and covered with a watery, greyish film, comes back into focus to register, sharply, her situation. She has found this, in reality, over the past few days: she either sees things in such bold relief that it sends a hard cramp over the outer edges of her face causing little clusters of wrinkles, arrow-like, to flare out from the corners of her squinted eyes, or at other times everything just floods hazily into view, monotone, dingy, silent.

As far as possible, Martha also avoids her flat. She does not answer the phone if it rings, although she couldn't have said if it did or not. The three flats in her care are where she mainly roams. It seems to her that they are nowhere near as clean as they ought to be. In the large flat, subtle pale smears of something greasy have settled on the skirting. More workmen have been in making repairs, and there is a fresh film of dust over everything, as well as assorted debris, shards of plaster, crumbly rubble pieces, paint-pots. It looks like the scene of a fight. An abandoned grey tool-box that spills spanners and pliers and complicated knots of wire indicates that they have more work to do and intend to return. She notices that the electrician has begun to install some new light switches and disconnected some of the ancient sockets that still use two-pin plugs. One or two new pieces of furniture, a small chest-of-drawers in a gleaming amber wood with fancy diamond-shape inlay and a footstool, have arrived. They sit squarely in the entrance hall, loosely bubble-wrapped.

Martha sets to work with a cloth, wiping away at the smeared woodwork, sweeping, hoovering, dusting, polishing, washing and rinsing, the air thick with sharp, dry detergent smells. As she works she examines her cleaning cloths, sees them turn in minutes from sunflower yellow to black, from perforated white and feather-light to grey and sodden. She squeezes her cleaning rag into her bucket of soapy water watching the grey bubbles fizz and dissolve. Sooty spots settle and dry on her forearms, like dark freckles. She scratches at the spaces between her fingers that are pink and a little raw from too much contact with detergent until blood comes. The cuts sting and fizzle when she reaches into the bucket of suds. There are smut marks round her mouth and streaking her forehead, and she looks despairingly at the high pile of filthy cloths. In order for the woodwork to gleam a cloth must be sacrificed. You can't get those kind of marks out again. It seems to her then that all cleaning is a lie, a pretence, all you can really do with dirt and grime is move it on, displace it. You can't be rid of it.

She lingers in the bed and bath section on the fourth floor of the department store, fingering a new line of Italian bedding that has just come in. It is top of the range and comes in large, padded presentation boxes, covered in blue and white striped cotton ticking. They contain thick and crisp king-size hem-stitched linen sheets. A pair with four pillow cases costs more than five hundred pounds. It is meant for matrimony, she thinks, or for wrapping the dead. The dead need the softest of fabrics next to their skin. Of that she is certain. Flesh that is not still alive chafes more easily, falls away from the bone.

She scuttles off, down four flights to the food hall, surveying the different nations' food counters, the jars of sugared almonds in twenty different colours, the pyramids of yellow rice studded with dried cranberries, the tangled nests of green and white and black noodles, the huge tureens of glossy red sauces, the portions of fish in pastry, the meat in aspic jelly, the diamond-shaped canapés, arranged on silver trays and colour-coded, salmon, asparagus, caviar.

Everyone she sees is celebrating something, clutching flowers and wine and boxes of cakes, holding little quilted polystyrene trays of golden Lebanese sweets in the flats of their hands, clasping tubs of exotic salads and pastel-coloured purées to their chests, for picnic life. In the corner, by the bakery, sultry Arab couples balance on the high stools of the oyster bar. 'Buy something nice to eat, whatever you fancy,' she says out loud, but nothing calls to her. She investigates other departments with which she is unfamiliar: men's accessories, belts, cufflinks, underpants, wallets, red button-on braces, sports equipment, the gardening centre, maternity-wear and millinery. Empty-handed she strolls back home, colliding with a serious female shopper, whose brisk, intense, purposeful strides almost plough Martha down, scoring her legs with her sharp-edged plastic carrier-bags.

When night falls she grows estranged from her bed, which strikes her as hostile and mocking, and she drags herself and several layers of thick padded bedding into the show flat next door. She switches on the light in the hall and immediately catches her reflection in a long gilt mirror that leans casually against the wall. In an ancient cotton tracksuit, the top baggy and the bottom shrunken, she looks mis-scaled, unlike a person. She scours the flat for different sleeping places to try: she crouches on the new parquet but it creaks alarmingly and the glue smells of fish, and the marble in the bathroom is icy even with blankets on it. In the small bedroom there is the outer structure of a sleigh bed, with huge scrolled wooden ends, but no mattress has arrived and when she climbs over the wooden frame and lays her covers on the floor below, it feels false, like a trick. So she drags the bedding out of the show apartment into the children's room in the family flat, installing herself in the top bunk and then the bottom bunk, squeezing in beside the boxes and bin-bags, stepping on sharp toys and squashy dolls as she moves between the two. From the lower bunk she can see new things in the rooms she has failed to notice previously. Against the wall behind the door horizontal smudged pencil marks indicate the changing height of the family over the years. Opposite, an assortment of stickers fills the wall space between the sleeper's head on the lower and the upper bunks. There are pale brown fingermarks on the walls also, and a darker patch that could have been left by years of hair brushing against it. As she drifts towards sleep it becomes increasingly clear to her that something tragic has befallen this family, causing them to abandon their life, their dressing-gowns and swimming certificates. Hounded out of the flat she sees them being marched off, beaten, the children shot in front of the adults, the woman and girl attacked. She wakes and drags herself to her feet, trailing a thick train of quilt behind her.

In the kitchen Martha squeezes into the cosy-looking space between the new cooker and the new fridge, feeling the latter's low warm hum vibrating against her back. But this buzzing electric nook is the wrongest place of all. As she withdraws from it, tripping on her quilt and falling against the wall she feels something sharp and spiky on her bare leg and immediately a stinging jolt of electric current throws her across the room, landing her, stomach first, flush up against the new worktops. She cries out in defence, as though it is a person who has flung her violently out of his way. Dizzy and breathless, it takes her a few moments to work out what has happened. She clutches on to herself, wrapping her hands tightly round the tops of her arms for support. She turns and sees three cut wires sticking sharply out of the wall, next to the fridge, where the power point has been dismantled and the cable left uninsulated. On her leg, inches below the ribbed cuff of her shrunken trousers, there are several narrow red lines that look like the veins on the underside of a leaf. When she strokes them they are warm to the touch. Afraid she may still be live she continues to stand in the middle of the room, taking care not to connect with anything wet or metallic. Her breaths come fast and unregulated, but she remains breathing and standing for ten minutes before it feels safe to move. Then she drags herself and her belongings, carefully, into the other flat, the squatters' one, where a large section of pale wallpaper has been removed and it lies, damp and festering, in a pile in the corner of the smallest room. The walls, smooth and plaster pink have had holes freshly drilled into them at intervals, for what she does not know. In the largest room a white toilet, basin and bidet, lie, plastic-wrapped, secured with black masking-tape. They look bizarre, arranged casually, all bagged up and unconnected; their gleaming silver fixings twinkling in the street-lights, like science-fiction eyes. But they do not seem like bad company. Scanning the room briefly for danger she settles herself and her heavy bedding in a pile on top of the raw floorboards, adjacent to the ceramic pedestal under the window. There she sleeps, and she chooses the same place the following night and the night after that. She eats sweet things in the morning on waking, bits of stale cake, hard currant buns, plain biscuits, left behind by the builders, she supposes.

Five

Three days after the birth of her father's new child,
Martha approaches the grey stone hospital near Regent Street,
trying to gauge her mood, only she isn't entirely sure that she
has one. She hovers on the opposite side of the street, lining
up the building's square corners with her eyes, transposing
sections of the façade, in her mind, from one side of the
hospital to the other, altering its lines slightly, making it taller
and narrower or more squat, more symmetrical. Peering at
the dribs and drabs of customers who enter and leave through
the soundless automatic doors, she marks out the smudge-faced
women stroking their vast bellies, the insubstantial-looking men
with a pleasant agitation to their step. A soft, elderly lady with
omelette-coloured hair and a large gift-wrapped box goes by.
Ten minutes pass. It is a mild day for November, but Martha
has so many different layers of clothes, vests, T-shirts, her green
and white polka-dot dress, a jumper and a pair of cardigans, a
jacket and her herringbone coat, that she feels a bit divorced
from her person. The announcement had come through the
night before, over the telephone. Stephania's voice was hoarse.
She sounded older, dryer. 'It's a little boy, Frederick Marco
Brazil,' she said. 'Six pounds and four ounces.'

'How you feeling?' Martha inquired politely.

'It is crazy, believe me, but I keep thinking the day when he gets married, it will be the worst day of my life!'

On the hospital steps Martha fixes the scene in her mind, as she has done many many times before: the quality and warmth of the welcome she will extend, the powdery milk smell, the well of feeling she's already nursing for the tiny red-faced infant with the long dark silken fringe and pink knotted fists. She hopes it will lie happily murmuring in her arms for a while, that it will feel something for her. She sees herself perched on the lip of the bed while the hapless parents rest elsewhere, off-stage. She'll hum to it softly, baby songs, nonsense rhymes, lullabies, smoothing its loose light clothes over its chest, tracing the outline of its button toes: the baby's skin warm and smooth against her bare forearms, its body a small crescent encased in woolly lace. She may bend forward and kiss its head, stroking tenderly the pink, crusted patches on its scalp where it suffered from cradle cap. 'Hello, darling little body,' she will whisper. 'Hello, boysy.' Then, more loudly, 'Hello, my handsome fellow.' She will grin broadly at the child, whose thin little raw-edged almond eyes flicker and close, then peer open again. 'My lovely sweet precious one.'

She takes the lift to the fifth floor, to the baby department, unpeeling the many layers of clothing as she ascends, unbuttoning furiously the jacket and the jerseys, pulling the T-shirt speedily over her head, a pile of warm, discarded clothing accumulating at her feet. Say a green young doctor climbs on board on the next floor, sees only a pink-white flash of jaw-line, the rest of her face encased in maroon-coloured wool, her elbows crossed over her head as she tugs at the narrow neckline, a jacket and another jumper, wedged firmly between her knees. A twang of bra strap! She giggles and frees her head, finally peeling off the sleeves of the cardigan, straightening up, smoothing down her hair, which has turned static due to the mini travelling striptease, brushing herself down, picking one or two bits of stray thread and lint off her person then folding all the garments and stowing them in her bag. She is dressed for the occasion now, or undressed, in her best clothes and newest shoes, the herringbone coat slung casually over her shoulder. Brushed hair — that really was a turn-up. As she was dressing, as she was brushing, she had the strangest sensation. She thought: If I were a man I would be putting on a suit now, my shirt ironed crisply for me, tying and retying a tie.

A nurse with thick glasses, sitting whispering on the telephone at the nurses' station, directs her to the third room on the left, without looking up or terminating her conversation. Martha taps gently at the door. She taps again. Her father ushers her into the large room, which is thickly carpeted and painted magnolia. It contains a large high bed and a broad window which is open two inches and shaded by light-coloured Venetian blinds that rattle and chatter slightly in the breeze. The woman is in bed in a long-sleeved nightdress which, in truth, does little for her.

The child lies slumped in its mother's arms. Her jewelled hands stroke its head, which is misshapen and lumpy-looking after a nineteen-hour labour. Martha peers at the little baby: the bald and lustreless, pale-coloured sluggish thing that doesn't open its eyes or make a sound.

But her father! He is all carnivals and camera angles and bonhomie. Physically he makes himself useful and kind, producing flutes of champagne, feeding flower stalks into vases, fetching soft-backed chairs. These movements are assured and they are carried out with smoothness and ceremony. The shape made by his excitable features, the avidness and candour combined, it even puts Martha in mind of a *fleur-de-lis*! He plays host at the birth of his new son with the utmost pleasure. 'I rather think he has my nose, don't you?'; 'The nurses were marvellous';

'More wine?' he calls out, from the shallow swinging seat of a nursing chair that sits on clumsy-looking wooden rockers. A rocking chair!

He had witnessed the whole thing, had proud red crescents on his palms where she had clutched at him with her nails. (Spare me the details, please.) He was like a child himself, soupy with joy and exhaustion and relief. For the first time, Martha saw him in clothes that were not quite immaculate, that were very slightly crumpled. Suddenly, when he turned to fetch something for the baby, she saw on the back of his shoulder some dry, cream-coloured streaks. Baby sick, was it? She couldn't believe it.

The woman appeared older, it was inescapable. She looked to be somewhere between forty and forty-five, this person who at the wedding had seemed scarcely older than Martha herself. *His* face was riddled with sentiment that was unadulterated by anything stern or cool. His ice-blue eyes, damp-lashed and misty, focused squarely on the new life. His thin-lipped smile rose with feeling at its edges. His legs seemed almost electric with pleasure, as they skipped about, from the knee down, even when he remained in his chair, as if already he was entertaining a child on his lap. His ears were prone and alert to the thinnish murmurs the child started to make. That odd manner he had, his way of suggesting, without apology, that he wasn't quite present for you in the way he was for himself, would never be, because it just wasn't on the menu, well, it certainly was that day. It was the speciality of the house!

Martha withdrew slightly from the family scene, edging silently towards the patch of wall that was next to the door, looking closely at the aluminium light switch and the crimson alarm button and the annotated dial that regulated the room's heating. She laid out the gift she had brought on the hospital night-stand, a sky-blue velour sleeping-suit with mother-of-pearl buttons and jaunty little feet that sprang and danced about when you picked it up. 'Hello, my sweet fellow,' she'd said fondly to it, when she'd held it up in the baby section of the department store. 'Hello, my darling little body.'

The pores in the skin on the woman's face seemed enlarged, the complexion coarsened. Was it possible that, in childbirth, she had actually lost her looks? Even her hair, which had impressed Martha at the wedding with its glossy, luxuriant appearance, the rich and dark patina, well, it looked a bit frazzled, heat-treated, burnt out. But Anthony Brazil looked down at her, lying with the baby clasped flatly to her chest, as if there could be no limits to what he felt for them, the parched-faced woman, the unfortunate-looking little child. The woman turned to Martha and smiled warmly and with love. 'Thank you so much for coming, it was so kind of you.' Her eyes fell on the present and she felt it with her fingers. 'How lovely,' she said. 'You are very kind.' Then something awful happened. The woman started to cry. Large, sparkly tears came coursing down her face, settling in the lacy white cotton of the baby's shawl. One even landed on the baby's forehead. Then she was sobbing and the baby started to scream. Her father took her hand and smoothed his fingers over her fingers. 'Come on now,' he said to her stiffly, but with gentleness. 'Come on now.'

In two or three months, she never quite remembered the actual date, her father would be sixty-nine. A child has value to a man of that age. Martha slipped out of the door, leaving them to their awful little scene.

Behind two porters and a wheeled hospital trolley (empty) Martha squeezed into a dark corner of the clanking lift, which stank of the murky, cooled water in which greens have been boiled. The rattling apparatus descended at an unbearably slow pace. It seemed to Martha, at one point, that it had broken down, stuck, and she would be suspended for ever between the mother and baby department and the radiology suites. In the confines of this bizarre, jolting metal box Martha felt at sea, abstract, random, uncertain things popping in and out of her brain, little sparks of feeling, half-remembered incidents, lost sounds. For a moment she tried to position her mother and her father next to each other, in the same frame. It was something she found impossible. The woman: blunt and brave, with all her strenuous concerns flapping about her, the sincere red hair and then the effort she put into things – it was so physical, this handsome, clumsy person who could not fill a kettle without soaking her sleeves, right down to the elbow, to the shoulder-blade. Then on the other side, the man: withdrawn, private, elegant, alone, hyper-intelligent; severe, yet endlessly fanciful, when you thought about it.

One thing she did know. Being married to her father had made her mother, for a short while, ill. There'd been an incident when Martha was almost three when her mother had gone away for some weeks. Her hair had started falling out in great furry handfuls. Soon there were matted clumps sprouting on the backs of all the chairs, and in the middle of the dining-room carpet, small orangey-brown hairballs clustered, like dead pets. A lady came. She gave them cake every afternoon, different sorts to 'ring the changes'. Almost every day she took them to see the giraffes in the zoo, because it was the only thing they said they wanted. 'Mum's not herself,' was what the lady told them. ('Her hair's ill,' Matt offered his sister as further explanation.) The lady was very kind. One of the giraffes had had a little baby. They stared at it for hours, its pale blotches, its downy, elegant neck that curved in shyness. It didn't like it when you left, not at all.

Then shortly after her mother came back they moved out to the new house. As the removal men dragged boxes down the stairs, packing up their goods with blankets and old newspaper, huffing and puffing, 'Ea-sy, Ea-sy,' slumping against the van in the street for a few minutes after each journey down the five flights, with beakers of tea and cigarettes, breaking at half-time for sandwiches and sticky meat pies, the man just carried on writing in his office. They lingered on the doorstep, clutching their last bags in the shadow of the leafy trees that soared above, taking long, sober looks at the impossibly tall cream house they were leaving, that had banished them, Martha tying and retying endlessly her shoes, pulling at her sock, Matt kicking gently at the black railings; but the man for some inexplicable reason did not come down to say goodbye.

Standing outside the hospital gates now, where a thick-set flower-seller sold bouquets to prosperous-looking men in a hurry, the wetted Cellophane squeaking and crackling as they took the blooms in the crooks of their arms, it came to Martha in short uneasy bursts that if there were ever any kind of dispute between her parents (there could be no flare-up in reality, only in her mind, because her parents' worlds had contained no area of overlap, hadn't done for more than twenty years), if it should happen that a tug of loyalties arose or a question of affiliations simmered to the point of a reckoning, well, she would always always always take her mother's side.

The strange thing was, the very afternoon of the hospital visit a man came into her life, a real one! She did not quite understand where he had sprung from or why he had, nor could she have said exactly what he meant to her, although she knew it wasn't nothing, and then he was a very solid-seeming person, that far she could see. He wasn't shadowy in any way, or at least although he came and went a bit, there was nothing flimsy about him. He was a good size for one thing, tall, broad-shouldered, slightly wide-looking if you went in for proportions. He liked his food very much, that was another thing. One of the cupboards in his little grey galley kitchen was crammed with chutnies, pickles, sauces, relishes, three types of onion marmalade, 'I'm a bit of a condiment junkie,' he confessed. This had made her laugh uncontrollably. Of all the vices!

Also, he had a job and a tiny house with a garden with some kind of ornamental water feature installed by the previous inhabitants, and then sisters, hundreds of them, their photographs laid out in an album, with different hairstyles, in baggy childhood swimsuits at the seaside, and every stage thereafter, all the way up to their wedding days. Some of them had children themselves: gangs of freckled, curly-haired girls and jam-faced boys in pirate costumes with eye patches and peg legs and skull and crossbones hats.

The man went by the name of Francis. He had seen her, daily, in the food hall for quite some time now, buying food for his evening meal as she wandered about, familiarising herself generally with the stock, her face marvelling at the plenty, notching up eagerly, and with deep appreciation, any new lines, and then one day, the day she had nipped in on the way back from the hospital, he had decided to smile at her and ask if she would come with him to a film sometime. 'Can I telephone you?' He spoke the words so that they were light as feathers. She watched, nervously, as her hand, which clutched at his pen, shakily, scribbled twos at the beginning and end of the line of figures, when the truth was these numbers were, in reality, sevens.

Undeterred by this, the next evening Francis had telephoned (how had he?), proposing an outing for the following night. He had tickets for a show, he said. They'd have a drink first, maybe something to eat after, if it wasn't too late. She wrote all this down, their little romantic schedule, as he spoke, in red pen on the back of an envelope. Meet at seven at the café opposite.

TICK. Might be five minutes late because of meeting. TICK. Look forward to seeing you. TICK. Might grab a bite after. TICK. When she put the phone down it occurred to her that she had never been invited out with such ceremony, where arrangements had been made for liquid refreshment and conversation followed by entertainment, and crowned by an opportunity for nutrition.

In her red and white button-through stripy dress with collar and elbow-length cuffs she did have a slight look of a land girl, in celebratory mode, or a fancy-dress nurse, but it *was* a look. She imagined talking to the man about her work, about the things she felt close to discovering. An image of the American poet kept coming back to her, the shadow he had cast on his deathwards plunge; one passer-by thought he had actually been waving as he hurtled through the air. But he couldn't have been waving, it was too much. What the witness had seen, it was all it could have been, was just a man, life in his teeth, clutching at straws. In an early sonnet he'd had a quarrel with a lady-friend ('yellow she was wearing') because she'd been outraged at the selfishness of a suicidal man who'd jumped from the Empire State Building, landing splat on some poor person's car. As if a man like that had had a choice, the poet had insisted, shaken by his love interest's disgust. It was one of those early differences of opinion that could colour a whole romance.

Francis arrived at the semi-French café, slightly breathless and with beads of sweat on his upper lip, his blue shirt exposing his ample neck where a few pale hairs were clustered. Oh! Martha thought, with distaste. He pulled out a thin wooden chair, laid his coat over the back of it and sat down squarely, raising his eyes towards her. He was bearing tickets for a silent film that was almost three hours long.

'Great.' Martha's voice was limp. It seemed to her one of the drabbest offers that had come her way, possibly ever.

'Is that . . . do you . . . ?' Francis's face had fallen slightly, his hands were fluttering about.

They sat opposite each other in the wine bar beneath a terrible oil painting of a lady's red high-heel entwined flirtatiously with a man's flabby desert boot.

'I'm sure it'll be fine,' Martha said. 'How much do I owe you by the way?'

Francis shook his head. 'Let's have a drink, shall we?' He sighed. 'I might have a little snack as well,' he added, asking if she would like something. He ordered the drinks and a steak sandwich. The minutes dragged. Why was their talk proving such a spectacular failure? The sandwich arrived – it was huge – and Francis smeared mustard on it and finished it speedily. There was nothing wrong with his table manners, but still the whole thing was actually a little bit disgusting. Disappointment, thick and bitter, solidified in Martha's gut.

Francis paid the waitress and they gathered their things and left the bar. Martha walked very slowly. In her extremely high-heeled black suede peep-toe mules, which had been designed to be worn without a stocking, walking did not come easy to a person in tights. The shoes made ugly clanking sounds. But Francis seemed to understand the difficulty. This impressed her. Briefly, as they walked along together, she envisaged a sudden reaching round of arms, and huge feelings of health.

'Oh, it's just here,' Francis said, as they approached the rounded entrance of a venue that specialised in dance performances.

'But I thought you said a film?'

'Well, I suppose as the film's got a new score, played by the London Philharmonic, they thought a theatre would be more . . .'

'A new score? And they play the music in time to the film?'

'That's the aim.'

'Nice!'

The lights dimmed at almost the moment they took their seats and a man in baggy beige trousers and a navy blazer walked on to the stage.

'It has taken six years to bring this edition to you in the splendour that it was first seen in 1928. Tonight we not only have one of the best orchestras in the world playing the specially arranged score, but as a special treat, the star of the film has flown over this evening to introduce it.' He went back behind the crimson curtain and an ancient, tiny lady, with an impish expression but the bones and bearing of great elegance, like a dancer's, appeared on the arm of a much younger man who was in evening dress.

She stood, fragile in shimmery garments, emitting great beams of grace into the auditorium as the audience clapped and cheered. 'When I meet the director for the first time, he tell me, "Let others make films about gay old Vienna. I will make films about sad old Vienna, not because Vienna is sadder than any other city, but because the world is sad."

'Imagine what it feels like to be me. It is so beautiful tonight. Seventy year ago I make a film. You are all so beautiful to be here. All you who come you are so delicious and beautiful. I will remember this moment for ever, I will cherish it. The love I feel . . . I knew when I make this film my life was different, better for ever. The whole film has such a special flavour for me. Imagine to be me, how it feels. To be here tonight. To be here with you, in this magical place. And all the musicians,' she made a frail open-handed gesture to the orchestra pit, 'you not know how old I am, but I am much older than I look.' (Francis whispered, 'The youngest she could possibly be is ninety-four.') 'It is so beautiful. There have been so many changes. I don't recognise the world as it is now. But in the film everything is so beautiful. The apple blossom. The light. They do tricks with the light from behind, and they make me a plain Viennese girl, they take me and they make me look beautiful. This has always been my most favourite film, whenever any one ask me. It was made by a genius, but he was my admirer and that gave me freedoms. He made this film, this beautiful film, that is so magical, in essence a love story. For me that is the only story worth telling, because it is the story of the world, the story of life.'

She bowed her head and made her way carefully off-stage, the beads on her dress weighing heavily on her tiny frame, her right side slanted stiffly against the arm of her companion. Behind her the screen started to flicker. Martha whispered to Francis, 'I'm having such a lovely time.' Francis smiled. The film began.

In the film, the hero, a young impecunious Viennese aristocrat, is told by his grisly father and his chic, worldly mother that he must marry for money. A seasoned *roué*, despite himself he falls in love with a simple, modest girl, whom he meets among the apple blossom in the early hours of the morning because it is then that her parents snore the loudest and she can get away. But the nobleman's father, drunk, in a brothel, betrothes his son to the daughter of a corn-plaster baron, a lovely, fading beauty who walks with a limp and is worth twenty million. Against his heart the hero marries her in a grand, religious ceremony, leaving his apple-blossom love crying outside the church, condemned to a life as the wife of a violent butcher who eats raw slabs of meat for breakfast.

After the film they returned, in small excited steps, to the same café for another drink. 'Wasn't it great,' Martha's eyes flashed with enthusiasm, 'when he came to see her in hospital with a huge box of chocolates and he said, "I thought you might like these," and she says, "You thought I *might* like them!"'

'It was wonderful.'

'They don't make boxes of chocolates like that any more.'

'Oh, I think they do, you know,' Francis said, 'if you know where to look,' and the way he said it for an instant made her think that he was hinting, although hinting was perhaps too strong a word for it, that somehow, one day, such a box of chocolates might find its way to her.

The café was almost full now, all its patrons indulging in their noisiest, briskest talk. They took their seats at the same table, only the table had been dressed for night, with a white cloth and a candle in a glass holder and a withering lone iris in a bud vase that occupied the centre point. Martha shifted friskily in her chair, which made gruff, scraping noises against the wooden floor. Assorted couples sat at other tables with white candles and irises between them to thicken their plots.

They both drank a brandy.

'Thank you so much for arranging it. What a huge treat.'

'Oh, it was great you could come.' Just then an enormous sound of clattering plates and cutlery came from the kitchen, followed by some swearing and a clanking of metal on metal.

They both looked down. 'I'll definitely remember it for the rest of my life,' Martha said again.

Suddenly, Francis raised his eyes to speak and with a terror that he was going to come at her with some genuine, unmatchable declaration or . . . or . . . *phrase* of, well, of romance, Martha sank lower and lower into her chair, wrapping her legs round its legs, pressing her back into the back of its seat. She had to secure herself, she thought, as grave echoes of mistakes made and almost made sounded in her heart. 'Thing is,' she began, 'I don't in any way want to presume anything at all and things, but I am in a bit of a funny way at the moment.'

'Oh?'

'I'm just in a slight state of confusion about things.'

'What sort of things?'

'Well, everything really . . .'

'Oh?'

'So I mean, well, you know . . . I mean, I don't really think I could . . .' Something almost ill-willed had crept into her tone, which was actually a bit ugly, she thought, a little bit disgusting.

'Sure,' he said kindly, absently. 'Sure.' He nodded a couple of times and then looked dully away. Neither of them spoke for almost a minute. The candle flame made a tiny lapping sound as a small draught from the opening door made it flicker. Then it blew out.

'Now, how about another drink?' she suggested.

'No, I think I'll be heading off. I'll get a taxi, and drop you on the way.'

'Oh, OK.'

When they walked outside on to the gloomy narrow street a taxi came straight at them. 'Oxford Street, Marble Arch end,' he told the driver, 'and then Vere Gardens, please.'

In the safe darkness of the taxi, with the roar of the radiator blocking out all other sounds, Martha surveyed Francis as he peered out of the window. He looked thoughtful, and somehow amused. The car went past a parade of shops that included two fish-and-chip outlets.

'I always like to have chips, champagne and chocolate on my birthday,' Martha said.

'Quite right too. Did you have them on your last birthday?'

'I think I did, yeah.'

'When's your birthday?'

'February' she said evenly. It was actually on 14 February, how embarrassing was that? 'What did you do?' she asked quickly.

'On my last birthday?'

'Yeah.'

'Well, I . . . I . . . it's just . . .' He looked flustered.

'Don't say if you don't want to.'

'No, it's all right. I went out for dinner with my then girlfriend, she'd booked this fancy restaurant weeks in advance, and said she wanted to give me a really special treat, which was very kind, and we had lovely food.'

'What did you have?'

'Well, I had this risotto with truffles and green herbs. It was so delicious, it really made you . . . well, it made you think. It was called *tartuffe à la trufe au risotto vert*.'

'*Tartuffe à la trufe au risotto vert*,' she repeated. The cab approached a pelican crossing and waited for the lights to change.

'Anyway, near the end of the evening, when I was having my pudding, this amazing caramel and pistachio soufflé, she suddenly said, "So, when are you going to ask me to marry you?"'

'Oh, no!'

'Well, it was completely out of the blue and I didn't say anything for a while, and then she said, "Say something," and I said, "Well, I don't know what to say," and then she got up and left.'

'Just like that.'

'Yes.'

'Leaving you with the bill.'

'I didn't mind that, but it was awful, though. I felt – I phoned up quite a lot after that, left messages for a while, but she didn't get back in touch.'

'What, not ever?'

'No, I haven't seen her or spoken to her once since that night.'

'Not at all? Not even one time?'

'No, I've run into friends of hers who tell me she's all right, but that she just wanted to make a clean break.'

'Oh, I see.' And then suddenly Martha didn't want to talk about this other girl any more. For a moment she actually wished this other girl was on the other side of the world, unhappy somewhere, that she was unwell, that she was dead. Then she felt ashamed, and under her breath she whispered briefly, inaudibly, 'Sorry.'

'What was that?'

'Oh, nothing. Just a pile of old rubbish. The usual!'

Francis laughed kindly. The streets were still deserted but as the taxi turned the corner into her road Martha spied a group of boys in the distance, walking towards them, kicking their feet along the ground. One carried a black guitar case which he clumsily switched between his left and right hands.

'I can't stop thinking about the film,' Martha said. 'It was so great when the actress said at the beginning that she'd remember this moment for the rest of her life, as though she were quite a youngster.'

'That's right. You don't really think of amazingly old people saying that, do you?'

When the taxi reached her building Francis asked the driver to wait for a moment and he climbed out with Martha, leaving his case inside the vehicle for security as he walked the eight steps from the cab to her door with her. They stood kissing in the street opposite a half-lit clothes-shop window, which threw strange images at them, bizarre headless models dressed in swimwear, with synthetic bouncy wigs sprouting out of the ends of their necks. Large beach balls with red and yellow and green segments were stuck crudely to the end of their toeless feet, spades and buckets glued to their palms and fists. Martha closed her eyes against these peculiar women. She felt the mechanisms of Francis's breathing working steadily under his jersey, and her own heart rocketed under the papery fabric of her stripy dress. His fingers were warm against the back of her cool neck. His kisses were hot and lulled her gently into even, drowsy pleasures that built in her shoulders and her feet and the joints of her elbows and legs, which felt naked and foolish.

Gradually, though, her thoughts began to stray. They strayed on to the loneliness of various straggly passers-by, who dawdled singly at bus stops and kicked at odd pieces of cardboard boxes that flew across the pavements in the dry whistling wind. She braced herself, painfully, for the moment when her own public show of happiness, the long, slow, moody kissing she was physically involved in would strike a lone and bloated-looking woman who was approaching them from the other side of the street as a kind of violence. Her thoughts turned to Francis's grasping old girlfriend with her bullish request for a marriage proposal. It would have been far better to have simply come out with, 'Will you marry me?' The 'So, when are you going to propose?' was actually a little bit like a threat, Martha thought, vaguely.

And then suddenly all she could see was the ungainly white head of her father's new baby, and her father capering round it like an excited little goat. She felt tears, like cruel slits, stinging her eyes, but she bit hard on these feelings. You had to throw yourself into something else. You had to grit your teeth, shunt these nasty pictures out of your mind.

She decided to concentrate strenuously on the dynamics of the kissing, saying in her mind the word 'kissing' over and over again and bringing to mind, with some force, the spectacularly kind things Francis had said and done that night, and little by little the kisses did start to hold her and the grimy asides, the clawing gratuitously after illusions of anxiety, deserted her. And then the kissing was entering a new phase, rising up faster and faster and with more and more pleasure, the pleasure rising, sheer and concentrated, and the feeling of some startling new beginnings came with the kissing, and the feelings grew and rose and their arms held on to each other tightly, tensely. She did not know who exactly or what or where she was, but something amazing was taking place, and it was happening to her and with her consent. It caught her up in ways she hadn't deemed possible. Their eyes blinked open sometimes and spilled over with strong glances that meant important things, responsibilities. The street, the long and straight shopper's paradise, was flooded with shop lights and street-lamps and the growling refuse trucks that roamed up and down, preying on rubbish, crunching glass, leaving rotten fruit smells lingering in their wake. A new café called Bon Appetite came into view and outside, although there was no one about, a man stood supporting a large wooden placard saying GOLFSALE.

Francis smelt good, like a pillow smells, and it dawned on her suddenly that she would have happily just stood there all night holding him and sniffing tenderly the sandy strands that covered his scalp. The taxi beeped gently, and Francis made a conciliatory motion with his hand, without stopping what he was doing. The driver took up a newspaper and started to read it. He was smiling, he had faith in them somehow, and still the meter was ticking away.

They drew apart for a moment and gazed at each other, weighing the things that newly lay between them. Martha took fright for a moment.

'I better get back,' she said. 'It's late and I've had quite a day, what with one thing and another . . .' She stopped talking.

They linked fingers and Francis led her to her door.

'I don't know the wisdom of saying this, but I've—'

'No,' Martha put her hand to her face and shielded her eyes, 'please,' then she let it drop and suddenly she was overtaken by a coughing fit and she coughed and coughed and spluttered and fought to gain her breath . . . She took a few steps back and a deep breath and then, 'Good night, lovely!' she called, and ran from him into the entrance of her building, coughing as she went, all the way up the stairs to her flat, not looking back . . .

They went to Regent's Park the following weekend, meeting in the rose garden. 'I used to live in that house there,' Martha pointed to a large, tall building standing in the central curve of a pale crescent, overlooking the park, 'until I was three or four.' The front door was black, as were the doors of all the houses. A broad railing framed a strip of garden separating the house from the main road. On the grass two girls in dark blue coats with velvet collars were playing. 'My father still lives there. We used to be very big on the ducks,' she said. 'Some of the ducks really really made me laugh. I used to like these funny black and white ones with bizarre teddy-boy-style orangy-red quiffs.'

'Was it amazing, the house, inside?'

'It was pretty great. Always think I had my heyday when we lived there. I was slightly sophisticated as a child.'

'Why, what did you do?'

'I don't know. I mean, I just used to sit upstairs,' she pointed to the sitting room on the first floor with three long, high windows that were draped with elaborately arranged sky-coloured fabric, 'on my own, with a book, looking out of the window, reading and writing things down in little notebooks. I didn't make a sound. I thought I was very grown-up.'

'What did you write?'

'Well, first of all just squiggles and then I used to write over and over again, it's a bit embarrassing, but I used to write "Martha Brazil is my name comma and my game."' She pronounced her surname Brazil, as it was meant to be pronounced, to rhyme with 'frazzle'. This was something she seldom did, as people always took it to be an affectation. Francis smiled, but he did not say anything. They followed a softly curved path through the rose beds, stopping to look at the names of the different blooms, which were displayed on small rectangular green notices.

'They've got some mighty odd names, some of those roses.'

'I know.'

'"Starlight",' he read out. '"Splendid Renate". "Noblesse". "Pensioners' Pride".'

'I learned to read here, pretty much. People like Gina Lollobrigida I really thought were just roses, for years.'

'Of course!'

'My dad had this huge office. It was on the landing. He pretty well lived in it. It had this double insulated door that had all grey . . . felt, I suppose it was, on the inside of it, and then when you opened it there was another, thinner, door as well.'

'Sounds like he didn't want to be disturbed.'

'Oh, we didn't disturb him. No one did, really. It was such a big house. I can hardly remember anything. I mean, I remember a few things, but they're mostly things I put together in my mind afterwards.'

'What like?'

'It's weird but I remember passing my father on the stairs or in the hall or something and having a really strong feeling that he was hoping I wouldn't see him.'

'I suppose he had to concentrate very hard, in his line of work.'

'Yes. But there was never a question we would have disturbed him. Anyway that wouldn't have been enough. I think my mother had to arrange things so that it didn't seem like there was anyone else in the world, let alone in the house. But then I think, How could I have thought that when I was three?

'People fascinate your father,' it had been remarked to her, over the years.

'They do?'

People who were unstimulated by her own straggly personality, older people, teachers, the parents of her friends who spoke to her in stilted wavering tones, well, suddenly, huge soaring peaks of interest, warm and urgent, got injected into things, when they learned of her connection to the writer they *so* admired. 'You must be *very* proud. What was it like growing up in such an *artistic* and *rarefied* household? He's made such an exquisite study of human nature,' they said. 'There's so much delicacy! So much fastidiousness! It feels as though there isn't a stratum of cultured human activity that doesn't capture his imagination.'

'Oh, I know! He's, er, certainly . . . um . . . got that well . . . um . . . in his . . . under . . . his stride.'

'What, dear?'

So, when they had outgrown their duck talks, she thought up for her father, instead, special questions about aspects of the human race, about rare personality kinks, particular sorts of social afflictions, crackpot hare-brained theories about semi-sanity that came to her at odd moments. His books were littered with doctors and psychoanalysts, she had heard or read somewhere. Mental wards, sanatoria, clinics, West End practising rooms with panelled walls, and in *The Lock*, an airless doctor's waiting room with fitted carpet that extended right up into the fireplaces.

'I was wondering,' she'd venture, 'do you think it's likely that a person who was very religious until they were twenty-one and then went completely the other way and things, do you think that person would be more or less likely to be happy?'

'Do you suppose if someone is really really depressed, clinically, I mean, not . . . not for any specific reason, and then something absolutely dreadful happens to them, a shocking thing, a real thing, do you think that there's any slight chance that they might actually be jolted out of it in some way, start to feel better and things, like a blind person who has a terrible accident and his sight comes back?'

'I was just thinking, I don't know if you have any experience of this, but if you take an unhappy person and take away all the circumstances and facts of their unhappy life and transport them to a happy person's life with all the . . . the trimmings that a happy person's life would have, do you think they could just settle down and be . . . be happy, or not? Would the sad person's insides remain with them, d'you think? Could they go through with it?'

Much thought went into the framing of these questions. It seemed to her once or twice that she had managed to capture his interest a little. The frail scenarios she put to him suggested themselves at the oddest times, like when as a teenager she used the bathroom after her mother, and inhaled the slightly ripe, woody smell that lingered there. The strange thing was she never actually listened out for the answers. Her father spoke at length on these matters but, strangely, exactly what he was saying was not something she wanted to hear.

The man, the new man in her life, who sauntered with her across the grass was speaking tenderly. 'I'm only now realising what amazing luck I had with my parents.'

'That's a lovely thing to say.'

'I had very flat feet until I was about eight and Nicholas, that's my father, he went on these evening classes and learned how to make me these special shoes. They were unbelievably comfortable. Like walking on air.'

'Really?'

They reached a shady, deserted patch next to some trees. 'Shall we sit here?' he asked.

'If you like. Pull up a blade of grass.'

Martha flattened some white paper napkins on to the small patch of grass that measured the distance between them. She began unwrapping the packages she had brought, arranging buns and almonds and the thin slabs of fruit cake into little piles. It was a coolish day but the sun was high and bright above their heads, whitening their hair. She unscrewed the lid of her Thermos flask, and poured out some tea into the cream plastic cap, which had a little handle attached.

'So did things change much when you left the big house?'

'They changed so much I felt like a completely different person. I mean I was a completely different person. I had the life of a completely different person. It was slightly mad.'

'In what way?'

'Well, my mother, I think the way we lived in the big house was very much my father's way, very grown-up, and when we moved we lived more in my mother's way.'

'And was that less grown-up, from your point of view?'

'Well, she's actually a little bit great, my mum, but she's quite wild. She's like a delinquent teenager crossed with Joan of Arc or someone. Mother Teresa.'

'Sounds interesting.'

'Well, she doesn't like a quiet life, in any way.'

'No.'

'How can I put it? She . . . she's very, very good in a crisis, but . . .' A huge wave of loyalty washed over her. In a second all the very nicest things her mother had ever done for huge numbers of people, some of whom she'd very genuinely rescued, flashed in front of her eyes, and she lost her thread. 'But . . .' she said. 'But . . .'

'Good in a crisis, but not so good out of one?' Francis suggested.

'Yeah.'

Martha woke early next morning in Francis's bed, before it was light. Her arms and legs felt hot and smoothly foolish. Her hair had twisted itself into little snail-like knots. His arms were cool, his face warm. On his milk-white chest were some untidy, sand-coloured hairs. She peered across at them, tried to read them like tea-leaves. All she could make out was a few giddy villagers processing towards a small thatched hut. His thinly lidded eyes were slightly open although he slept.

Suddenly she likes her body immensely. The parts of it that touch his body she especially admires. She breathes out softly, feeling the air expelling warm and spherical through her parted lips. She strokes her shoulder with the flat of her hand, to and fro, to and fro, appreciating its strengths, trailing her fingers down to her wonky elbows, past the bluish inside of her forearm to her narrow little wrists. There are so many different levels of pleasure in her flesh, along the sloping lengths of the low soft surfaces as well as at the leaner sharper portions. She is delighted to be awake. Her eyes stray on to him; she examines him carefully, half clothed by a crumpled sheet, from all angles, his resting genitals, the blond and jovial hair, the skin pinky mauve, in places brownish, mottled with dark veins. He is fairer than she is, his skin tone light and freckled. She thinks how well his skin fits him, there are no areas of slack or surplus, but neither is it stretched tightly over his bones, the funny lumps and peaks that he has.

Even the space between their enjoined limbs hangs shapely,

rich with curves, the diamond chink where his left knee and her right knee go their separate ways, the tiny triangle his elbow makes, indicating like an arrow her breasts, which fall sleepily together into a creamy, double-humped shelf of flesh. She lies still, looting their dual treasures with her eyes. She likes her body when it is with his body, she thinks, suppressing, now and then, little chuckles of excitement, feeling her smiles, bursting fresh and pink on her mouth and cheeks.

She had explained sex to him – that it was slightly something she didn't quite go in for, just at the moment, that it wasn't something she could take on board quite yet and could that be all right, for now? And he hadn't made anything of it, at least he hadn't set up any discernible objection. His response was one of serious nods and small, permissive hand movements. All she knew was that if that squished-up little baby crept into her mind at the wrong moment, or the grasping old girlfriend demanding marriage . . . or her brother's snarling reproachful glance, or . . . or . . . No. No.

During the night sometimes the birthday scene in the restaurant that Francis had described did come back to her, the rejected girl furiously spooning soufflé into Francis's mouth, a huddle of conflicting desires, cooing and hissing in turn, kissing him one minute the next wishing he'd choke on his food. The shame! To be so open about your desires and receive such a crushing blow in return; because there was nothing worse than silence when there was something you really wanted. Neglect was harder to stomach than abuse, because with abuse at least the other person was taking you seriously.

She pictured the girl at length, striding wonkily out of the restaurant pride in tatters, make-up falling gloopy on her gritted face. Martha tried to bat this image away, her fascination with it struck her, after all, as the slightest bit unsavoury. When it persisted, beyond her control, hammering at her, the little picture of perfect humiliation, of failure, she drowned it by recalling all the different items in Francis's condiment cupboard, reciting in her mind the huge list of exotic, bottled preparations, sometimes even saying the words out loud, her own kinky prayer: onion marmalade, anchovy sauce, mushroom ketchup, lime pickle, pickled pears.

Over the next few weeks, however, when the nights they had spent together numbered fourteen or sixteen, when Francis lay sleeping in her arms, Martha gazed at him, on his matted sandy-coloured hair, which gleamed in the winter sun that poured through his window, settling on his eyelids where the skin was so thin it was almost see-through, and it struck her that there was so much more weight and colour to everything around her now. Any little thing she did, when she made a leap in her work, or if a shaky, wax-faced man on the bus said to her wistfully, 'I've never had much luck with the female genre,' or the department store issued the women who worked in the bakery section with nursy pink gingham uniforms with button-down collars and epaulettes that were highly saucy, it was all deepened and enriched by the fact of this Francis character being in her life. And then, suddenly, the other things in her world, the things that were not him, did not need to mean so much, hardly needed to count for anything at all, because even without them her day was to yield her incalculable reward or charm or unqualified delight, just through the fact of him existing, whether at work or in his flat or in hers, a phone call away, 'Coming round in half an hour, till tonight or see you in the morning.' Even from a distance, if they had to be apart, there he was just quietly and steadily underwriting everything she was about. Because of this, of course, it was obvious, it was almost unfair, all the things, the work and the costumes and the people she met, they all meant so much more to her anyway, because they didn't need to count for anything at all. It was quite harrowing how much she'd clawed from these things previously, how much delight she'd squeezed from the little squares of colour in her day.

When she cast her mind back to the past concerns of her heart and its shabby clientele, arranging and naming, in her thoughts, her co-stars in the near-unbroken chain of sour romances, it was truly astonishing how she had soared to her present heights, how she had swept her heart clean and entered an unprecedented realm of human activity, with this large, kind man, where a phone call arrived to say when a person would be *ten minutes late* and good turns were repaid in kind, often within the hour.

There was just one awful thing. They were in their fourth week now and the shadow of the old girlfriend still dogged her for an hour or two each day, but however much she batted away at the image each time it came, still the little scenes played in front of her eyes: the heartfelt entreaty in the restaurant that fell on stony, deaf ears. The utter humiliation. The bruised retreat. The spikes of shame that would last a lifetime. It wasn't impossible to live with, but it *was* hard. Martha calculated the percentage of her day that was spent agonising in this bizarre fashion, her brain on hot coals, her nerves jangling appallingly. It was only 10 per cent, 15 per cent. Of course, this figure doubled if you set the time killed against your waking hours rather than the hours in each day, but you didn't need to push it too far.

Sometimes in dreams and day-dreams the searing disappointment had a different flavour to it. Turning the girl down, it transpired in dream time, was something that Francis reviewed increasingly with private agonies of regret. Martha's behaviour grated against him when her predecessor came to mind. He and this girl had evidently been extremely close. It made Martha cringe with all her skin, winded her, sent her hands shooting up towards her face in her sleep. Still, these melancholy workings Martha contained as best she could. She legislated against them, drawing up little strategic lists. She divided them up, setting them firmly against each other with 'The Bad Thoughts' hovering grimly on one side of her brain and 'In Reality' towering huge and proud on the sweeter side of things, a land in which she told herself she was 'slightly more herself'.

One Saturday afternoon, after a spectacular morning spent cradled in Francis's arms, Martha goes off cheerily to meet Stella at the Dear Friends. She pauses at the steamy window of the café to observe her friend, to try out in her mind one or two ways of announcing that she finds herself in possession of an exceptionally good mood. But Stella, through the plate glass, across the matrix of empty sky-blue table tops does not look well. She sits on the edge of herself, spine curled, head in hands. Martha scuttles into the café. Stella has pressing news. Martin, the sportif-complexioned man from the party, had that morning declared he did not believe in their relationship any more. He had given no reasons, just a patronising smile and a consoling light squeeze of the hand and then he was gone. Stella was making huge efforts to control her feelings, but the wonky tremors of lip, the slumped posture, the wet that kept trickling out of her eyes, the colourless face, apart from the red nose, all denoted an extreme state. It was actually a little bit terrible to witness. 'Let's get you something to drink,' Martha said, stroking her friend's fingers, curling a stray lock of hair out of her eyes and behind her ears, pulling some paper tissues from her bag, wrapping an arm round her friend's waist.

For a second Martha thinks of her own happier circumstances, and almost instantly she shrivels from herself. The contrast, the crass pleasures she imagines unbuttoning in the face of another's distress, well, her own thoughtlessness left shocking, stinging marks criss-crossing her heart.

And another thing – the thin waitress seemed to have grown

hollower and sallower, even since the previous week. Now her skin boasted a strange, colourless hue: papery-looking, the cheekbones, in the absence of any flesh for them to support, had become so prominent that they lent a bizarre, haughty aspect to what was so obviously a desperate state of mind. She looked as though standing up, for her, was almost torture. Martha thought: Not only has she not eaten for a long time, she probably hasn't even had a drink of water. The hollow look stirred some memory in her mind, another face, monkey-like, caved-in, despairing, but forbidding also, proud, her brother's face. She winced as thoughts of him sidled up to her, bitter, extreme. For the first time, possibly in her entire life, she had not given him a single thought for nearly a week.

'Oh dear,' Stella said, gazing in the waitress's direction. 'She seems to be going downhill, pretty rapidly.'

'D'you think we should say something?' Martha asked.

'Like what?'

'I don't know. I suppose that we're worried about her.'

'No, I don't think so. It's not as if we know her or anything.'

'I know. It's just that if I was very obviously in pain, in an awful lot of pain and I had made a decision to wear that pain very publicly, like a uniform, I think I'd want someone to remark on it.'

'Would you, though? I just don't know that we can presume that.'

'But, you know, fellow feeling and things.'

'Maybe. But I wouldn't want to intrude. It seems too personal somehow. She's really ill. I mean, she probably doesn't weigh much more than five stone now.'

The waitress came over to them. She moved slowly, stiffly, as though she had to protect all the sharp edges of her bones. She seemed so weak and drawn that she shouldn't be standing at all, let alone working. The huge smile that broke out like sunshine on her face when she delivered large oval platters piled with chips and golden omelettes and puce-coloured bacon rashers, though — it was actually a little bit macabre. Her shrunken face was at its most ghostly when she smiled: the smile was out of proportion to the surface area of the face, the head was too big for the slight frame, the narrowness of her back. She was like a mis-scaled child. The black clothes, a whole wardrobe of them, some thick and some lacy, clung to her body. There must have been five or six layers, leggings, trousers, a narrow knee-length skirt, vest, T-shirt, jersey, cardigans, but the vain attempt at bulk, of course, just suggested its opposite. Her eyes seemed drained of light and too wet, too glossy, like animals' eyes. 'Can I get you anything to eat? We've got tarts, treacle tart, lemon meringue, Bakewell tart, cherry tart, chocolate gateau, paradise cake, millionaire's shortbread, macaroons and iced buns.'

'What d'you think?' Martha asked Stella.

'Not hungry,' she said.

'Neither am I, really.' The girl's eyes rose and dipped sharply. 'I'll have an iced bun,' Martha said quickly, adding when the girl had moved away, 'we don't have to eat it.'

'She needs to go to hospital,' Stella said.

'D'you think? I actually find it a bit heartbreaking looking at her.'

'D'you want to go somewhere else?'

'Oh, no. It's fine . . . I mean . . . at least she hasn't given up completely.'

'How d'you mean?'

'Well, she's still coming into work and things.'

'That's not what she needs. Unless she faces the fact that she's got a life-threatening illness, and drops everything, she could, well, she might not be around for that much longer, you know?' Stella's tone was combative. Her nerves were strained, her whole person adopting slightly unnatural contortions.

'Anyway,' Martha said.

'Anyway.'

Stella tries joking about the break-up. 'Sometimes,' Stella confides calmly, 'I thought Martin was a little bit pompous.'

'I suppose he did have a hint of the after-dinner speaker to him.'

'Yeah.'

'Touch of the Peter Ustinovs?' suggests Martha.

'Yeah. Orotund,' Stella concurs.

'Yeah, Orotund, moribund, cummerbund!'

Stella laughs grimly, and then with a more open heart. 'Oh dear.' She sighs and wipes her hand across her face to catch the drips from her nose. 'It's pretty embarrassing,' Stella continues, 'but once in the street he described this large woman as looking really ang-ry. But I couldn't see it and I asked him to explain what he was on about and it turned out he meant she looked Ingres-y, as in like a painting by Ingres.'

'Oh, no! That's obscene!'

Stella giggles deliriously, she is almost bent double, she has to hold on to the back of her chair.

Martha left the café, feeling crushed and ill at ease. She had wanted to say to her friend, 'Very big things are happening in my life, huge, slightly great things I hardly dared to hope for, love and everything.' But big things were happening all around, things that meant you starved yourself to death or laughed hysterically when all you wanted was to cry. She reproaches herself bitterly. You know you're not the only one living life and it's actually a little bit disgusting the way you carry on as if you are. Her heart sank at the thought of Stella's disappointment, it sank in thick, agonising lurches that shocked her and took her breath away. Gradually she saw her mood darken all around. She thought back briefly to the comfort and peace she had felt in Francis's bed as though they were events in her earliest youth. Then she considered the old girlfriend, the one from the restaurant, lying in the same bed feeling those self-same feelings, perhaps on the very eve of that final, gourmet humiliation. Suddenly her mind fixed violently on to that unfortunate-looking baby, its bland little visage quite unequal to the difficult course it was going to have to start negotiating, if it was to survive. It was too much. The whole thing. It really was.

On her way home, as a pick-me-up, she looked in at the department store and on a whim she tried on a skin-coloured floor-length silk evening dress, only the strange thing was, the colour did not suit her, not at all. 'Very few people can get away with flesh,' the assistant said sympathetically.

Francis's old girlfriend flashed into her thoughts again. 'Oh, go away!' Martha mumbled wearily, but the girl would not go away. And then to her dismay, the next morning, when Martha awoke, the girl was lying next to her in bed, smirking triumphantly. Martha sprang up and dashed into the kitchen, but there the girl was ladling out porridge into shallow soup plates, leaning away to avoid the steam. Martha locked herself in the bathroom and caught her breath, but the girl was staring sourly at her from the slick porcelain of the wash basin, her tight, sarcastic eyes narrowing and taunting from the rim of the toilet bowl. Out into the street Martha ran but she was there with her at every turn, jeering, crowing, snatching at her nerves one moment, the next touting viciously for sympathy: a girl-shaped stain in the sky, her slight figure hurtling out at Martha from everywhere, shop fronts, doorways, side roads, mirrors, the slender crazed body fizzing with endless recriminations and regrets.

Martha wandered up and down her street, completely at

a loss, making her self as small as it would go in order that the shoppers treading down the backs of her plimsolls and ploughing into her person — one time, knocking her two feet into the road — did not seem quite so powerful, as they buffeted her continually from one side of the pavement to the other, grabbing at her shoulder-bag, their elbows in her ribs, her breasts. Back home she cleared the remains of her breakfast from the kitchen, wiped it down and spread out some writing things on the table top. She picked up her pen with no idea of what it was she was going to write and suddenly the words came flooding from nowhere and she filled the sheets rapidly with rows and rows of snarling, spiky characters, which she scarcely recognised as her own.

My then wife was a shop assistant in a large department store in the West End of London. She worked in haberdashery, and spent most of her day matching up buttons and cutting ribbon. As well as basic sewing equipment, pins, hooks, coat-hangers, pinking shears, hat boxes, tapestry kits and assorted trimmings (feathers, lace, sequins), other things were dispensed by the haberdashery department that you would not have thought would have come under its jurisdiction. Moth spray and breast pads for nursing mothers, shoe inserts to stop foot odour, sanitary dressings, fluid for cleaning out telephone handsets.

My then wife enjoyed shop work. She liked the pleasant little exchanges you got from the people who bought things or made inquiries and although the words 'Cash or account?' tripped off her tongue automatically she prided herself on sending each customer off with a personalised pleasantry, a good wish, an expression of hope that the weather would hold for the wedding or that the insect problem would soon be under control. Her nature was friendly and sensitive, in fact these were the qualities that initially drew me to her on that eventful Friday lunchtime when I had gone into Betterton's in search of a reel of black thread.

My then wife had been extremely helpful the first time that we met, quite beyond the call of duty. She had not only helped me track down the reel of cotton and advised me in some detail on the best way of sewing the small tear that had appeared at the seam of my jacket pocket, but as the department had been virtually empty and her supervisor was nowhere to be seen, she had undertaken to perform the task for me, swiftly making a row of tiny stitches, and in order to thank her for this attention I had invited her out to lunch the following day.

My then wife had arrived at our chosen rendezvous thirty minutes late in a state of considerable anxiety. Her face was pink, she was out of breath, and one of her own buttons had come off her blouse, although fortunately it was not a button that was crucial to her modesty. She apologised for her lateness at great length and finally gained some measure of composure, smoothing the creases in her skirt and repinning a stray wisp of hair that had detached itself from her rather severe coiffure. As far as the food went, my then wife ate little. Something evidently troubled her but she was too polite or reserved to mention it to a virtual stranger in a public place and for this I admired her. She seemed to have a very busy inner life, something that I felt indicated a measure of independence of spirit, a disinclination to rely or depend on others and this warmed me to her further. On the basis of this discovery and several pleasant exchanges, after a few months I asked her to become my wife. Our wedding was a quiet affair, neither of us having any family to speak of and even fewer friends.

During the six months in which we were married my wife seldom spoke. When not at work she busied herself with the making of minor repairs and alterations to my clothing, beginning with my suits and shirts, progressing to the darning of my socks. Her *handiwork, in this respect, really was a form of art: over a hundred threads of cotton would re-create, exactly, the texture and finish of the fabric that had worn through . . . My then wife was also a master of invisible mending. Once or twice I made a joke about it being perhaps the only skill that the better one got at it the less likely it would be that one would ever receive much in the way of acclaim. I forget whether she laughed.*

We muddled along in a smooth and pleasant enough manner, maintaining the usual courtesies that properly exist between man and wife until one day my wife intimated to me that she was with child. I was taken aback by this as it was not something she had ever mentioned before and I believed that I had made my wishes clear on the matter. I explained to her that any such experiment was out of the question and when she became hysterical in her efforts to thwart me and it became clear that reason had no part to play in her quarrel with me, I was left with no alternative but to employ force. Unfortunately, things ended badly for her.

These days, if a garment of mine sustains a rip or a tear it languishes uneasily in the ironing basket for weeks. When buttons are lost they no longer magically reappear.

My present wife does not know how to recognise one end of a needle from the other and would be quite unable to say what the difference between mercerised and unmercerised yarn was. Coming from a wealthy background she lacks a sense of industry. Sometimes when I come home from work I find women's magazines hidden down the back of the sofa, and last night an empty chocolate box caught my eye, stuffed into an old cereal packet at the very bottom of the rubbish bin. I must have words with her about it this evening.

That night, after Francis had cooked for her, in his flat, doing energetic, fiddly things at the stove, turning the entire procedure into a little carnival for her, tossing vegetables high into the air, swerving away to escape the spitting oil, expertly grilling fish, slicing into lemons, he looked at her seriously for a moment and made an announcement.

'I'm really sorry about this, but I've been told I've got to go away for work next week, for about three weeks. There's a meeting first thing on Monday morning, and I have to get the last train on Sunday night which goes about nine fifteen. It's a conference on branding and then a tour of all the branches. They only told me this evening. It's terrible timing, but I hope to get away for a bit the weekend after next, or perhaps you could come and stay at the hotel one Saturday night. It's infuriating,' he said. 'I hope you won't mind if I telephone you the whole time and I'll write every day and——? Martha? Martha?'

Martha pushed her food to one side. Why did he always cook quite so much? It made no sense. Four times a week, and often at quite inconvenient times, he went for a run, running five or six miles at a go. But, she wondered, why didn't he simply run less, and then he wouldn't have to shovel such violent amounts of food down at every available opportunity? It wasn't exactly hard to work out. And what was it he was running from, anyway? She imagined making the charge at him, triumph ringing bitter in her voice. There would be so many ways to hurt him now. She wouldn't know where to start. Watching him eating, sometimes, the amounts, not the style, actually made her feel like being sick. Still. It was certainly no affair of hers. He was saying her name, asking her things, apologising, making little flinty promises. She'd have to answer him. She thought of the old girlfriend's face, the glossy fringe, the mouth a huge hoop of pleasure and kindness, but the eyes slitted with fury.

'As you like,' she said coolly. 'Whatever,' although what she was feeling was, Let's just forget it, shall we? sucking hard at the pockets of flesh that lined her mouth until the whole area went numb. I think we'd best call it a day. Thinking: You see, the mistake you make is, I just couldn't care less what you do. I never have, and I never ever will.

Francis was visibly upset. He must have been because he dragged himself away from his food for once in his life and went to her and fed a shaky arm around her shoulders. Outraged, she threw off his advances. Silently, she faced him with it. 'Nothing you do will ever affect me in the slightest. What you get up to in your spare time, you see, it's absolutely no concern of mine.'

Then suddenly, without ever quite deciding it was a viable course of action, she stood up, batted her plate of food off the table with the side of her fist and watched the dainty fish fillets, the delicate sauce, the stupid little baby-vegetable medley soaring into the air. The plate smashed with a huge clatter and she slammed herself out of the flat, racing down the stairs and hurling herself on to a bus that would take her back to her own building. She was so angry she could quite easily have killed someone. She stormed into her home, thundered up the last flight of stairs and bashed open the front door to her flat, knocking into the telephone as she raged along the hall so that the innocent-looking receiver now hung dangling forlornly from its tangled spiral cord.

Six

Martha awoke from a nightmare, breathing heavily, clutching at her arms, her face freckled with sweat. She leaped out of bed; if the only way she could rid herself of the shame was by turning her back on the place where it had been born, then that was what she would do. She had to get out of the flat. Things were quite simple. It was five o'clock in the morning and cold and night dark. She dressed speedily, pulling on an odd assortment of garments, trousers, skirts, a grey Shetland jersey belonging to Francis. She had put him out of her mind, but everywhere there were all these little sharp pointers. She shrugged her coat over her shoulders, leaving her arms free, and raced out of the house.

She went westwards, striding at top speed through Hyde Park, letting her hands and face fully absorb the cold. The extreme temperature soothed her, took her out of herself. She felt her skin contracting round her cheeks and thin lines drying at the corners of her eyes and there was a deep stinging in her nostrils where the chill bit. Gradually, her pace slackened. She observed the elderly, lumpen trees. The broad paths in the park, lit by street-lamps, were iced over and littered with fallen leaves that lay yellow and crisp-edged in clusters. A clock struck six. Light began to feel its way along the streets that still smelled musky and of night. Almost no one was about. She exited the park, walking briskly. A library and a police station went by. These deserted streets seemed vastly inferior to her own where, even at this hour, there would be no shortage of people. Cleaners of all sorts abounded at this time, in her road, arriving in armies to prepare the buildings before the onslaught of custom. Some wore uniforms under tightly buttoned coats: you could glimpse a square of pink-checked overall, a flash of sky-blue nylon. She knew the signs, she was a cleaner herself, after all. Suddenly she heard someone taking shuffling steps behind her. She turned and locked eyes with a young man with curly grey hair. He called out to her something she couldn't hear, but it felt like some kind of suggestion to do with nasty sex.

Martha slipped her arms into the sleeves of her coat, fastening it at the neck only and began to run. She ran and ran until her calves and ankles ached from the high jabbing of her heels against the hard pavements. She entered a small, dimly lit café, whose walls were painted a bright green gloss, and ordered a cup of tea and a toasted bun. She rubbed her elbows through the sleeve of her coat. Over the last few weeks, as a reaction against the high turnover of detergents her work entailed, she had developed some patches of rough, inflamed skin, which burned at night, some hardened, pinkish itchy areas on the underside of her arm, which were raw and uncomfortable. Where she had scratched, the skin had broken and a thin, brittle crust had grown. At night she had to concentrate not to claw away at her forearms and the spaces between her fingers – she steeled herself against the urge – but in the morning her arms were more painful than ever and she realised she must be scratching in her sleep. Sometimes in the morning there were spots of blood on the pillows, and dark sickle-shaped ridges under her fingernails. She'd seen this on the women who arrived at their cleaning posts in her street, with their crimson, flaky finger-skin, their scabbed hands, pink and raw. In places, now, her nails looked as though they'd been pushed back to their roots. Francis had noticed her ailments and she'd laughed them off, saying they wouldn't last the week. She'd felt embarrassed at her hurts, but he had viewed the sensitive skin, and the shrunken, cracked nails with great kindness, patting them gently, kissing better the little sore places.

'Is it eczema?' he asked. 'It looks so tender. Poor you.'

She crunched the teacake, brushing crumbs from the front of her coat with her hands and drained her drink, leaving coins on the edge of her saucer. Her dream, which she had frozen out and hidden away, came seeping back at her in the warm room: grotesque, macabre. The baby, her father's baby, had been watching over her as she slept, then had crawled over to her, dragging a huge pillow in its gummy mouth and with its body held it over her face. She bit at the pillow, filling her mouth with the bright striped ticking, grinding through it until her throat filled with dry choking feathers and she had coughed and spluttered and tried to free herself, but the baby was strong, it held her head down, it held the pillow down on her head until her breathing stopped altogether. 'Sorry,' she said out loud to the empty café. 'I'm sorry.' She repeated it three or four times.

She paid up briskly and walked the mile and a half to her home. Her street was already swelling with noises to greet her. The gas board cheerfully drilled holes in the pavement opposite her building and a large electric road-cleaner, operated by a squat man in orange overalls, roared its way up and down the kerb, its rotating circular brushes sucking up dirt. The bin men were in evidence also, flinging mauve and black sacks into the whirring mouth of the rubbish truck, its insides thick with viscous black dust and dank, rotting smells. She drank in the sounds.

One of the bin men said, 'I've been divorced for six years now, longer than most marriages!' mirth ringing richly in his voice.

In her kitchen the fridge hummed loudly in the corner to show her she was home. The kettle wheezed and purred. She rubbed at her arm through her shirt sleeve and peered at the plates on the dresser, their turquoise, white and gold pleasing and correct.

Inspired by her fellow workforce Martha rummaged in the cupboard under the sink for her metal bucket of cleaning things. She fetched the vacuum cleaner from its nook by the front door and looped the large bunch of keys to the other flats over her thumb. The show flat looked especially pristine this morning, but she hoovered the bedroom carpets, ran her duster over the marble. She saw that some new furniture had arrived, a dramatic large plate-glass coffee table supported by what looked like huge, smooth logs. When she extended a finger out to them, the logs were cool to the touch, made of brass. On the table was an oval silver dish that had been filled with brightly coloured fruit sweets. Two Louis Quatorze-effect sofas, blue watered silk on fancy gilt frames, had arrived and had been arranged in one corner of the room, in an L shape. Ten small cream raw silk cushions with claret-coloured piping had been balanced on their points around the seating. Mmmm, she thought, taste!

Martha buffed up the cushions gently. In the kitchen a basket of exotic fruit with a high rounded handle covered in Cellophane sat on top of the counter, the mangoes and nectarines radiant and waxy under the shiny clear paper. She checked to make sure it was real. It was. How had it got there? She inspected it for a card or a label, but there was nothing. She wiped down the kitchen surfaces, pressing hard with cloth and detergent, working away with vigour, as though the surfaces she was cleaning were not already spotless. She covered the taps in white metal polish, massaging them into a high shine. Soon they gleamed. She mopped the floor violently, rinsed it, then wiped it over with a clean cloth. The Versailles parquet she did not touch. Well, she swept it, cheerily, but she was awaiting further instruction as to its upkeep. She did not want to harm it in any way. The task completed, she surveyed her handiwork. The room sparkled. 'Oh, yes.' She said the words out loud.

A rounded man, well spoken, in a brown leather blouson, had come to take photographs of the splendid apartments for a brochure that was being prepared. He made notes about the double aspect receps, the entertaining spaces, the sumptuous bathroom suites, the wealth of features boasted. When she said she was studying literature he tried out a few of his phrases on her. His terminology was stunning. Ambassadorial opulence, interior-designed to within an inch of its life, silk, gold, marble, all came as standard. No stone unturned, no hinge unhinged, something like that anyway. An oasis of tranquillity and splendour, a Mayfair haven of luxury in the throbbing heart of London's glittering West End . . . How did it go again? A marriage of the inimitable style encapsulated in the word Mayfair itself, with the lifeblood of the heart of the city at its best. Dazzling parkside views – that *was* pushing it. If you had X-ray vision, maybe. A gateway to the shops and restaurants envied by the world. Oxford Street, that magical thoroughfare full of mystique and memories. Modern glamour. The essence of the spirit of the capital. Was that too much, did she think?

World of London was on sale, at the minute. Its royalty section was being cut back, there just wasn't the demand any more, and on the high shelf where decorative gilt-edged cake platters had once been arrayed in little clusters (The Windsor, The Balmoral, The Clarence House, The Kensington Palace) there was now a row of adult magazines. It had also introduced a *bureau de change* kiosk: a chubby Arab lady sat in the little glass-walled booth, grumpily swapping hundred-dollar bills for fifty-eight pounds' worth of filthy notes to eager-faced tourists.

One thing was sure. Someone would be coming soon: a young bachelor prince, say, new to London, who thought this was how people lived, with Cellophane fruit baskets and marble toilets as far as the eye could see. And why not? Good luck to him. She calculated that the fruit would stay fresh for another five or six days.

She passed the door to the family flat, wiping down the wooden panels, moistening the tiny specks of dirt with a damp corner of her cloth then removing them with a dryer portion. The flat was now entirely devoid of all furniture and personal effects, although where they had gone she could scarcely bear to think. Suddenly, from inside the flat, she heard some odd shuffling noises. She paused, listening very carefully, face pressed hard against the door. She peered through the letter-box. In the far room, the one that had been the children's bedroom, she saw the tail end of a bottle-green sleeping-bag stretched out on the floor and next to it some discarded clothes, a striped sports shirt and some black socks and shorts, and next to that *in the middle of the brand new carpet* half a packet of sliced bread and a gaping, ill-balanced carton of milk with blue cows on it. Her heart sank with jerky, angular thuds. It was only eight o'clock in the morning but she went back into her flat and telephoned Mr Quinn's house. The phone rang and rang but nobody answered. She thought of going in, conducting a little investigation of her own, but she was afraid. It could be the squatters from number eleven back again. She didn't want to get into any situation she could not easily handle. She sat in her kitchen drumming two fingers against the Formica table top. She did not know what to do. Francis would know. She telephoned the hotel number he had slipped in her pocket, before their . . . their quarrel; her hand shook, she felt breathless and riddled with anxiety. What could she really say to him anyway. Sorry? Did she feel sorry? She knew that no other word would be acceptable considering the turn of events. Thankfully there was no answer from Francis's room even though it was only eight fifteen. The hotel receptionist tried to have a joke with her about this, but soon gave up when he heard the worry in her voice. She left no message. She left it emphatically. Where the hell was he? She tried Quinn again and this time an answerphone came on, but the voice on the machine sounded shockingly bleak. She left a message for him to call her. She tried to make her voice sound casual.

She took herself back into the kitchen and spread out some of her work on the kitchen table, the sheets and sheets of notes, the box files, the texts she was studying. She reread some notes for her essay.

This poem is exceptionally bleak. The despair it contains is of such an intense quality, that it seems sublime, almost holy. The guilt that resides in the poem's hero is so heavy that it forms a whole new character, one who is able to threaten the hero's life by suffocating his heart. Yet this stifling guilt is not presented as a freak occurrence, anything out of the ordinary; on the contrary, the poem's hero is so prone to it that the merest thing, a distant cough, or a smell or a noise, can set it off at any time. The poem has a nightmarish quality to it. In order to suit his mood the hero of the poem dreams up the worst crime he can imagine, being a brutal murderer, and then he accuses himself of it, in the foulest terms. He needs to believe that he is the monster, the scapegoat for his own sense of sin. It is as though he asks, 'What does being bad mean, what does it actually count for if you don't commit enormous, heinous crimes?' In this way, in order to justify the side of him that is wholly absorbed with his own shortcomings, he convinces himself he is guilty of the foulest imaginable murders. In the mental landscape of his dream-world, only the worst is good enough. In this way the hero betrays himself as a rather unusual kind of perfectionist.

Martha tries to imagine how it would feel to lie in bed convincing yourself you were a murderer. To need to.

The moment it opens, Martha takes herself off to the department store. She feels slightly safer there, fingering fine merino blankets, less jittery, lifting up sparkling silver cream ladles and cruet sets in the basement. She examines an elegant sterling silver masher. Wouldn't it turn the potatoes green? On the ground floor she strokes a grey Balmain tie patterned with tiny navy squares. She takes the escalator to the children's section to look for a present for her father's new baby. She feels sorry about it. She cannot even remember its name. Her eyes fall upon a tiny blue tweed coat with navy velvet collar, half-belt and covered buttons for a hundred and fifty pounds. Children did not really wear things like that any more. She sees a rack of clothes designed specially for premature babies. She imagines a room full of clear incubator tanks each housing a tiny pallid slug-like form, fighting for life. Those bodies would need these little blue and white garments, carefully knitted with love and supersoft yarn. They'd need them, perhaps, more than anyone. She imagines herself as the mother of a dead baby then quickly shunts the image from her mind.

At noon she meets Stella for coffee at the Dear Friends. They settle into their seats, straightening their clothes, unthreading their scarves.

Stella was pensive. They drank their drinks and crunched their fruited buns. Martha looked up and cast her eyes about the room: not many of the other tables were occupied but there was a pair of old men and a youngish couple, the girl in mittens with thick white-blonde curly hair. Then the waitress's face came into view and Martha saw that she was crying. Suddenly her weary frame slid silently down the front of the chilled-food cabinet into a tiny crouched heap on the ground. 'Look!' Martha whispered, sharply.

Stella sighed.

'D'you think we should call an ambulance?' Martha eased herself from her chair and went over to the girl. 'Are you all right?' she asked, gently touching her fingertips against the girl's shoulder. For all the droopy black garments it was like ice. 'Shall I get a doctor?' The girl said nothing. 'It makes me sad seeing you looking so unhappy.'

'I know I'm ugly, you don't have to throw it in my face,' she hissed.

'I'm sorry . . . I . . . I didn't mean—' Martha stumbled.

'Well . . .' the girl growled. 'Well . . .'

Martha helped her to her feet.

'I'll get your bill,' the girl said, and returned seconds later, pushing the grey scrap of paper on their table. 'Drinks × 2. Sundries × 2. £1.60. Thanks for your custom. Call again soon.'

Later on, when Martha returned home, pushed the landing door and drew her keys out of her purse, she heard more sounds coming from the family flat, but she scuttled past, covering her hands with her ears. Again there was no answer from Quinn's telephone number. Had he said he was going away? She had a distant memory. Then a terrible thought came to her. What if it was her brother, who had made himself at home next door? Hadn't the stripes on that discarded sports shirt looked a little familiar?

If it was him, well, he would have a few of his cronies with him by now. Every room he had ever lived in had boasted the same kind of thickened, dank atmosphere, regardless of the dimensions or the natural advantages of the property, or the area. Once when one of the people he had fallen in with still had a bit of money remaining and lived in an elegant apartment in a Regency building with high ceilings and long windows, well, six weeks later seven of them seemed to be inhabiting one room, the smallest room, and the amount of debris and the stultifying atmosphere, the airlessness, it might as well have been underground. Suddenly she feared for the eleven thousand pounds' worth of carpet in the flat next door, saw it smeared with ash and dotted with cigarette burns. Francis would know what to do, she thought.

One piece of information she had gathered, but, well, she did not quite know what to do with it: stuffed down the side of Francis's little suitcase, all ready for take-off, she spied a book with a black and white cover called *Coming Off Drugs*. She had not mentioned the sighting. She felt to do so would have been unkind, exposing his concern for her and her family, as though it were an accusation she was making. She had no wish to humiliate him after all. She telephoned Francis's hotel, but there was no reply from his room.

She tried Quinn again, only this time it was Linda's voice on the answerphone, sunny, clipped vowel sounds, cheery, business-like. Martha left no message. It had occurred to her that she could be blamed for her brother taking up residence in Raven Court. Quinn might think she had extended an invitation to him, taken advantage of his good nature. The thing to do would be to get rid of him before Quinn found out, make any repairs necessary. Could she be liable for the damage Matt did? Was it her responsibility in the eyes of the law?

She tried Francis one more time, half forgetting in her panic how uncomfortably things lay between them. They had not spoken since the incident at his flat. They would not speak again, Martha had decided. But Francis was good at straight answers. He had a flair for rationale, a facility for knowing what the ordinary responses were. His married sisters put to him all sorts of ridiculous questions, such as 'How much money is it all right to spend on clothes?' and he'd reply, 'Oh, I don't know, say twenty per cent of your disposable income. Twenty-five tops.' That would mean about a pair of tights a week for Martha, but still, you couldn't deny it was a great answer. They'd had a spectacular phone call once before, when he was away for the night, before everything had fallen to bits.

'I wish Stella could meet someone really nice.'

'I know you do.'

'It's a shame you don't have lots of nice single friends.'

'I know, I am sorry about that. I can see it's a failing.' They had had this conversation before, but there was only a thin trace of 'Here we go again' to Francis's tone, and even that was largely underwritten by humour. This was audible, even though they were talking on the telephone, two hundred miles apart and with forty-eight hours of separation under their belts. Francis was stretched out on a squishy bed in one of the orange and brown upper rooms of a Travellers Lodge Hotel, north of York. Martha was lying on her sitting-room carpet, phone pressed so close to her face that it was leaving funny round indents in her cheeks and neck.

There was a lull in the conversation in which Martha took a wet swig of her tea, missing, partly, her mouth, and Francis sipped some icy water from the mini-bar.

'How did today go?' Martha asked, wiping her chin on her sleeve.

'Pretty well, exhausting, though. I went to look at this new supermarket. They want me to help with developing the brand . . . of the supermarket, I mean.'

'No, really?'

'At the moment I'm looking at things from the point of view of the shopper.'

'Oh, so am I, so am I. And, um, did it meet with your approval, this new supermarket, then?'

'It was amazing. You'd have loved it.'

'Would I?'

'They've been pretty playful with the design, not gratuitously, but they've put a lot of thought into it.'

'Yeah?'

'Yeah, it's as though each separate area is . . . For example, the area where the eggs are sold has a little brown roof with these little chickens on top and there's a button you can press that makes little chicken noises, and then by the milk area there's a cow—'

'Life size?'

'Bigger than life size, but it's just the front half of the cow and it's sticking out of this milking stall, at the same level as the product, and there's some landscaping, hills and meadows and so on, painted on a backdrop. And it's really cleverly lit so you suddenly see this cow but it doesn't look surreal at all, it looks, sort of, what you'd expect.'

'And what's it made of?'

'Fibreglass . . .'

'And do you think having these models and things and making shopping into a bit more of a carnival, do you think that's going to catch on?'

'Oh, yeah. The thing is, buying food is something that

touches the life of every single person in the country. Finally, I'm a socialist, I'm not trying to get people to spend more money, I just want to enable them to get hold of the things they want in the most enjoyable and economical way.'

'So what's your favourite supermarket?'

'In the UK or in the world?'

Martha beamed at this answer to her question. 'The world,' she said dreamily.

'Well, there's a store called Meijers in Champagne, Illinois. It's a Mid-west chain, mainly in Illinois, Minnesota, Ohio. They own about sixty stores.'

'And what's so great about it?'

'Well, the range of product for a start. It's a 150,000-square-foot palace to retail, a bit like the high street but rolled out. They sell everything: clothing, bulk foods, small-quantity foods, dry goods, wet goods, live pets, DIY, toys . . .'

'Like a French hypermarket.'

'Not really. It's more accessible and departmental, there's more emphasis on category management strategy, and I suppose the technology, in-store, is far greater.'

'Really? That sounds wonderful.'

Francis laughed.

'If someone gave you, I don't know, fifty million to build a superstore,' she proposed to him, 'let's call it Frankworld, and you could be in charge of everything from the architecture to the uniforms of the checkout staff, how would you, what principles would – would guide you? Or is that an annoying question?'

'No-oh.' Francis sounded weary. 'Well, I suppose, off the top of my head, I'd want it to be a very exciting, stimulating store, pretty eclectic in design, more so than a conventional supermarket, by which I mean I'd like the tone of voice in the store to vary a lot, from department to department. I don't mean just for the sake of it, that would be nauseating, everything would have to be highly relevant.'

To be having a conversation where supermarket departments boasted a tone of voice! Martha could scarcely conceal her delight. In fact, she did not. She stroked between her fingers where she had been scratching. The skin was thickening down there.

Francis continued, 'If you look at the blink rate of shoppers, it drops considerably when they are in supermarkets, they drift on to autopilot. That's why so often you get to the checkout and you haven't got the very thing you came in for. I suppose what I'd be pretty much working towards would be making shopping for food as exciting and stimulating as eating is. I think it's sad that getting the weekly shop in is such a chore for most people. People shop for clothes and luxuries for pleasure. I'd like getting the groceries to be like that. A treat, almost.'

'And the architecture?'

'Well, it would put more emphasis on the experience itself.' He paused for a second. 'I'd want to give people value for time, so that the actual shopping was more pleasurable and also quicker, and then value for money, obviously, and then value for product, by which I mean the most appropriate produce sold in the most appropriate way.'

'That would be your three-fold value promise.'

Francis agreed. 'No one does it that well at the moment. All the supermarkets are pretty much the same, there's no individuality, no risk-taking and—'

Martha had an idea. 'And would it reflect quite directly your own personality, the store?'

'I'd be destined to failure if I did that.'

'Oh, no!'

'If you've got a billion genuine friends in the world that might work, but otherwise – I'd turn the whole process on its head and concentrate on separating out the differences between needs, wants and desires, within the shopping experience. I'd want the store to be unique and unreproduceable. I'd use architecture in interesting ways to make statements or to make no statements at all . . . I'd . . . I'd . . .'

Suddenly it occurred to her that talking to him in this way was probably a little too close, for him, at this late hour, to a day at work. 'I'll say good night. You must be exhausted.'

'Well, I am a bit on the tired side. Missing you terribly, though.'

'Me you too.'

'There's a sign outside my window on the back of a pub saying, "Take Courage".'

'Well, there you are, then. Outside my window it says, "Kebabland".'

'Well, that's not a bad place to be.'

'I s'pose.'

'Bye for now.'

'Bye for now. All my love.'

Well, there would be no more where that came from.

Presently she heard some sounds right outside her flat and went out to investigate. Mr Quinn was hovering on the landing, his back turned to her doorway, hands stuffed deeply into his pockets, one of his shoelaces dragging sadly behind him in a little coiled pile: thinking.

'Am I glad to see you!' Martha almost laughed as she came through the landing door. 'How are things?' She decided to come clean about the mystery guest. 'I suppose you realise we've got a bit of a problem here. I only discovered it this morning, I've been telephoning all day, but I only got the machine and I didn't like to—' It suddenly occurred to her that Mr Quinn had not even turned round. She tried again.

'Mr Quinn?' she said. 'Mr Quinn?' Louder and louder. She reached out a finger and tapped him very gently on the shoulder.

Mr Quinn almost jumped out of his skin. He swung round, his expression startled. He looked awful, his face bloated and bleary-eyed, nervy, with sharp stubble discolouring his face, like some kind of insult.

'Are you . . . ?' She chose her words carefully. 'Did you want to see me about something?' He remained silent. She moved towards her flat and turned the key in the lock. His eyes stared at her imploringly — she could feel it even though her back was turned. 'Tea? I'm just going to make some,' she offered.

He followed her into the flat and she led him into the kitchen, which seemed unfamiliar and oddly stale, as though the air in it was somehow tinged with rust. He sat down, unbuttoning his coat, then overlapping the edges of the garment under tightly folded arms. She fished a few gingernuts out of the biscuit tin while they waited for the kettle to boil, arranging them on a saucer and placing them before him.

'Is . . . um . . . everything all right?' she asked.

Mr Quinn shook his head. Her eyes darted briefly to his eyes and to her horror she realised that he was having some kind of collapse. His cheeks flashed pink and hung slack and blotchy, growing looser and looser by the second, his mouth sagging open, his head shaking sadly from side to side, his face now ashes and crimson, in streaks. Martha stood up calmly and went over to the cooker where the kettle was reaching boiling-point. Suddenly Quinn's body jolted forward in his chair, his face crunched up with pain, or the memory of pain. His whole head started to shake furiously, his teeth gritted and then his arms jutted out, flailing impotently above the table top, trying to reach something. Then, after a short while, the features relaxed again and spilled open, tears splashing down on to his plate, mingling with the biscuit crumbs, making little oily brown smears.

Behind them the high whistle of the kettle started to sound and Martha lunged towards it, hugely relieved that something was finally going right between them, something ordinary was being interposed. She grabbed the kettle blithely, lifting it off the gas ring, delivering it over to the counter where the cups were waiting. But in an odd sort of time delay, she realised suddenly that the skin on her bare hand was recoiling at the extreme heat, crimsoning, blistering round the curved steel handle that was cutting into her like a switch. She winced at the pain, biting down as it stung into her, as she tenderly unfurled her crimson fingers, but she didn't make a sound. She ran some cold water into a large mug and dangled her hand in it casually, taking her seat back at the table. 'Is something wrong, Mr Quinn?' she said, in her smallest, gentlest voice.

Quinn sat silently weeping and quaking in his chair. Something about his crying seemed to loosen the fibres in his clothing so that a thick scent of old sweat and alcohol rose up. Martha wiggled her hand back and forth in the cup of water which seemed to have heated up rapidly; in fact the water in the cup was almost boiling now. She got up again and refilled it with cold.

'Shall I give Linda a ring? She could come and collect you.' Quinn let out a long, low howl, and actually started sobbing: whoops of despair filled the room. With her good hand Martha pushed the plate of biscuits towards him and he made to eat one or two, but in the end he just broke bits off and lined up the huge crumbs, between sobs.

'Would it help to say what has happened, at all?' she ventured. Then she shrugged her shoulders. 'Or not really?'

He shook his head. 'I just don't know what to do,' he said. He had made his voice hard. Then he said it again.

'Has there been some kind of . . . some kind of problem?' she tried again.

Suddenly the muscles flexed hard and purple in his neck, and he brought his fist down heavily on the table with a loud bang. His plate sprang up into the air and landed with a crack on the floor, breaking neatly in two. He jumped to his feet. 'Oh, God. Look. I'd better go. Don't tell anyone I've seen you,' he said. She nodded and he crept away.

That evening she heard him pacing up and down, up and down in the luxury flat. Once she heard the sound of something smashing and a loud crash against the wall. Soon he will go home, she thought. He'll have things to see to. He's just having a bad day. But it got later and later and still the sounds drifted through, rustling, despairing sounds. She went to bed at twelve, pulling the covers up over her head, but still she heard him. His movements were slower now, leaden, and this heartless, creeping navigation of the rooms of the flat was much worse than the angry crashing and fuming. Unable to sleep she ventured on to the small landing, coat over her nightdress, feet unshod.

She peered in through the open doorway, across the parquet and the marble, which were gleaming perfect, gold and ice. In the hallway, on the left as you came in, a large gilt and green marble console table stood grandly, at its centre an engraved silver tray, on elegant clawed feet. On the floor was an open suitcase that spilled tangled shirts and worn underclothing, and some running shoes and a large navy wash bag printed with anchors. Among the clothes were some dog-eared magazines. And then she saw in the distance the bottle-green sleeping-bag she had earlier spied in the next-door apartment. It was Quinn who had moved in! He'd had some rift with Linda and was using Raven Court as a sanctuary. Of course.

She went back into her flat and silently pulled the door

to. She locked it. She came into the kitchen and saw the crumbled biscuits, the plate cracked, everything about her life interrupted and interfered with. The flesh on her palm was scored with a thick red welt, the skin split at the edges. She felt it, tenderly gauging the dimensions of the raised crackly wound. It would make cleaning difficult, that was for sure. From next door drifted some grunts and grazing sounds of furniture being moved about roughly. 'Don't scratch the marble! Mind the chair legs on the parquet!' she wanted to yell, banging on the wall. Although it was not exactly to her taste, the perfection of the show flat really stood for something. The skirting-boards were eleven inches high and had been freshly repainted in white eggshell the day after the flooring was laid.

There was no use trying to sleep. She slipped her coat on over her nightdress again and went to confront him. Sitting in a little pile on the marble in the hall, Quinn held his chin in one hand; the other hand was smoking. The door was ajar and she squeezed her body through the gap. A crimson bell of ash fell from the tip of his cigarette and shattered on the slick chill grey surface. Martha shook her head.

She went and sat down on the floor about three feet away from him. He looked utterly sunk.

'Whatever it is you're going through, I'm so sorry,' she said.

'Sometimes it seems as though you're the only one who understands,' Quinn replied sadly.

Martha altered her posture so that it was more upright, 'What? What? Is it something to do with the building?' she inquired gently.

'Oh, no! No, it's not that at all. I don't care about *that*. It's Linda.' And he uttered her name as if it were the most mournful word in the English language. Suddenly his clothes looked tragic on him, ill-fitting of his character, for they were, really, the apparel of a younger, happier man.

Martha smiled down on his trouble. 'Poor you,' she said. 'It sounds so painful.' Quinn turned his face from her for a moment. Martha got up gently and walked over towards the window. 'I'm so sorry . . . Would this be a terrible moment to tell you my favourite joke? It's pretty cheering.'

'Please! Go ahead!' Quinn said, and there was so much sweetness in his voice that although it was obvious he was only being polite she went ahead anyway, genuinely believing that a little distracting might somehow do him good. 'All right. Well, it's quite long, but a friend of mine moved into a flat the other day, rather a nice flat in the basement of a tallish building. Anyway, the morning he wakes up there for the first time, everything's still rather a mess but he decides to go for a little wander around, see where his local corner shop is, buy some milk and things, but it looks quite overcast, the weather outside, so he opens the window and sticks out his hand to see if it's actually raining, and suddenly a glass eye drops into his hand from directly above. Well, naturally he's a bit taken aback but then it occurs to him that someone in the building may have dropped it out of an upstairs window, so he goes to the ground-floor flat and rings the bell and introduces himself, asking if anyone is missing a glass eye and the gentleman who comes to the door looks at him as if he is slightly mad, so he tries the floor above, but no one there knows anything about it, nor on the floor above, or the floor above that, but when he rings the bell of the top-floor flat a lady answers wearing a black négligé and an eyepatch. Well, he shows her what he has found, and she thanks him profusely and disappears for a moment and returns with the eyepatch off and the glass eye in place.

'"Thank you so very much," she says. "You are so kind and

I am ever so grateful to you. I was just about to help myself to a Martini, could I offer you one as a way of showing my gratitude?"

'"Be extremely nice," my friend said, "thanks very much," so he followed her into the flat and took a seat on her sofa, which had many sumptuous cushions on it, and the drinks flowed and the conversation and they were getting on like a house on fire, and after an hour or so the lady said, "I am sure you have another engagement, but if not, I have a crown roast of lamb in the oven. It's far too big for one and I wonder if you would do me the honour of sharing it with me?"

'"Well, thank you very much, I can't think of anything nicer," my friend said, genuinely delighted, and so the two sat down for dinner, and delicious wines were served and an exquisite pudding and coffee and liqueurs and chocolates, even some vintage Armagnac, and a cigar was produced and they were laughing and joking and having a lovely time and then the lady said, "I hope you won't think me too forward but I was wondering if . . . if I could invite you to spend the night here with me?"

'"Well . . . to be perfectly frank with you it would be the greatest of honours," my friend said. And so they spent a night of beautiful passion and romance together in each other's arms. Then in the morning when the man awoke the lady was no longer in bed but presently she came into the room with a huge tray of silver dishes, containing bacon and eggs and a jug of hot coffee and fresh toast and orange juice, and she placed the tray at the foot of the bed and said to him, "There's no hurry at all, I'll just leave your breakfast here and then whenever you want it, please help yourself."

'And the man said, "Thank you so much for all the wonderful kindness you have shown me. The last twelve hours have been like a beautiful dream. I have never known anything like it in my life. The welcome and hospitality you have extended to me really have been beyond my wildest imagination and I just can't believe what a delightful evening and night I have just experienced. Only one thing worries me slightly." He paused. "I do sincerely hope that you don't treat all the tenants in the building in this marvellous fashion?"

'"Oh, no!" the lady says, shaking her head. "Only the ones who catch my eye!"'

Martha stopped talking and waited for a reaction. She felt shy and a little foolish. 'Anyway, anyway, anyway,' she said.

Quinn had brightened marginally. 'Oh, that's very good,' he said, 'very good indeed,' but there was no danger of him laughing.

They were quiet for a while together, then after a minute or so he added, 'I'm so sorry about all this. Made a colossal fool of myself, not that that's at all unusual. How are you getting along, though? Everything all right?' He barely had the strength to look up, but she appreciated that he was turning the conversation round.

'I'm all right, you know. Yeah. I'm fine, really, if the truth be known,' she added, somewhat uncertainly. 'Nothing spectacular to report, but then I mean . . .'

'No . . . well . . .' Quinn agreed. And then, 'Saw your brother the other day.'

'Where did you see him? Not here?'

'At your father's.'

'No! Really? What sort of state was he in?'

'He was having a bit of a scream-up but he soon calmed down. She's not the most confident mother in the world. It's as though she doesn't know what to do with him, doesn't quite trust herself. But I'm sure she'll get the hang of it.'

'Oh, you mean the baby.'

'That's right. Linda never wanted children,' he began. 'I'd

have loved some but she insisted and finally . . . and then now she's gone and I – I – She'd have loved your joke by the way but I don't think . . . I just don't . . .'

Ridiculously, Martha's eyes started to cry. Her hand throbbed with beats of hot pain that shot up her arm. She could have stopped herself, but what was there really to lose? You could smell singed skin, like wrongly cooked meat, wafting in the air. The smell of herself made her gag. Quinn was standing near to her now. One of his hands was on her face and the tip of his thumb caught a tear from the apple of her cheek. He held up the tear to the light, as though it were something of great value.

'We're very alike,' he said. 'You and I.'

'What?' Martha said. 'Are we? D'you really think that?' Quinn suddenly extended a stiff arm around her, and moments later he was smoothing her shoulders with his fleshy fingers, the firm, clumsy movements having the effect of rocking her to and fro.

'There there, now,' he said. 'Easy does it. It's all right. Come on now. That's right. That's right. Now, it's not the end of the world, is it?'

'No,' Martha murmured wearily.

Now Quinn's large flat hand was stroking her back, up and down, up and down with little arrhythmical pattings and rubbings in between. 'We're two of a kind,' he said. He smiled at her attractively and gazed into her eyes. 'I must say I do love the way you're so confident and so unconfident at the same time,' he whispered hazily.

'*Merci beaucoup*,' she replied, smiling through tears.

'I know, I know.' Amazingly, just then, he cupped her chin in his palm and bent to kiss her. She was so astonished that before she knew it she had taken the tiny, delicate kiss and another and another. Pop pop pop went the sound of these dry minuscule lunges, Martha thinking, vaguely, all the while: You can't blame me, I *am* doing my best.

Suddenly it dawned on her: wasn't her deepest fear that, in the neutral, scathing eyes of the world, her mother and her father in their very particular spheres were neither of them actually good people? That she wasn't either? Could it not be said that none of them were quite the people they thought they were, each with their own carefully carved-out set of high standards and that, in the end, possibly what each of them most authentically stood for was nothing at all?

The second dream of last night came back to her, the one in which, silently, in a side room, with no mess and a degree of modesty that could smash your heart, her father's new baby had committed suicide.

She'd taken to buying it presents now, most days, just a teeny pair of socks or a bonnet, or a little pink terry rabbit or a sailor-inspired matinée jacket, and once a green and white striped knitted garment called 'overalls'. She popped them off in the post, gift-wrapped, beribboned.

She would not stand for misery in her children, crunched up in their bedrooms, the naked glare of the Anglepoise lamp bearing down hard on their despair. No fear. You had to take steps against it. Every time. It couldn't just go on generation after generation, the legions of unhappy infants gnawing their nails and wringing their hearts into the night. If her turn ever came, each night she'd ask them, tucked up in their pyjamas before she dimmed the lights (after the story), 'Is there anything worrying you at all, darling? Is there anything you want to tell me?' The quality of the listening, it would be designed to stun!

The effort she would plough into everything, the complicated models with the silver paper and fabric paints and glitter and icing nozzles and coloured pipe-cleaner figures and the potato clocks and the pin-hole cameras. The packed lunches she'd prepare would be the envy of the school, never the same thing two days' running, and the after-school treats, the weekend outings, the blue and white striped mercerised French cotton underwear, the in-depth homework service she would provide, the sleepovers, the waxworks, the biscuit-making, the tea-time feasts, the pyjamas and puppet shows, the party clothes, the birthday cakes, the balloons, the merry-go-rounds and clowns and magic shows and zoos and parks and swimming and picnics . . .

And suddenly, she was entirely awake to the sensation of Quinn's thick tongue in her mouth, slimy, insistent. 'If you want, my . . . my love, I could get a room at the Selfridge Hotel.'

With that she came to her senses. In her mouth was the worst flavour she had ever tasted: dry ashes, bitter rancid milk, last week's alcohol. She drew back, took two steps away. 'Thanks very very much,' she said, speaking rapidly. 'You're ve-very kind, and it's a lovely offer and I couldn't think more highly of you as a person as you've only ever shown kindness and been lovely to me always, every time but – you know, we're not really thinking straight, slightly not ourselves. I – I, there's Linda to think of – and you know, I'm slightly involved myself and . . . but thanks *so* much. I – I must be mad, and you're so very kind—' In the face of a sexual threat, excessive politeness was a natural recourse.

She looked at Quinn, her imploring eyes begging him to let her off the hook. 'It's not fair!' he protested. 'It's not fair!' in a narrow, childish whine. His face had reddened further, his hands were shaking. 'I don't want to make a nuisance of myself, but you came here in your nightdress in the middle of the night. With *jokes*.'

'I'm so sorry,' she said. 'I'm so sorry. I was worried about you. And . . . and I have got my coat on as well,' she pleaded.

Quinn clambered to his feet, shaking his head, confusion lining his face, thickening his breathing. 'I don't understand,' he said quietly.

'I'm so sorry,' she repeated. It's . . . it's me. I'm just not myself at the moment, I mean if I were, then obviously, *obviously* . . .' Then suddenly all was quiet. Quinn had taken himself off into another room. She took the hint and made her way back to her own flat. She wiped the table, mopping up the little piles of biscuit mush and shaking the sticky cloth out into the sink. She dried the Formica surface with a clean tea-towel. Moments later she heard the sound of an envelope being passed under her door. She examined the note, sitting at the kitchen table. In the envelope were four rose-coloured fifty-pound notes. 'Please wipe what has happened from your memory. A million apologies. You are a person of the highest calibre. Q.'

Martha got into bed, smoothing the covers round her shoulders for the last time that night. Underneath the window she heard raucous laughter and then some bilious Irish voices. She strained her ears to listen. A man said, 'I'm so hungry I could eat the arse off a nun through the convent gates.' She smiled, exhausted after her little escapade. The Selfridge Hotel indeed, she thought vaguely, as she drifted off to sleep, it was less than a hundred yards away! That was a curious piece of delicacy. As if at Raven Court they were lacking in rooms! Where did these people get their ideas?

Seven

Martha awoke to the sound of the phone ringing. It was her father. It never rains but it pours, she thought.

'I . . . um . . . wonder if you could come and sit with Stephania and the baby for a bit this afternoon. Be awfully kind.'

'Something wrong?'

'No-oh, not wrong exactly. About two, could you come?'

'Yes, if you like.'

'Thanks very much.'

'It's all right. Will you be . . . um . . . about yourself?'

'Probably not. No. Unfortunately.'

'Well, if you say to her I'll be along about two-ish, then.'

'Thanks very much. Bye.'

Later on, Martha stood on the pavement, facing squarely, through the railings, the creamy crescent of large houses, with their haughty Nash columns and rows of high windows and uniform black-painted doors. Noisily she trailed a twig she had stooped to pick up against the parallel black iron bars that marked out the strip of communal gardens as private property. One or two of the houses had domes or ghostly figurines looming down from the roofs.

It seemed to Martha then that something of herself remained in the house she faced, some small piece of her, not an essential element but some kind of extra that, ever after, she had never again quite been able to afford. She'd been left with the basics, certainly, all in working order, chugging along, without undue extremes of feeling, but sometimes she wondered, wasn't it those extras, the unnecessary side portions and little decorative flourishes that marked you out from the next person?

For instance, what had happened to all those muffled sounds that house specialised in, the times when she had bitten her lip to stop her teeth chattering, hushed her bones on the creaking stairs, swallowed sneezes and silenced the swish of her swinging pony-tail? Where had all those smothered gestures gone? Were they being repaid to her now with interest by the buses and taxis and dustcarts and motorised road-sweepers that roamed her street, the shoppers, the late-night revellers, the knock-off scent-sellers, the small-hours vomiters, the mouthy caramelised nut-vendors, the clacking heels of the crisp-bloused women who worked in the beauty halls of the department stores?

Maybe the disappearances had predated the failure of her family for hadn't they begun earlier, right from the start of things? Maybe, from her earliest beginnings, she had never been fully herself. Imagine that! And maybe, maybe, wasn't it after all possible, that in some bizarre way, this was actually a good thing, a saving thing?

Something Stacey had once barked at her, in frustration, when she had stolen into Martha's room to borrow shoes, catching Martha in bed at four p.m., shivering and staring into space, following what was probably the worst romantic encounter of her life: 'He didn't leave you, stupid. You left yourself. *Years* ago.' Stacey watched an awful lot of lunch-time talk shows, the ones with the psychological slants, but still.

Her father let her in hurriedly, on his way out, and directed her upstairs, slipping out of the door, speed-walking along the pavement. He was like a man leaving the scene of a crime! Stephania was sitting in the first-floor sitting room, slumped in a blue chair, the longest finger of her right hand in her mouth, her face pallid and drawn, her thick dark hair slightly wild.

The room differed from Martha's memory of it and this was not any failure on her part: certain aspects of it had actually changed. There was no longer a cool expanse of blue carpet, a huge shimmering woollen lake in the vast L-shaped room. The floor was parquet now, not golden like the flats in her building but a deep pinkish brown. She peered at the marble fireplaces, with their little Regency details. A wood fire burned in one of the grates. That would be a problem once the baby started to crawl. Had they thought of that, she wondered?

But the thick air-blue curtains still hung at the windows, a little faded but still beautiful, still inviting, the slightly loose threads in the fabric poignant with age. Would the baby be curling himself up inside their silky folds one day? She bit her lip and turned again to Stephania. Gradually her eyes and her ears opened fully to the whole scene and she took in the baby lying at its mother's feet on a blanket, and the fact that the baby was crimson and heaving and screaming with all its might.

'Um . . .' Martha said. 'Umm.' It was clear the baby wanted to be held, but there must be a reason why he was being left to cry; perhaps he did not like another's touch. Still, 'May I pick him up?' Martha said. The woman nodded, gnawing on a bit of inflamed skin that was hanging loose at the edge of a fingernail.

In Martha's arms the baby stopped crying immediately. He seemed like a modest soul. His mother looked awful, grey, weary, shaky and full of anxiety. She lit a cigarette, and sucked hard on it at tiny intervals

'How are things?' Martha asked, wandering over to the other

side of the room, where the smoke wouldn't reach them. Her shoes sounded echoey on the parquet: ancient and far away.

'Oh dear!' Stephania whispered. 'Nothing I do is right. I try everything, but he won't stop. Nothing is enough. He wants more and more and more from me. I don't have any left to give.'

'It sounds . . .' Martha began '. . . it sounds very overwhelming.'

Stephania nodded. 'And the worst thing, it's terrible to say, but I don't think he, after all I do with him . . . I don't believe he really likes me!'

'Oh, no! Of course, I mean, you can really, really tell just by the way he looks at you.'

'Ah, you are just being kind. Everyone is being kind.' She hissed the word as though it were a sort of curse.

'It must be hard for you,' Martha was searching around for something helpful to say, 'not having your family in this country.'

'The lady who comes here to clean, I know she thinks I am a bad mother. She finds fault. I think she steals my clothes, you know, because things just vanish and I don't know where they go. He's good with *her*, he sleeps, he is smiley-smiley, but with me, ugh! He isn't good for me. The real thing is – I don't know how to feel good when I am not working. I don't know if I . . . As she spoke her accent became thicker and thicker and then she started talking in Italian. Martha could not understand. The woman was growing hysterical.

'How long has it been now since you were able to work?'

'It's twenty-nine days since I picked up my violin. It's too long.'

With a flash of regret, it dawned on Martha that that was all the baby's age meant to her, all it would ever be, a period that had slipped away from her, unworked, wasted, never to be regained. Still, she could see it was serious. 'Could we feed the baby and then I'll take him to the park for a little bit and you could have a quick . . . ? And if he's not happy I'll bring him straight back.'

The baby had gone to sleep in her arms with a grin on his face. 'Could you? Would you, really?' Stephania's eyes were huge, imploring.

'No problem! Does he have a coat, or shall I just button him into mine? A hat he'll need surely?'

'Whatever you like,' Stephania said, gesturing towards a basket on the landing outside in which some baby clothes were stacked in a neatly ironed pile. Martha rummaged around, drawing out a little scarlet bonnet with a tassel, a fawn, hand-knitted cardigan with pearl buttons, a small woolly shawl. She wrapped him up in these garments.

Finally Stephania stood up.

'What about food?' Martha asked.

'He'll be fine until an hour and a half,' she said. 'There's a bottle in the fridge. You can give it to him when you get back.'

'Sure?' Martha said, regretting it instantly. Just then she noticed that on the back of Stephania's gathered pale skirt were three or four dark bloodstains and that above her upper lip quite a lot of dark hair was growing. Also, there were several ladders in her tights. It was time to say goodbye. Martha wanted to make some vote of confidence to the woman, reassure her in some enduring, satisfying way, but it seemed impossible. In the end, she held out her palm towards Stephania and, gingerly, the two women shook hands.

In the park she drifted over to where the best ducks were, which was on a little mossy bank directly under a curved bridge. They looked spectacular today, their orange crests, their snow-white bibs, their dazzling petrol-blue tail feathers. Most people with new babies feel tried to the limit at times, Martha remembered someone on a bus telling her. She practised saying this out loud to Stephania. 'It's a huge change for anyone. Everyone finds it a strain, doesn't know what's hit them, and then suddenly you're not quite your own person any more, and it's mighty odd.' But she had felt fear in the sitting room with the woman, as though she had no faith in her own power to be a mother, and that, well, possibly the baby was not entirely safe. Did she know all the things you were meant to do and not to do? The hygiene things? The emotional things? She gazed into the baby's eyes. He was a creature of the highest calibre, entirely perfect, pure, lovely and loving.

A woman wheeling a very elderly dozing lady in a wheelchair approached. She put the brake on the chair, for they were standing now at the crown of the bridge. 'You make a lovely pair,' she said. 'How old is your little boy?'

'Twenty-nine days,' she said.

'Aaaah. He looks just like you. Going to break a lot of hearts that one.'

'I certainly hope not!'

Martha walked on with the baby tucked in her coat all the way across the park until she reached Portland Place. The pale stone mansion blocks looked cruel in the harsh sunlight. But she fancied that the baby's rosy head, bursting out of the tweed of her coat, among her collar and green scarf, gave him the look of a little flower. She sang him a song made up of endearments, linked with short passages of whistling: 'Hello, my darling little body,' she crooned. 'My sweet precious darling angel. Little one. Boysy. Tra-la-la.' He slept on.

She turned into Regent Street, arranging her scarf over his ears so that the traffic wouldn't wake him. He stirred drowsily, blinking for a second, but then resumed his sleeping. She walked speedily along the streets, not minding anything much, the warm flesh of his hands soothing and velvety against her heart, the warm little breaths, the clenched fingers. She checked her watch, forty minutes had gone past. She'd take him back in another forty, no longer, in time for his next feed, give the woman a proper break.

She imagined the busy shoppers wondering about her and her child. Would they think she looked too young to have sole charge of a baby? Too strict? Too indulgent, with all her cluckings and strokes? One thing she knew for sure. There was no treatment that was too good for a baby. Babies deserved the very best always.

The sheer breadth and weight of the love she was developing for this child who was in some regards her relation, of her own blood! It seemed to double every ten minutes or so. Where would it end? She folded her arms over him, so that if one of the shoppers came bashing her way, he would be protected.

Approaching her building, she felt a huge sense of ceremony. The baby was awake now, but he didn't cry. 'This, my dear fellow,' she announced in singsong tones, 'this is where I live. This is the shop underneath my building,' she said, as though reciting a nursery rhyme, crossing the threshold of World of London, holding up a tiny crown-jewels pin-cushion, for him to see. 'This is the Queen of England,' she sang to him sweetly as they came face to face with a celebration cake platter (fifty per cent off) bearing that august lady's visage. 'This is Mr Sherlock Holmes.' She pointed at an arch-looking plaster figurine, in deer-stalker with intrepid expression. At Holmes the baby smiled. 'Guess what?' she exclaimed merrily to the nestling child. 'He plays the violin, just like Mum!'

She decided to take him to the food hall, show him off to the men at the fish counter. She couldn't resist. 'He's as good as gold, isn't he?' the man in his navy and white overalls said. 'As happy as Larry. Happier!'

'Oh, I know, we're very lucky with him.'

Once, Martha's mother had told her, when she was pregnant with Matt she felt so lonely that she wrote to him every day about how she was longing to meet him and all the lovely things they'd do together, the places they'd go, as soon as he'd hatched out.

'Wouldn't mind swapping with him,' another man said, as he laid out a huge slab of cod on the marble board, washed it down, teased out the pinbones. Martha blushed, the baby's head was using her bosoms for pillows, after all. On cue, the baby smiled. The man stopped his work, washed his hands, rubbing liquid soap deep into his palms, dried them off on a bit of rag and came round the front of the counter. 'May I?' he asked, and stroked the baby's head gently, just the once. 'Good little man,' he said. 'Looks like he could teach us a thing or two.'

'Oh, he's ever so good,' Martha cooed, her voice sure, motherly. She'd never detected that tone in herself before. She liked it. She crossed her fingers. 'Sometimes at nights when he's sleeping in the cot next to our bed I just look over at him and wish he'd wake up so I could play games with him.'

'Do you, love? Do you really? Aaaah. Soon grow out of that!' The man slipped back behind the counter, started ripping the ink sacs out of some giant squid, carefully removing the transparent, feather-shaped backbones.

She took him up the escalators to the toy department to buy him some kind of cuddly animal. She picked up a rabbit, a bear, an ostrich, a woolly lamb, but none of these things caught his interest. Finally a little pink towelling lamb seemed to capture his imagination and she bought it for him, ripped off the labels and tucked it inside her coat against his chest. How the assistants cooed and smiled. The compliments they lavished on his tiny head, his smiling eyes, his sweet face. She could barely tear herself away. She looked in at Boots and bought a small packet of nappies, a pack of three sterilised bottles and some ready made-up formula, just in case. They cost a fortune, but still. You had to do these things properly and it would be mad to run to a whole sterilising unit just yet, wouldn't it? *Wouldn't it?*

'And this is home,' she said, climbing the steps to her flat. 'These are the stairs. There's fifty-eight of them, one, two, three, four . . .' she counted. 'And this is where I live,' she said. 'This is the kitchen, these are the plates, this is my bedroom. Are you hungry, my sweet fellow?' she asked. She unbuttoned her coat and held him up in the air to sniff his nappy, as she had seen other mothers do. 'Nothing wrong there,' she said.

'Now, what would you like to do this afternoon?' she asked, settling herself with him in her arms into a kitchen chair. Just then she heard one or two tiny sounds coming from the bedroom, a halted footstep, some breathing, and dimly she sensed the presence of another person in her flat, at the other end of the hall, and suddenly the sounds stopped, like a person held in suspension and then she heard a definite footfall and she ran into the hall to see what crazy game Quinn was playing at now, but there was no one about and then, suddenly, she heard a creak in the floorboards and she swung round and there, stealing towards her front door, was Matt. Martha tried to soften the horrified shock that smarted on her face as she glimpsed his features, sharper and emptier and more colourless than she had ever seen them. His cheeks seemed to have fallen away altogether and the pallid hollows in their place were haunting, skull-like. One result of this was that his dim eyes were huger and sadder than she would have thought possible in a person, but his mouth was wild. Looking at him was actually a little bit frightening, like looking at a vicious dog, or some kind of crazed ape.

'Oh, hi,' he said. 'That your baby?'

'I'm looking after him for someone.'

'Right. What's up with you?'

'Nothing. How did you get in here? What are you after?'

'I need a bit of money, Martha. It's serious this time.'

'I can't,' she said. 'I don't have any.' But there were four fifty-pound notes sitting on the kitchen table, the ones that Quinn had delivered, after their . . . their . . . What should she call it? Their tryst? Matt moved round so that he was positioned about two feet from the money.

She slipped her body between him and the table.

'Oh, come on, Martha. If I don't give them money tonight, they're going to hurt me.' He rolled up his sleeve to reveal an arm that was covered in thick purple bruises and underneath the bruises were puncture marks and woven in among them odd little scabs and crimson sores. Martha took a step back. 'They've done it before. They say I've got till six o'clock. They're serious, Mar. Thugs. They've killed before.' Both sets of eyes were fixed on the notes on the table, burning into them with their different claims.

She clutched the baby closer to her. 'Don't be so theatrical,' she said.

There was a slight note of menace in Matt's voice now. He moved towards her. 'What? What? Please, Martha. Please.' He was making his eyes cry, but there was genuine fear in there. He might be telling the truth.

Suddenly she snatched at the money before he could do anything and she grasped it tightly, crumpling it in her fist and wrapping her fist around the baby's back. She took two steps away, then scuttled round the table in nervous little sideways steps.

'It's not a good time. It's not my money, for one thing. It's the landlord's. There was a misunderstanding. I can't keep it. I've got to give it to him later. I can't do this now. I'm looking after the baby. Can't you see I'm looking after the baby?' The baby started to make tiny frightened sounds. He could sense her grip on him wasn't entirely secure. She took another sideways step round the table, away from her brother. 'I've got the baby to think of,' she said.

'Do you want them to kill me over fifty quid? I'll give it back. I promise. Please.' His face was shaking, he was gearing himself up for something. 'Just don't be stupid, OK?' he said. He had made his voice hard. He took a step towards her, round towards her side of the table. She took a step round, he took another step. The baby looked up at her, his tiny eyes appalled. He started to whimper, painfully. The noises, muffled frightened sounds, clawed at her heart. There was nothing for it. You had to put the baby first. There was no contest. She threw the money on the floor at his feet, in disgust, and to her dismay he grabbed it all, even snatching a few silver coins off the table.

'Cheers, me dears,' he said, bounding out of the flat, slipping down the stairs.

'Don't spend it all at once,' she called after him, sourly. 'Cunt.'

She swore under her breath to protect the baby. That was it now. That was *it*. She shook her head. She was so angry she could actually kill someone. The baby wriggled in her arms. She slumped in a kitchen chair and waited for a few moments. Waited to feel better.

She must have dropped off holding the baby because suddenly she saw on the kitchen clock that it was almost four. Stephania would be out of her mind with worry. She had to get the baby back. She had to talk to her father. Stephania needed help. They'd have to employ a nanny, some kind of nurse. She could telephone, but she only knew the fax line and by the time she'd organised a fax . . . She raced out of her building and jumped into a taxi. The baby was wailing now for his mother, for food, for home. Martha held him, comforted him, tried to persuade him to take one of the bottles but he refused. She performed little games to cheer him as best she could, 'This is the way the gentlemen ride,' but the sharp bolts of shame she felt for what he had just seen, the pathetic little piece of melodrama they had both just witnessed, well, she would never forgive herself. The traffic crawled along at a snail's pace and by the time they turned into the park it was nearly four thirty.

'Looks just like you,' the taxi driver said.

'Most people say he looks like my husband.' (It couldn't hurt, could it?)

'Oh, right, must be a good-looking chap!'

'Well, what did you expect!'

When the taxi drew up at her father's house, pulling into the narrow, private, milk-coloured crescent there was an instantly recognisable sense of commotion brewing in the street. Her father was pacing up and down outside the house, in his shirt-sleeves, clearly agitated, his cuffs flapping in the wind, his hair askew. Had she ever actually seen him without a jacket? Martha wondered. She was fairly sure she had not. He looked insub-stantial, narrow, frail, his legs all spindly like old man's legs.

What would she say to him? What would she do? She had never had him angry with her before. How would she explain? Her breaths started coming uneasily, and when she looked down she noticed her hands were trembling. She held them fast against the baby.

But her father was hugely relieved to see her. 'Thank goodness you've got him. Is Stephania with you?'

'No, she's not. Is she not inside?'

'No. Did she say where she was going at all?'

'No, well, she said she hadn't worked for twenty-nine days and she needed to work right now.'

'But she's not at the flat.'

'Is she not?' was all Martha could say.

'She's been finding it all rather a strain.'

'Yeah, I gathered as much.'

'What did she say to you? Do you remember her exact words?'

Martha reconstructed the little scene, her father nodding throughout, occasionally questioning a particular phrase or two, probing the fall of a certain cadence, asking about a look, whether it had significance, until Martha realised that what he was really doing was clutching at straws.

They sat together, stiffly, in the first-floor sitting room, waiting for Stephania to come home. It seemed like hours. They started off on separate chairs, yards apart so that any shaky comments Martha might venture had to be half shouted, crassly, across the room. After a while she took a seat on the sofa to be nearer her father. It seemed to her that he was afraid and she couldn't tell exactly what he was in fear of, except that it was certainly, in some very profound way, 'the worst'. Was he worried that his new wife might never return? That the difficulties she was having might preclude any realistic married life, and that he, that she, Martha, would be left holding the baby?

Martha mused on the state of her old room, right at the top of the house, next to Matt's, and hadn't there been a bathroom each with squeaky floors? She pictured the baby set up in one of the rooms and the night visits she would make to him, laden with muslin cloths and musical toys and pale woolly shawls for that little pinkish fellow she had only recently met, but the degree of love she felt for him, well – she actually had not known she was capable! Just now he lay sleeping peacefully in a corner of the room swaddled in shawls in a Moses basket. It wasn't impossible that she should become his chief caretaker. She did know one or two things about looking after babies. Well, her knowledge was limited to theory, but it wasn't worthless. She knew that nothing was too good for them, that parents of all people had to require an awful lot from themselves, all the time. The thing was, it seemed to her, that if you could only start them off in the world, the babies, in an atmosphere of smooth care and safety and listening of the highest calibre, well, then all you'd have to do was watch them thrive!

She saw the two of them taking him out for a stroll in a large hooded perambulator, the huge apparatus stiff and unwieldy as they swerved to dodge the pigeons in the park. She pictured elderly women peeking into the pram's interior, catching a glimpse of their charge. She heard their aahs, their milky-hued cooing sounds.

In his bluish armchair it was clear that the waiting for his wife was grating on her father terribly. His hands made strained, nervous flutterings in his lap, but he seemed unaware of his body, blind to the anxiety building in his rapid finger movements because, Martha presumed, it was all dwarfed by the sharp, frenzied activity of his brain. At intervals he drew himself up and paced the room. Finally at six-thirty the police were alerted, and because of her father's reputation they seemed to rouse themselves quite eagerly to the challenge. She heard her father pause before reading out to them his telephone number, something Martha did not herself possess. She noted the digits, storing them up for a rainy day.

Martha made tea, and at a quarter to seven she prepared some formula for the baby, in accordance with the directions on the packet. It was so tricky, so many points at which you could get things wrong. The kitchen had been entirely remodelled. It was marble and white-painted wood now, modernish with a long slip of window running the length of the wall, giving on to the small paved garden with the high ivy-clad walls. Gone was the old-fashioned green kitchen of her own reign. She asked her father if he could face eating anything, but he just shook his head. As she came upstairs with the tray balanced carefully on her forearms, her eyes fixed loosely on the sad, brown teat of the bottle. Martha wondered to herself, was there something about her father that drove women crazy?

In the sitting room, they sipped their tea in silence, hers weak and milky, his weak with a lemon slice. Seven o'clock turned into eight o'clock. They barely spoke. Martha made up more formula for the baby, feeding him with the bottle when he woke, holding him in her arms until he nodded out, his face falling flabby and disconnected, like a man who had taken too many drugs. Her father regained some of his composure and between them they made some stabs at conversation.

'D'you see anything of Quinn ever?'

'You could say that.'

'Oh?'

'He crops up now and then, you know.'

'But he doesn't make a nuisance of himself?'

'Oh, no! He's the perfect gent,' she offered.

Her father gave a brief smile. 'Can't help being quite certain he's got absolutely no head for business.'

'Well, there is that. But things seem to be going all right with the building.'

'Oh. That I *can't* believe.'

'Yeah, no, I think it's all right. Well, I don't know, really. I mean, I don't know about the letting side of things, the selling side or the budgets or anything. Maybe it's not going so well, but I mean it's looking great. You – you'll have to drop by some time, you know, if you're passing.' She paused. 'I expect I'll have to be moving on soon myself.'

'It caught my imagination rather. I was thinking about it last night. Seemed rather full of possibilities somehow, that ugly great building being got up to the nines.'

'Oh, we're *well* beyond the nines now, make no mistake. There's talk of grand pianos.'

'Oh, how funny!' Her father shook his head. Suddenly he looked hugely old for his age, weary, time-worn, just an ordinary elderly gentleman hovering in a wing-chair.

'Yeah, I suppose I ought to be looking out for a new place,' she murmured again.

'Any news from the dope fiend at all?' her father asked at ten past nine, and just as Martha searched for the right words in the circumstances, the key turned in the lock and in walked Stephania.

'Hello?' she called up the stairs. 'Hello? Anyone home?' They ran down to see her.

'Are you all right?' Anthony Brazil asked, voice steady, eyes composed.

'Much better,' she said, 'much better.' She took the child from Martha and wandered into the kitchen. 'I am starving,' she said, throwing open cupboards, pulling out ingredients, swinging open the fridge door. 'I will make dinner for us all,' she announced, a saucepan in one hand, Frederick balanced on the opposite hip. She looked happy and peaceful. 'Leave us to it,' she said. 'It will be ready in forty minutes. I'll call you.' She smiled kindly.

Martha and Anthony Brazil shuffled upstairs again. 'Funny thing is, she can't cook for anything,' he said. 'Never even tries.' But he looked hugely relieved. 'I hope you can stay,' he said to Martha. 'You must be hungry.'

Martha thanked him, but said she ought to get back.

Her father nodded. 'Thanks very much. You've been marvellous.'

She nodded, and he nudged the side of her ear slightly with

the edge of his hand and turned away for a moment. She saw his hand reach deeply into his pocket. He pressed a large number of notes into her hand. 'Thanks very much,' he said again.

She stuffed the notes into her bag, too embarrassed to look at him. 'Thanks . . . What will you do?' she asked him, her left knee brushing the skirts of the sitting-room curtains as her father lingered three or four feet away.

'I'm not sure that I know.'

'Please, whatever you do, please do it properly,' she started, 'because whatever it is, it will really matter.' She felt her father shrivel from her as the words came out. Suddenly he was at the other end of the room, at the very furthest point from where she was standing, without actually stepping through the far window on to the little back balcony.

But what he said was, 'I do realise it's rather serious,' and they stood there on their opposite sides for some moments, drinking in the moon and the stars, and the sounds that drifted over from the park, night birds, the odd fast car in the Inner Circle, the distant noise of audiences clapping the cast of the open-air theatre (was it?) as they took their curtain calls under pink and amber lights.

Thirty minutes later Martha was clambering into bed. The phone rang twice, but she ignored it. The third time it rang she got up in her half-sleep and knocked the receiver off the handset. There wasn't room for more words. She went to sleep in her clothes and slept for eleven hours. Then she got up, unhooked her bra under her jersey, feeding the straps and the cups through the end of her sleeve without removing the topmost garment, and went back to sleep again. She awoke refreshed, renewed. It was late afternoon. She felt the money her father had paid her thick and warm in her pocket. She counted out the rose-coloured notes. There was nine hundred pounds.

Pulling her coat on over her stale-ish clothes she wandered in the dim evening light over to the department store. With the money in her pocket she felt madcap and carefree. The shop was heaving. She took the stairs to the second floor. A red and white checked halter-necked dress, a sort of glorified silk apron called out to her, a long pink A-line skirt with row upon row of ribbon frills caught her eye, a black silk jersey shirt-dress, a rose-coloured cotton peasant-style blouse with irregular navy dots. A shop assistant gathered her choices and led her into a fitting room. Each outfit looked spectacular. She felt Italian and sort of sultry, fresh from the beach, and Christmassy also. But she couldn't go through with any of the purchases, not quite, not yet, so she went down to the food hall. She bought ten cocktail mince pies at thirty-five pence each from the bakery counter and in the beauty hall a curvy green bottle of scent called Honeysuckle Splash, which was eighteen pounds. That would do for now. She headed home, sniffing at her wrists as she walked.

Quinn was hovering outside her door. Oh-oh! she thought. The Rover Returns.

'Quick,' he called out. 'Your mother's on the telephone,' he said, handing her his cellphone, then disappearing thoughtfully into his own flat. 'Sounds important.'

'It isn't fatal,' her mother began slowly. 'He's still in one piece, still very much alive, but Matt took an overdose yesterday lunchtime, and while he's still not himself, the hospital seems to have got him to agree to going to a treatment centre for a bit. It's rather handy that I couldn't get hold of you for so long,' she added. 'I thought that was it, at one point, that it was all over, that we'd lost him, but now it looks as though something good may come out of it.'

'Something good?'

'Well, obviously there aren't any guarantees, but at least,

for now at any rate, he's safe, where he is. Even if it's just a temporary escape from the people he owes money to, at least . . . at least . . .'

'What happened exactly?'

'Seems he'd got hold of quite a bit of money Thursday afternoon, blew the lot in one go, his friend said. Turned out to be purer than usual, or something, the heroin.'

'Right. Oh, God.'

'We'll go up and see him next week, shall we?'

'Yeah. If you like. Whatever you think.'

'I'll certainly keep you posted, if I hear anything. I imagine he'll just lie low for a few days and then . . . take it from there, really. He'll have to attend a certain amount of meetings, every day, I think. Some of it might sink in, you never know. He might be ready by now. I think his life has become pretty unpleasant. He's very ashamed.'

'It must have been awful for you. Were you on your own at the hospital, all night?'

'Oh, well!' she said.

'It must have been really, really terrible.'

'It wasn't . . . Well, it wasn't . . . great.'

'I'm really sorry I wasn't there to help you with everything. That you had to go through it on your own. I wish I had been there.'

'Thank you, Martha. Thanks. I appreciate that.'

'How you feeling now?'

'Pretty shaky, but life goes on, I suppose.'

'Yeah. I suppose.' Then she paused. 'Does it, though? Things have pretty well wound up at this end.'

'You see, I've got someone coming to stay this evening and I think she might be a bit of a handful, and . . .'

'You couldn't put her off for a day or two?'

'You know what, perhaps I could.'

'Might be worth a try.'

'Yes, no, thanks, I think that's a good idea. I'll give a ring now, see what can be done.'

That evening the Christmas lights were to be switched on. Martha watched the whole thing from the large window in the luxury flat, mince-pie in one hand, mug of tea in the other, as she slid from side to side on the marble in her socks, a warm moustache of raisin juice and pastry crumbs spreading happily on her upper lip. She saw the crowds amassing at half past five, the huge heaving mass of people bristling with their own brand of static anticipation. A brass band was working its way mournfully through Christmas carols. 'The Holly and the Ivy'. 'In the Bleak Midwinter'.

Stella was brilliant at Christmas. Last year with the knowledge that Martha would be waking alone she had put together and delivered the most spectacular Christmas stocking, crammed with multi-coloured crackling packages – and the gifts themselves! Eighty metres of 1950s polka-dot ribbon on its original card, a miniature Stetson-shaped bottle of bourbon, home-made ginger heart-shaped biscuits, their middles embossed with pink-icing Ms.

At a quarter to six the local mayor arrived, all red robes and clanking gold chains, smoothing his hand thoughtfully over his festive drinker's jowls. At his side, an ancient Pearly King and Queen bobbed about, the watery, pale buttons on their black coats glistening softly in the last of the light. At five to six, three stars from a soap opera, got up in gorgeous filmy red and green evening gowns, arrived to flick the switch: a blonde, a brunette and a redhead, something for every taste. They made brash-looking jokes between themselves, egging each other on. Then there was a hush for a moment in which the actresses expressed their extreme gratitude to be performing this task and then whoosh! The sky was ablaze with white lights and bright lights and red robins and jade-coloured Christmas trees and golden choirs of angels. Some of the decorations were less than eight feet away from where Martha actually stood. She opened a window and stretched out an arm towards a small white neon pile of Christmas parcels that hung suspended in the air, level with her shoulders. She could hear the lights fizzing slightly in the cool night sky, and the oohs and aahs of the chill crowd gathered below. And then suddenly the people were beginning to disperse into the large, warm stores and the traffic was starting up again, and in fifteen minutes the streets were choked with the usual hissing cars and buses, the clogged, livid vehicles dragging at a snail's pace, taking people home with their Christmas shopping, the large carrier-bags stuffed with kaleidoscopes and jerseys and electric kettles. Briefly she closed her eyes and out loud into the street air she asked, quietly, for a bit of peace, just some anonymous unhurried time over the next little bit so she could get herself back. And as she made her wish, she drank in, in no small measure, her spectacular surroundings, the magical location, the gold, the crystal and the marble, the gleaming parquet, the downy carpets and, with the very last of her strength, she found herself shaking her head from side to side in the alien face of this perfect dwelling whose beginnings had been so unfailingly forlorn.

Eight

The straight and narrow drive that leads up to the clinic is austere in the extreme with its absolute flatness, its perfect dark green boxy hedges, its spotless slate-grey track, the bone-white sky, and the total absence of any kind of nature, bird life, squirrels, rabbits – this was the countryside, after all. There are not even any sounds on the air, just the low whir of tyres on the flush, brand-new road surface, and the various clanking of the miscellaneous items in the back of her mother's red van. At intervals, soaring neat trees have been planted whose leaves are pointy and a dark correct evergreen.

But the clinic itself, when it suddenly comes into view as the drive curves radically for the last twenty metres, looks like the invention of a madman facing his second childhood, or a fairground attendant's fantasy dwelling, or a filmstar's bolthole for sipping champagne out of ladies' slippers. A low-slung, heavy-set pale pink Victorian building, it has four medieval-looking cone-shaped turrets and a jaunty, rough-hewn crenellated frontage that smacks of fairy-tales and children's drawings and dream-time. A large black and gold sign bears its name: Castle Hall. An adjacent board holds a glass-fronted map, with arrows pointing to the swimming-pool, the fitness centre, the Eating Disorders Unit, the stables, as well as Outpatients, De-tox, and Colton and Pennington wards.

The day before Martha had unfolded the two sheets of thin paper that crackled in her hands.

Dear Martha,

I have met some very good people in here who seem to think I may be worth helping. They are very tough with me and do not miss a trick. We are all in the same boat here, and so no one gets away with anything, which is good, but also it makes things hard. We are all basically telling the same stories. It's going to take a long time and a lot of hard work. There is so much to learn.

I have got a lot of making up to do, I know. It has always meant a lot to me that I meant a lot to you. I sometimes feel I can never put a foot wrong where you are concerned but I realise by now this must be wishful thinking. I don't know if this is still the case, but I hope it is, or will be again one day. Please know how much I care for you, how much I want to prove it when I'm back on my feet. You don't know how sorry I am about everything.

Love Matt.

Martha had dreamed of such a letter. If they were going to get him back, well, that would be a miracle. Some old words of her mother's came to her: 'Sometimes it's like living under a fascist regime when someone you love disappears and you just don't know how to reach them.' Her mother had received a letter too, although they had not, as yet, compared them in detail. It felt too tender.

'I had a really really wonderful letter from Matt.'

'I did too.'

Neither woman wanted to have unrealistic hopes, hopes that might overwhelm him, or bring the wrong sort of pressure to bear on his highly emotional state, or lay themselves open to their own scorn, that shrill, mocking voice that taunted, *Of course nothing will ever change, only a fool could believe it might,* the familiar low ache of boredom and lurching crisis combined. They were dangerous, they took your appetite away, and dulled all your other desires, as mourning does, those little clutches of hope; they lunged towards you only to swing rapidly, and with no warning, out of your grasp. But even still.

Martha smoothed the edges of the paper, where the letter had been folded. If when she saw him there was even a hint of his old self, well . . . Her eyes wetted at the prospect and a warm, sore knot lodged at the back of her throat. She swallowed. Caution was required. She knew what she needed to do was to be ordinary with him, not hysterical or emotional, just balanced and . . . and sane. It was not wrong to show your feelings but she did not want to drown him with them. It was his meeting, after all. They must not do anything to tip the balance away from this. The burden of this hung heavy over her as they circled the car park in the rickety old van, searching out a visitor's space.

She thought of his old self. She thought of his old self and her old self, as they had been, splashing about in the bath. He had shone for her so in his boyhood, well up until his middle teenage. When he was nine he could turn fourteen cartwheels down the street, bandy-legged and curly-headed, and he would come to a final standstill, brush down his clothes, cool as a cucumber, without a trace of breathlessness. Her hands stung with all the clapping. She remembered again, as she often did, too often, really, the time she had been ill and he had brought her breakfast on a tray, and the toast was cut into fingers and on each separate finger a little face and the outlines of jaunty garments had been painted with a paintbrush in different-flavour jams, and all the faces were different, and the hairstyles too: curls, plaits, a bald egg-headed man. It was a family, she realised. He made up a story about them, about their adventures, their spry, toasty antics in a magic land.

And his prowess on the skateboard, careering across the pavements at top speed hurtling up home-made jumps, rocking across concrete half-pipes at the skate park, soaring into the air and turning, 360s, 720s, 1080s, his cream wheels, with the gleaming Independent trucks, his Toni Alva customised deck, which he'd worked fourteen Saturdays in the local fishmonger's to pay for. He'd come home on Saturday evenings stinking in an apron stiff with blood and bits of bone and scales and purple innards; even fish eyes attached themselves, eerily, to the large, low-slung pocket that stretched out in a broad smile below his waist. And then another ten Saturdays to get his navy blue rubber-soled suede high tops with the white swoosh. The trips she and her mother made with him to the skate park, the look of admiration and wonder in the eyes of the younger boys as they watched him soaring into the air, his long, lean legs shooting off his board as it hurtled up above him, only to jump back on as it passed him on the way down. The smoothness of the manoeuvre, the style, the grace. He was even in time to the loud music that belted out of the skate-park office. She had not pictured him on a skateboard for years. It was oddly painful to recall, all that soaring, the great swoops, the endless, fearless application of himself to life, the hours of practice in the street after school, leaping up after every knock, improving, perfecting his turning and honing his jump technique. The girls waiting about on the street corners tried to catch his attention sometimes, in their unseasonal skimpy attire, but he had no eyes for them. He had a job to do.

Once, she'd heard it said that the recovering addict needs to return to the point of development at which the drugs took over — to do his teens again, that would mean. To be a thirty-one-year-old man, starting again, greenly, at fifteen, making good and recovering those years that had been skipped over. It wasn't an enticing prospect. It was actually a little bit horrific. No wonder his whole life was spent in ensuring he would never have to embrace that poignant, wonky time travel. If you spent seventeen years avoiding something, what kind of knock or blow would it take to make you want or need to pick up again? How dreadful would today have to become for the collapse and the restart to seem preferable? She understood fully why he shied away from it. It was not right, but there was some degree of twisted sense to it. The strength you'd need to make the leap. If you had that kind of wherewithal, it was unlikely you'd have fallen so low in the first place.

Her mother parks the old red van at the back of the car park, the ancient engine spluttering and groaning at the prospect of a rest cure. Once in a clinic in Shropshire, Matt had found some magic mushrooms growing in a far corner of the grounds and brought them back into the television room and it was midnight feasts all round. The next morning he was on the first train back to London, her father several thousand pounds poorer, her mother distraught. It was the night before her exams began, and she and Matt and a friend of his who'd been ejected with him had all been treated by her mother to takeaway kebabs from a Greek restaurant. What was all that about?

Martha hops out of the van and makes her way towards the hospital gates, but it is impossible to proceed. Rapidly retracing her steps, she busies herself around the back of the vehicle, pretending to look for something she has dropped by the wheels in order to calm herself. An earring was it? A stick of gum? She asks her mother for the car keys and scouts about under the seat for this lost thing that does not exist, a scarf or an old shawl, something to cover her up, because in a skirt and jumper and coat she is too exposed. All she comes across is a knot of greasy engine rags. She tries to take even-length breaths, but her breathing is growing faster and faster. Her mother waits for her patiently by the gates, pretending to examine the hedge, finally breaking off a tiny rosemary branch and rubbing one or two of the fine green needles between her fingers and then holding her fingers up to her nose. Martha makes to join her, but holds back again, and bends to shake a stone from her shoe, only she cannot find anything there. She needs some kind of insurance before she can go in. All the signs are good, better than they have ever been before, but if it all comes to nothing again, as it always does, every single time . . .

'You know Dad's been rather a hero,' Martha's mother said, 'paying for all this again.'

'Right.'

'I didn't actually speak to him, I spoke to his secretary, which was rather a relief, but he seems keen to be involved, which is good.'

This was very generous, Martha thought, because if there was a single person in the whole world that her mother absolutely loathed it was her father.

'I . . . I was looking through some of his books the other day. For the first time. Bit of a new departure for me.'

'Had you not really crossed paths with them before?'

'Rather kept out of their way.'

'Oh,' her mother said gently. 'D'you know? I can't remember if I ever read one. Isn't that mad?'

'No. Not really.'

'I feel like I must have done, but if I try to think of a cover or a plot or anything, sitting in a chair with one, my mind just goes blank.'

'Oh, well, perhaps they're not as good as people say,' Martha offered.

'Well, I don't know about that!'

'I mean, it's not as if it's a great big thing, either way, you know, in my life, I mean.'

'Yes, but it's not nothing.'

'No, it's not nothing,' Martha agreed. 'Mum?'

'Yes, darling?'

'I do hope and . . . and pray, with Matt I mean, that all this,' she gestured vaguely with her hand at the vegetable garden at the side of the clinic, at the swimming-pool block to the rear, at the royal blue sign ahead that announced RECEPTION, 'I hope that it's not too good to be true.'

Her mother patted her shoulder and said, 'I know, I know. I don't know if I could take another disappointment.'

Martha blinked. The two women took small steps into the main reception area, where a nurse sat at a desk, her face half hidden by the arm of a beige-coloured Anglepoise. The pale carpet crackled underfoot muffling their shoe noises, but it seemed to muffle every other sound also. Hospitals are echoey places as prisons are, with constant clanking sounds, squeaking of trolley wheels, clattering dishes, hollow lift-shaft noises, flapping sheets, babies' cries, sirens floating in and out of hearing, but the silence here weighed heavy in the air as though the carpet ran up the walls, extending over the lowish ceilings, covering the mouths and faces and the feet of the inmates.

'We've come to see Matthew Brazil.' Her mother pronounced the second word of her son's name correctly, to rhyme with 'frazzle'.

'And you are?'

'Mother and sister.'

'That's right. They're expecting you in the family room

in ten minutes. Would you like to take a seat, please?' She gestured to a right-angle of navy sofas opposite her desk, next to a bulbous mineral water dispenser. Martha drew a ribbed plastic cup from the stack and drew herself and her mother a drink.

'How you feeling, Mum?'

'Calm,' her mother said.

'Do you think he's serious this time?'

'Well, I don't like to project into the future. We'll have a better idea when we've seen him.'

Martha had had an incoherent phone conversation with Matt three or four weeks ago. She had spoken to him at her mother's house, listened to him ranting on about how the probation officer he had to go and see every week was forcing him to stay on drugs, because he could never come off drugs in England, and he couldn't leave England because of the probation system.

'So you do want to come off drugs, then?' Martha had almost said, but they were so present in the rhythm of his words and his slurred resentful tone that she couldn't face saying it, rehearsing the little nauseating dance of lies and recriminations (him) and excuses and apologies (her).

Afterwards, when the phone call had ended, after he had said, 'I'd love to say let's meet up sometime, but I can't face seeing anyone just now, especially not family,' she felt that she had let him down, because not once in the conversation had she referred to the fact of his drug-taking. She imagined him, reeling with contempt, 'I talked to my sister just now and it's all so polite, and she doesn't even care that I'm in this state.'

'The fact you listened for so long and so carefully, too, proved you care. You said you just wanted to hear his voice, show an interest in him,' Francis had consoled her, his eyes softening at her distress. That was before their big break.

'I was so weak, it was my big chance to say something important to him. I can't believe I was so wasteful. I just couldn't face any conflict.'

'How well could it have gone, realistically?' Francis said. 'It was brave of you to make contact at all. A way of saying, "here I am," being ordinary. And to let him know you always have him in mind.'

'Yeah, but what if he just twisted it into a sign of my not caring about him?'

'His illness might have encouraged him to do that, but as long as you know you're caring about him and thinking and always hoping good things for him . . .'

'That's all I can do, isn't it? Apart from not giving him money and getting on with my own life in the happiest possible way.'

Francis nodded.

The happiest possible way.

'I feel really bad suddenly.' Martha turned to her mother, who was leafing through the clinic's brochure.

'Do you?'

Martha nodded. 'I just—'

Her mother stroked her shoulder gently. 'Look, darling, even if the worst comes to the worst and everything slips back again, it's important to remember that, although it's not a life you or I would choose, he has got a life of sorts. Sometimes I wake up in the night and think about it all and I just can't bear it—'

'I do too.'

'But, then, there are things to be thankful for. For one thing, whatever he's done or not done, I still really love him and I feel very lucky in that.'

'Do you, Mum?'

'I do.'

'He's the lucky one.' Whatever Matt had put Martha through it was a million times better than what her mother had had to contend with, of that she was wholly certain. If someone's your son . . . How did you bear that without going out of your mind?

Martha's mother started to speak. 'It's a great loss to him, you know.'

'How d'you mean?'

'Being in the state he's in. He's had to give up so much.'

'It is his choice, though.'

'I know. But to choose to give up on life is a terrible loss too.'

'I suppose.' At that moment in the distance Martha saw a familiar face, a familiar wiry frame cloaked in many, many black garments at the other end of the corridor, even though it was boiling hot. It was the waitress from the Dear Friends! She was standing arm in arm with a black nurse in a royal blue uniform with white piping at the collar and cuffs. The nurse was helping her walk along. The nurse said something and the two of them started to laugh and slowly hobbled off in the other direction. 'Just seen someone I know.'

'Oh, no! It's all go, isn't it?'

Martha refocused on the matter in hand. 'So you don't feel too optimistic, then?'

'Not optimistic exactly, but I'm always hopeful.'

'You are *so* great,' Martha suddenly wanted to say, but she fought shy of the words, afraid her mother might somehow take them the wrong way.

The nurse from the front desk was coming over to them. She bent her head, gently, and spoke in a soft half-whisper: 'If you'd like to go along now.'

'Thanks.'

'It's on the second floor, at the end of the corridor, the last room on the left.' She pointed to where the stairs were. 'Or you can take the lift.'

'All right, darling?' Martha's mother said, outside the door. Martha smoothed an invisible strand of hair from her cheek and pulled down the front of her jumper.

'Yeah. You OK?'

'Yes. I think so.'

They heard clipped footsteps, fast-paced and even, at the other end of the corridor and Martha turned her head suddenly to see her father heading rapidly towards them.

'Oh, fuck,' said Martha's mother.

'Martha. Christine,' Martha's father said. 'Shall we go in?'

Matt sat on a low-slung orange tweedy chair with thin black metal armrests, his head in his hands, some of the curls peeping out between his fingers. Next to him sat a lady in a red long-sleeved T-shirt, on his other side sat a man in a green V-necked jersey. Opposite the little arc of chairs were another three chairs, arranged in a curve so that the whole made up a little circle. These chairs were exactly the same, but upholstered in green tweedy fabric and they had no armrests.

'I'm Jim and this is Joy,' the man said standing up.

'Anthony Brazil,' Martha's father announced, unfolding the full, suited length of his arm and holding out his hand to Jim, who shook it warmly. Anthony Brazil retracted it almost straight away.

As a child Martha had always been interested to note how many seconds it took for a smile to fade from the mouth of an adult. She had counted, silently, exactly the amount of time that elapsed between the initial flash of happy upturned lips and the return to the natural, slack, emotionless attitude. A lot of smiles dissolved so quickly that you had no choice but to doubt the sincerity of the practitioners.

'Martha,' said Martha.

'Christine,' said her mother. They sat down, Martha taking, automatically, the middle chair, flanked by her parents. It occurred to her then that the entire family had not been together in the same room for more than twenty years! Her father's long fingers stroked the sharp outline of the keys on his lap. Matt's head was still in his hands. She could see from the outline of his face, of his body, that he had filled out a bit. He no longer had that fallen-in, haunted appearance, but he would not look any of them in the face. Her mother sat squarely and calmly, and Martha's gaze flew between each of the assembled company in turn. Joy had huge bosoms that were worn low, in a broad, thick shelf. Jim fingered the triangle of his grey-spiked chin with his thumb and middle finger.

Jim spoke. 'Well, I'd like to thank you all for coming. We all know why we're here.'

For the first time part of Matt's face emerged from under his hands. He blinked rapidly several times, as though to shield his eyes from the light, then went back into hiding again. But when he spoke, he spoke like an angel. His eyes filled with tears, and for a while he could not speak at all although it was clear he was trying to. The pain he's in, Martha thought. To see someone you love in that much pain and not be able to do anything for them. She felt tears boiling and spiky at the back of her own eyes. She held her head in her hands for a moment as huge bolts of love for him gathered in her stomach and her throat, winding her with their suddenness and strength. She removed her hands from her face. She would start the talk.

She braced herself to try to sound as ordinary as possible, that was the thing. He was in a highly emotional state, after all, she could hardly just show up after all this time of not saying anything and dredge up all her thoughts (her feelings, were they?) in a thick and rapid stream. She asked Jim if she could say something.

'Go ahead.'

'Matt,' she said, and her voice crumbled in on itself and she began to sob and suddenly the room was echoing with her huge donkey sobbing, but she continued to speak in between the soaring and wailing. 'We just love you so so much. We'll, I'll always support you in anything you do.'

Her father's hands grasped his keys so hard they were leaving little jagged pink imprints on the flesh of his fingers. Martha thought he might actually draw blood.

Her mother was frowning.

'Matt?' Joy said gently. 'Is there something you want to say?'

'I just want to say . . .' He stopped. He blinked briefly and took a big breath. 'Yeah. I just want to say . . . it's like I don't know what you want from me, but I can't be, I don't know how to be the person that you all . . .'

'We just want you to be happy,' Martha said simply. Her tears had gone and she felt stronger now.

'I can't handle this,' he muttered. Matt looked anxiously at Joy and Jim, shaking his head. He seemed to be communicating something with his eyes, but Joy held up a small reproving hand to him. Martha thought he had been seeking permission to leave and Joy was telling him he had to stay. He covered his face again with his hands.

'Can I say something?' Martha asked again. 'I feel you are so angry and disappointed in us, Matt.'

Matt's look of unease evaporated, he exhaled sharply and

noisily, and shook his head. 'That's just typical,' offendedness ripening deeply in his voice as he spoke. 'You can't always turn everything around to me. It's too much responsibility. I don't know what to do with it. You know . . .'

'In your letter you said you were sorry about things,' Martha said, reeling slightly from the attack.

'Yeah, well . . .'

Martha swung round helplessly to look at her mother and then at her father. They seemed to be happy in their spectating roles.

'D'you want us to go, Matt?' she asked. 'Is that what you want?'

'Stop trying to make me feel guilty the whole fucking time. OK?'

'Perhaps your mother and your father have things they'd like to say,' Jim interposed. He gazed encouragingly but neither spoke.

'Fucking typical,' Matt was mumbling under his breath.

'I think I'll say a little about the work Matthew and I have been doing towards his recovery,' Jim said. 'When Matthew first came here, he was in very poor health. He was in trouble with his dealer, who was beginning to turn violent. He was having morbid thoughts and suffering from paranoia. He was involved in some small-scale dealing himself that he was not comfortable with, in order to support his habit, and in the last month two of his close friends had died.'

Oh, Matt, I'm so sorry, Martha thought, but she did not quite say it out loud.

'He was very hostile to me at first,' Jim continued, 'and suspicious, and angry with the whole set-up here, but he said he had made a decision never to touch drugs again, and that he knew that for this to work he would have to make not taking drugs the most important thing in his life every day, perhaps for always. Ten days later we're beginning to examine some of his feelings and thoughts surrounding his drug-taking, the ethical decline that went with it, the health risks, the self-deception and paranoia among many other things. In the work we've been doing it has become clear in Matt's mind that he cannot and will not tolerate the lifestyle he has become accustomed to. He has made a list of all the people he has harmed and has said that he wishes to make amends to them all.'

His father looked up sharply here.

'Will you tell us something about your ideas about recovery, Matt?' Joy asked.

'I don't really think any of them care.'

'Why would we be here if we didn't care?' Anthony Brazil's voice was icy and there were notes of sarcasm.

'You tell me,' Matt said.

'What could we do to show you how much we do care?' Martha's mother said.

'If you don't even know that, then what's the point of all this? What is the fucking point of any of us sitting here and . . . and . . .'

'I don't think that's very fair,' Joy adjudicated.

'Why do they see me as the only one in the family with any problems?'

'Why don't you explain what you mean?' Jim said.

'There you all are in your weird little separate worlds, stuck up your own arses.' He looked at Anthony Brazil. 'You haven't got the first idea about, I mean, you don't even know a single thing, and just maybe your actions actually affect other people, and that maybe you just hide away all day long doing whatever it is you do because you despise anything you can't control!'

Martha blinked hard and took a deep, loud breath. She blinked again. But Matt was tackling her mother now. 'I don't understand you. Surrounding yourself with the most miserable people on the planet. Does it make you feel strong? And Martha's fucking miserable, has been for years, and neither of you do a single thing to help her out, do you?'

'I'm not miserable,' Martha said brightly.

'Oh, no!' Matt said. 'Pardon me!'

'What do you mean, Matt?'

'You know.'

'This isn't getting us anywhere,' Anthony Brazil sounded weary.

'Sorry if we're not making enough *progress* for you. Like you care.'

'You're very angry with your family,' Joy asked, 'aren't you, Matthew?'

'Can you blame me?'

'You feel sorry enough for yourself, that's for sure,' Anthony Brazil said.

'You seem angry too. Would you say something about your anger, Anthony?'

'Oh, I'm not angry, I just observe, you know.'

'I forgot – you don't have feelings, do you?' Matt hissed.

'That's rather cheap, Matt.' Anthony Brazil said the words smoothly.

'Well, I think, from what Jim says, you've been doing marvellous work here, and that you should be congratulated for your sterling efforts,' Martha's mother ventured.

Matt smiled sourly and shook his head in disgust.

Suddenly Martha saw this conversation stretching out for hours, days, months. If any of them really wanted to unravel things, in any serious way, make a commitment to sorting out all the strands of this mess, then it might take years. This thought did not horrify her. Not at all. She was finding the whole thing strangely stimulating. The atmosphere in the room was so wild and highly charged, for all the straight-back chairs and views of clipped and groomed hedges, *absolutely anything* could happen. Why had they not done this before? She felt a sudden swell of pride that they were all putting so much into it. What she couldn't see was any kind of ending. But no one seemed to be wriggling in their seats, or making for the door. That they were all there for the duration was perfectly clear.

This was the world when you stepped into it. The thick charge of blame and assault and love and murder and unbelievable acts of kindness and the bitterest sunken levels of disappointment that you could imagine and then, quick as a flash, from nowhere, jokes! Suddenly it dawned on her that Matt and her father were shouting abuse at each other, they were both standing up, her mother's eyes glued to their faces, her head swinging, incredulous from one to the other, every feature agog, even her nostrils, which were puffing and blowing.

'You never did this!' Matt was howling at his father, swinging his arms around expansively, his face puce, sodden, shaking with fury. 'You never fucking did that.'

'I never knew you wanted me to. No one ever said. How could I have known?' Her father was actually screaming back, his whole face fuming and crackling with uncontrollable feelings. Martha had never seen anything like it in her life. It was like Shakespeare and Greek tragedy and gladiators and bull-fighting and clowns frolicking in the circus ring.

'Look what you've made me!' Her brother's voice was hoarse with all the recriminations. Her father's was too. Both tried to shout even louder and longer than the other. It was a matter of honour.

'I might have made you. But no one's keeping you there, apart from yourself. You're thirty-one. Why can't you take some measure of responsibility for the first time in your life? Think about someone else for a change!'

That's daring, Martha thought.

'*How dare you?*' Matt's voice roared. Joy got up quietly and closed the window that gave on to a courtyard below, because some frightened birds were squawking.

'You've never spared a single thought for another human being in your whole fucking miserable life,' Matt boomed.

'What do you want me to do then? What do you want me to say?' Anthony Brazil's rage was hitting its peak.

'I haven't got all the answers,' Matt shouted so hard, that the light fittings in the ceiling actually shook. Martha was convinced the ceiling was about to come down on the lot of them.

Matt was on a roll cursing them all, 'Cunts, fuckers, wankers, bitches, zombies, fascists, Nazis. Why does no one in this bloody family ever have any feelings?' he was bellowing now.

'Don't be so ridiculous, of course we have feelings,' Martha's mother joined in, starting up suddenly in her chair. 'Don't be such a drama queen. You men! I don't know. I really don't,' and then something extraordinary happened. Matt started to laugh. Her mother's face was half illumined by a grin. She tutted and swept her eyeballs up to the ceiling. Martha saw little merry twitches at the corner of Joy's mouth and she saw the efforts Jim was making to keep his face entirely straight. Then Martha's mother started to laugh. She said to Joy, 'If I wasn't laughing I'd be crying.'

The room went quiet for a moment. It was relief to every single person in it. It was airless and unbearably hot suddenly, what with all the shouting, and Joy opened the window again.

Some curious sea-birds circled the window.

'Exhausted,' Martha said to no one in particular.

'Well, quite,' Anthony Brazil added.

Matt sat, lanky and humorous, one leg hooked over the arm of his chair. 'When you get to know us,' he said to Joy and Jim, 'we're just like any normal family, really.'

Anthony Brazil drew a silk square from his pocket and wiped his brow.

'Same time same place next week, everyone?' Joy suggested.

Martha turned the key in the door to her building and gathered up her post. She was dimly aware that the days of her little coming-home routines, the stop-offs for scones, the browse round the bed and bath department, they were almost certainly numbered.

Tomorrow she would set about looking for a new place of abode, she resolved. Somewhere a little bit less busy, she thought vaguely. Maybe a room in a cul-de-sac in a suburb somewhere, or a nice cheap basement in an unpopular part of town. She pictured herself in the desert, on a high mountain, in a small white sailing boat. She still had the nine hundred pounds minus twenty, which would serve as a deposit and a month in advance. She did still have that nine hundred pounds.

She recognised Francis's writing straight away on the thin brown envelope. She ran her thumbnail under the flap and a postcard of the crown jewels arrayed on purple satin cloth fell out. She climbed the stairs as she read it carefully. She began at the end to see if he had written love before his name. He had. At the beginning there was 'Dear' too.

Dear Martha,

I've been thinking about things while I've been away and I feel strongly that I'm not going to allow you to make a quarrel between us for no reason. I don't know what's going on but it seems to me everything got all muddled up and I personally think it's worth unmuddling. Back on Friday. Sincerely hope to see you then, with love, Francis

'Glutton for punishment!' Martha said out loud, gazing out of the kitchen window at the Christmas lights, the thin little pink robins and yellow bells. 'Some people!' but she couldn't help noticing the huge uncontrollable smile that was practically swallowing up her entire head, dampening her eyes, dripping down her front, across her arms, swimming down her legs, and collecting in the thin soles of her shoes. She picked up a sharp pencil, felt with her fingers its hexagonal black and red ridges, and very slowly and carefully she began to write.

Now you can buy any of these other
Review titles from your bookshop or
direct from the publisher.

FREE P&P AND UK DELIVERY
(Overseas and Ireland £3.50 per book)

Hens Dancing	Raffaella Barker	£6.99
The Catastrophist	Ronan Bennett	£6.99
Horseman, Pass By	David Crackanthorpe	£6.99
Two Kinds of Wonderful	Isla Dewar	£6.99
Earth and Heaven	Sue Gee	£6.99
Sitting Among the Eskimos	Maggie Graham	£6.99
Tales of Passion, Tales of Woe	Sandra Gulland	£6.99
The Dancers Dancing	Éilís Ní Dhuibhne	£6.99
After You'd Gone	Maggie O'Farrell	£6.99
The Silver River	Ben Richards	£6.99
A History of Insects	Yvonne Roberts	£6.99
Girl in Hyacinth Blue	Susan Vreeland	£6.99
The Long Afternoon	Giles Waterfield	£6.99

TO ORDER SIMPLY CALL THIS NUMBER

01235 400 414

or e-mail <u>orders@bookpoint.co.uk</u>

Prices and availability subject to change without notice.